Null-A Three

A. E. VAN VOGT

SPHERE BOOKS LIMITED
London and Sydney

First published in Great Britain by
Sphere Books Ltd 1985
30-32 Gray's Inn Road, London WC1X 8JL
Copyright © 1984 by A. E. Van Vogt

Set in 9½ point English Times

Printed and bound in Great Britain by
Cox & Wyman Ltd, Reading

Dedication

To my dear wife, Lydia, an exceptionally beautiful woman, first, in gratitude for having married me in 1979, and then, when we returned from France, for asking me the questions that finally started me thinking about what a third Null-A novel should be about.

To Jacques Sadoul, editor of J'ai Lu, the publishing company, which has kept *The World of Null-A* and *The Players of Null-A* in print in France, who several times urged me to write a sequel — to no avail until a couple of years ago when my wife and I visited Paris, he urged her to persuade me to write a third Null-A novel. That's when it happened.

To Fred Pohl who, when he was editor of *Galaxy Magazine*, was the first person to ask me to write a Null-A sequel.

To the late John W. Campbell, Jr., who — as editor of *Astounding Science Fiction* (now called *Analog*) — when he serialized the *World of Null-A*, called it a 'once-in-a-decade classic'. That was in 1945. Later — in 1948 — he serialized the sequel, *The Players of Null-A*.

To the late Jack Goodman, editor of Simon and Schuster, who printed a revised *World* in 1948 — the first post-WWII science fiction novel put out in hardcover by a major publisher.

To Raymond Healy, 1940's west coast editor of Simon and Schuster, who recommended *World* to Jack Goodman. Healy now lives in retirement on the east coast.

To Don Wollheim who, as editor of Ace Books, printed the first paperback edition of *World* in 1953, and later printed *Players* under the title *The Pawns of Null-A*. Wollheim is now owner of DAW Books, Inc. in NYC.

To Berkley Pub. Co., which took over the paperback

rights of both *World* and *Players*, and has kept them in print ever since.

To Count Alfred Korzybski, the Polish born mathematician, who formulated the Concepts of General Semantics, on which the Null-A novels are based. Korzybski's major work, *Science and Sanity*, was first published in 1933, with the sub-heading: 'An Introduction to Non-Aristotelian Systems and to General Semantics'. The count died in 1950.

Science and Sanity is obtainable from the following:
Institute of General Semantics
RR1, Box 215
Lakeville, Conn. 06039

International Society for General Semantics
Box 2469
San Francisco, Calif. 94126
(ISGS publishes a quarterly journal, *Et Cetera*)

Introduction

What does ten, twenty, thirty or forty years do to a reader's recollection of a novel read during one of those distant times?

My first novel about General Semantics, *The World of Null-A*, was originally published in *Astounding Stories* (now called *Analog*) in 1945 as a three part serial.

In those days, editors of magazines that published novels in serial form either had a low opinion, or a correct opinion, of the majority of their readers to recall the early instalments. And so, I, as author, was expected to provide a summary of the first part as a preliminary to Part Two, and summaries of both parts One and Two when Part Three was published a month later.

In what follows I have combined the 'best' parts of these original magazine summaries for the first two installments and then added a summary of Part Three.

In the year 2560 A.D., the semantic philosophy of Null-A dominated human existence. Annually, in the games of the Machine, hundreds of thousands of young men and women competed during the policeless month and tried to become 'worthy of Venus'. The lesser winners were awarded all the good jobs on Earth. The top winners were sent to glorious Venus, there to become citizens in an all Null-A civilization.

Gilbert Gosseyn received his first shock on the eve of the first day of the Games. He was barred from the mutual protective group of the hotel in which he was staying — because a lie detector stated that he was not Gilbert Gosseyn. The hotel security forces promptly expelled him from his room.

Out in the night he rescues a young woman from marauders of the policeless period. He quickly suspects that she is not, as she has stated, a poor working girl, because she flashes a twenty-five thousand dollar-bejewelled cigarette case. He begins to realize that he has become involved in some tremendous intrigue when he discovers that she is Patricia Hardie, daughter of Michael Hardie, President of Earth.

The Games Machine also tells him, when he arrives for his first test, that he is not Gilbert Gosseyn. But it informs him that he will be allowed to compete under the name of Gilbert Gosseyn for fifteen days, although by that time he must have discovered who he really is.

That night Gosseyn is kidnapped, and taken to the palace-home of President Hardie. He is interviewed by Hardie, by a cripple with a strong personality whose name is 'X', and by a sardonic giant named Thorson.

He learns that the President of Earth is involved in a plot to destroy Null-A, and seize control of the Solar System.

The three plotters become very excited when they discover something in a photograph of Gosseyn's brain. And when, after being driven almost insane by torture, he succeeds in escaping from a steel-walled room, he is pursued and mowed down by machine gun bullets and flame guns. Thus death comes to Gilbert Gosseyn I.

Gosseyn awakens in a mountain hospital on Venus. He has full recollection of having been killed, and he realizes that somehow, some way, his personality has been preserved in another body that looks exactly like the first.

He swiftly discovers that he is illegally on Venus, and accordingly is subject to death, automatically. He overpowers John and Amelia Prescott, the doctors in charge of the hospital, half-convinces them of a plot to overthrow Null-A, and then sets out into the Venusian wilderness to escape the detectives they had previously called to arrest him.

Venus turns out to be a fantastic land with trees three thousand feet tall and hundreds of feet in diameter. It abounds with natural fruits and vegetables, and the climate is perpetually, marvellously mild. It is a land of dreams, the heaven of the Solar System.

On the sixteenth day a roboplane agent of the Game Machine rescues him, informs him that there is no chance of his escaping capture, and advises him to surrender to the pursuing detectives with a carefully prepared story. It tells him that fully half of the detectives on Venus are agents of the gang, and that it is taking him to a forest of one of the reliable detectives.

At the last minute, as he is getting out of the roboplane, it explains that there is a factor in the affair about which it knows nothing — an alien factor. But that whatever evidence is available, he will find it here.

Gosseyn finds the tree-house furnished but unoccupied. He discovers a curious tunnel at the back of the apartment. The tunnel leads into the depths of the tree, and after some strange dreams about beings and ships that have come from remote interstellar space, he decides reluctantly to explore the tunnel.

But it turns out to be very long, intertwining through the roots of the colossal trees, so he returns to the tree-house for food. He is captured and taken back to Earth.

There he sees the body of Gosseyn I, and realizes that he *is* in a second, duplicate body. He is invited to join the gang, and he has just refused when John Prescott, the Venusian, kills President Hardie and 'X' and drugs the other men in the room.

Gosseyn and Prescott escape, and Gosseyn seeks out a psychologist to find out what it is in his brain that has made him the center of an intrigue, which actually held up the gang's plan to invade Venus.

The psychologist, Dr Kair, examines his extra-brain, and for the first time he learns the difficulties that stand in the way of training that part of his mind. In the midst of the investigation, they discover that Prescott is really an agent of the inner group of the gang; and that he killed Hardie and 'X' for the double purpose of convincing Gosseyn of his bona fides, and of using the hunt for the assassins as a means of manipulating Earth against the Games Machine and Venus.

Kair and Gosseyn escape in a plane, after learning from Prescott that the Distorter is in the wall of Patricia Hardie's bedroom. Kair plans to take Gosseyn to the lakeshore cabin which he owns, but after the psychologist falls asleep, Gosseyn realizes there is no time to waste.

So he carefully turns the plane around and jumps in an anti-gravity parachute down onto the palace balcony that leads to Patricia Hardie's apartment.

He is captured by Eldred Crang, Venusian detective — and turned loose. After what Prescott overheard Kair discover about Gosseyn's brain, they no longer fear him. Indeed, the gang realizes they are expected to kill Gosseyn. They refuse.

Free, Gosseyn doesn't know what to do about himself. He goes to the Games Machine. And it tells him that Crang was right. He has served his purpose. He was used, first to startle the gang leaders, then to show them that their secret hiding place on Venus was known. It was all part of an immense political maneuvering, and it is up to him now to make way for Gosseyn III, whose extra-brain is already trained.

The Machine also tells him that Venus has been invaded and all its cities captured, and that therefore he must waste no time in killing himself. Gosseyn refuses to do so, but later, after boldly entering the palace, and sending the Distorter to the Games Machine, he realizes that he has no alternative.

He rents a room in a hotel, drugs himself with Coue hypnotic drug, sets a phonograph to endlessly repeat that he must kill himself; and he is lying there half-unconscious when he hears heavy gunfire. He drags himself out of bed, turns on the radio, and hears the Games Machine tell him not to kill himself because the body of Gosseyn III has been accidentally destroyed, and so it's up to him to escape and train his extra-brain.

Vaguely, Gosseyn hears the announcer say finally that the Games Machine has been destroyed. He returns to the bed, and slowly forgets what he has been told by the Machine. There is only the whining voice of the record repeating, 'Kill yourself, kill yourself! – '. This time he is rescued by Dan Lyttle, hotel clerk.

In the final third of 'World', Gosseyn's 'double' brain is trained, but he discovers it controls energy flows on a twenty-decimal level of refinement, thus transcending the time-space phenomenon.

4

The violent conspirators are confronted in the Semantics Institute on Earth, and suffer the fate they deserve.

In the final chapter Gosseyn, still seeking clues to his identity, finds himself looking down at a newly dead body, the face of which is a duplicate of his own. As his own mind probes the few, still living cells of the duplicate brain, vague clues come through. But he realizes that he has arrived too late.

He has won the battle; but he still does not know who he is.

The 1940's were easily the busiest years of my writing career; so, after it became apparent that *World* had made a big hit with most of the readers of *Astounding Stories* (about this time called *Astounding Science Fiction*), I wrote an even longer sequel: *The Players of Null-A*.

Players was published in the October, November, December 1948, and January 1949, issues of *Astounding Stories*; and it also had summaries of the earlier installments, beginning in the November issue.

The Players of Null-A opens with the introduction of a sinister new character, a shadowy being, called the Follower; and presently a strange history of human beings in our Milky Way galaxy emerges, and how they (we) got here.

Two million years ago, in another galaxy far away, the human race there discovers that a vast, deadly cloud of gas is enveloping all its planets. Not everybody can escape, but tens of thousands of small spaceships are sent out, with potential survivors aboard each little craft in a state of suspended animation. After the million-plus year voyage, the little ships reach our Milky Way galaxy, and begin to land at random on habitable planets thousands of light-years apart.

Gilbert Gosseyn, a clone descendant of one of the survivors has finally (in *The World of Null-A*) discovered the clues to his origin, and his special abilities. Here on earth of 2560 A.D. he has received Null-A training, and is accordingly entitled to live on Null-A Venus. He is, at first, unaware that, as a result of his newly discovered self-knowledge, he has become the target of the machinations of the Follower, a shadow-like being who comes to earth from a far-distant star system of the Greatest Empire – a vast interstellar civilization.

The Follower's purpose is to prevent Gosseyn from leaving the solar system. Which means he wants to stop him, first of all, from going to Venus, where there is a hidden – hidden underground – interstellar space-time distorter system for transmitting huge spaceships across light-years of distance instantaneously. The principal reason for trying to delay Gosseyn is that, if he reached Venus in time, he might accompany the sister of Enro, head of the Greatest Empire; accompany her and her Null A detective companion, Eldred Crang, to the Capitol Planet of the Empire.

The delaying action is successfully achieved by the Follower's human agent, Janasen. And, when Gosseyn later confronts Janasen, the latter produces an energized flat object, which has the appearance of a glowing calling-card. When Gosseyn finally, deliberately takes the card, he is instantaneously transported to a prison cell on the planet of the Predictors, a race of people who can predict the future. There, he meets, among others, a beautiful young woman, Leej, in whose presence – and with whose help – he has his first confrontation with the Follower.

Gosseyn has escaped from the prison cell by using his special abilities; and the Follower watched him escape, with the intention of learning his method.

As a result of this observation, the shadow being decides that Gosseyn is dangerous, and offers him a partnership arrangement – the purpose of which, apparently, is to take over the Greatest Empire from Enro and his sister, Reesha (on earth she used the name 'Patricia').

Gosseyn has the unhappy task of telling the schemer that Null-A people do not wish to conquer anyone except by reason. Whereupon the Follower tries to destroy him. The resultant battle between the two tells us a great deal about the special abilities of both.

They seem to be equally matched; for both escape.

Gosseyn, with the help of Leej, thereupon makes it to the Capitol Planet, where we discover that Reesha and Crang are trying to influence Enro toward peace; and the Follower, who

6

is revealed to be Enro's chief advisor when in human form, is urging Enro to destroy non-Aristotelian Venus.

Enro is alarmed by Gosseyn's special abilities, and, after a confrontation, he lets the Follower influence him in the direction of destroying the solar system.

However, Gosseyn, with the help of Leej, Reesha and Crang, aided by the special Null-A defenses of Venus, defeats the vast fleets that are launched against Earth and Venus.

But Leej, and even villainous Enro — it turns out — are also descendants of the survivors of the distant galaxy; and *their* special abilities will be useful, as part of a team effort, that has the goal of returning to their galaxy of origin to find out what happened there.

Players ends with the destruction of the Follower.

And so, now that the reader has become aware of what went on in the previous 'installments' (*The World of Null-A* and *The Players of Null-A*) the stage is set for *Null-A Three*.

Chapter One

Gilbert Gosseyn opened his eyes in pitch darkness.

. . . What, what, what — he thought. It was that quick. His instant feeling was that this was not where he should be.

During those swift moments there had, of course, been several awarenesses in him: he was lying on his back on something as comfortable as a bed; he was naked, but a very light cloth covered him. There were sensations all over his body, and his arms, and legs, as if at the point of each sensation a suction device was attached there.

It was the overall awareness of the numerous attachments that delayed the impulse to sit up. And so there was time for the Special Thought that only someone with his training could have:

Well, I'll be — this is it! This is the exact situation of life in relation to basic reality . . .

A human being was a head and body surrounded by — nobody knew for sure. Nobody had ever found out — for sure.

There were five principal perception systems that recorded the surroundings; and at least three of those senses had already provided him with tiny bits of information. But even that was based on information, and memory, in his brain. He knew things on the basis of previous indoctrination.

Essentially, the self is forever in darkness; and messages come in primarily by way of sight, sound and touch, which, like the antennae of TV or radio, are programmed to record specific wave bands.

It was an old General Semantics concept. But it was sensationally parallel to his present situation.

What was baffling about the condition was that he had no recollection of having gone to bed the previous evening in such a physical environment. But, since he felt no sense of threat, the lack of memory did not disturb him. Because — what a fantastic parallel it was.

. . . I, thought Gosseyn, as a self, am in actual pitch darkness. Almost immediately perception began. But it hasn't told me anything yet that shows any direct connection with the universe — with whatever the reality is . . . out there.

It was a typically human, fleeting awareness. Because, even as he had those thoughts, another reasoning process inside him noticed again that his situation did not fit the normal reality of the awakening of a living, intelligent person.

It was more than simple, unconcerned curiosity. It was a need to know because of a feeling that something was wrong.

Mindful of the numerous suction devices that he had sensed as being attached to his body, Gosseyn slowly raised his arms. First, then, he maneuvered the thin sheet downward, away from the upper part of his body. It seemed to be what he had sensed it to be: a loose sheet. It moved easily; and so, after mere moments, his hands and arms were free for their next action.

Carefully, he felt the bed itself. And, at once, found himself touching rubbery tubes. Dozens of them. They were what were attached to the suction devices on his body.

Actually feeling them was startling. He froze into motionless. Because . . . this is ridiculous!

Because — still no memory of how something like this could be happening to him.

Consciously, he braced himself, placed his arms and hands firmly on the cushiony surface underneath him. And with their help, sat up. Or rather tried to sit up. What happened: his head struck something cushiony inches above him.

He lay back, startled. But, presently, he was exploring the surface above him with his fingers. The 'cciling' of his long, narrow couch was made of a smooth, cloth-like material. And it was less than a foot above him. The walls on either side, and at the foot and head, were also cushiony, and also about twelve inches from him.

9

The situation was no longer merely ridiculous. Or puzzling. It was totally unrelated to anything he had ever known.

Lying there he realized that in some fashion he had, until this exact moment, taken it for granted that this was Gilbert Gosseyn awakening after a night's sleep.

Lying there he consciously made the cortical-thalmic pause of General Semantics.

The theory was that the reasoning — cortical — part of the brain could handle even a dangerous situation better than the automatic, feeling — thalmic — that simply reacted.

Okay, he thought wearily. Now what?

An additional realization came suddenly: of course! When I awakened, I knew who I was.

And that knowledge — that he was Gilbert Gosseyn — he had taken so for granted that it had faded from the forefront of his mind. But it was not a small realization.

To awaken and know who you are: it undoubtedly happened each morning to all human beings. Except, in this case it had happened to someone who was not just an ordinary human being. The individual who had awakened here was a human being with an extra-brain.

That was the acceptance of himself that he had awakened with. A casual memory of what he had done: the vast distances of the galaxy that he had traversed with his extra-brain's special abilities. The colossal events he had participated in, including the destruction of the Follower, and, even more important, saving non-Aristotelian Venus from the interstellar forces of Enro the Red.

. . . Knowing people like Eldred and Patricia Crang, Leej the Predictor woman, and —

Pause! Dismissal of those memories. Or rather, realization that there was no obvious connection between all those mighty happenings and this pitch darkness.

How did I get here!

It was not an anxious thought, but it was a valid question . . . Obviously no need for anxiety or fear of any kind. After all, at any instant he could visualize one of his numerous memorized areas: the surface of a planet, or the floor of a room, or a location on a spaceship. And be gone from this small bed, and this small, confined place.

The problem was, if he left he might never know what he was doing here, and where here was.

So there was the purpose again, in another form: examine his absolutely ridiculous environment.

With that thought, Gosseyn once more raised his hands and arms. This time, when he found himself pushing upwards against that cushiony ceiling — so close — he braced himself. And pushed hard.

A quick discovery, then. The cushiony part was about an inch and a half thick. And it was soft, and had give in it. But beyond that he could feel something as hard as metal.

Lying there he strained against it, briefly, with all his strength. But it had no give in it. After pressing at the walls and the foot and head cushions with equal futility, Gosseyn was convinced. Still not alarmed, he lay back.

Yet the thought had already come: what else was there to do in a place like this? It seemed a shame to leave without knowing. Yet the information available seemed so limited that, in fact, there appeared to be only one more exploration for him to make.

. . . All those rubber tubes my body is attached to: what am I getting from them?

More important, what would happen if the extra-brain transported him suddenly with the speed of twenty-decimal similarity?

It seemed a real concern: what would happen to whatever those tubes were transmitting into his body? Or — slightly belated thought   removing from his body: what about that?

Gosseyn allowed several tens of seconds to go by while he considered the implications. In the end, it seemed irrelevant. Because, out there, he didn't need any attachments. Every remembered area for the twenty-decimal method by which he travelled vast distances, when necessary, was in a location that was relatively safe for him as a living, oxygen-breathing life form.

Lying there, it struck him that the analysis, by itself, was almost the equivalent of a decision to leave. Almost — but not quite!

11

. . . Because, something happened to me that brought me here into this prison. That something had to be almost magically powerful to capture Gilbert Gosseyn, the man with the extra-brain.

Yes, capture him! And — worse! — the prisoner was not even aware of when or how it had been done . . . I should wait. And discover who, or what, this magical power is. Because, if he could do it once, then a second time whoever, whatever it is, might decide to take no chances.

For a while, as Gosseyn relaxed and allowed his body simply to lie, unresisting, it seemed real that he should wait. But he did have another thought:

Obviously there had to be a mechanism which opened what he was in. He was in an enclosure that, in some ways, resembled a coffin. But not really. They didn't make coffins as metallically hard, and resistant, as what he had touched through the cushions. True, a man who was buried in the ground would not be able to force open the cover of his coffin; the earth itself would be totally resistant. But it would not be a steely metal resistance. Coffin covers had 'give' in them, to some extent. A cover would give a little inside the box that coffins were placed in; particularly luxurious coffins like this one.

That train of thought had a short life in his mind. Because if this were a coffin, it was no problem to him. Five or six feet of packed earth on top of a coffin and its box was no barrier to twenty-decimal similarity.

Gosseyn actually shook his head, chidingly. The fact was, it was a meaningless thought for him to have had. People in coffins didn't have little rubber tubes stuck to several dozen parts of their bodies.

He was about to lie back again, when he had a thought that had no relation to anything. The thought was: 'This is Gilbert Gosseyn. I must have blanked out. What happened?'

Several voices answered in some way. What was peculiar about them was that although the thoughts seemed to derive from other persons, they came through as his own thoughts. The meaning was: 'Leej seems to have had a bad reaction, too.' The impression was of Eldred Crang speaking. Another meaning: '*My* impression is that something big happened, but I don't know what.' And the impression of *that* was that the words came from John Prescott. And Crang said, 'Patricia, dear, get the doctors in here. Fortunately we've got help standing by.'

'Yes,' — that was the first voice again — 'get the doctors. But right now, before we lose our impressions, let me say that at this moment I have the feeling that there are two Gilbert Gosseyns.' Pause. 'Anyone got anything to match that?'

Another thought from (impression) Eldred Crang: 'Oh, Leej is coming to. Leej, Leej, any impressions? Any predictions?'

It was a faraway voice that answered: 'Something happened. Something absolutely colossal. We didn't fail completely . . . I have a strange certainty about that. But — it isn't a matter for prediction. It's already happened, whatever it is. I, uh, don't get a thing.'

'Lie back, dear.' Patricia's voice was also, somehow, coming through another mind. 'Let the doctor check you.'

For Gilbert Gosseyn, lying there in the pitch darkness of what could have been a grave, but probably wasn't, the strange feeling had come to him that he was mentally unwell.

— Now, I remember, he thought uneasily, we were going to make the jump from this galaxy to that other one, but . . .

As his mind came to the vagueness of that 'but', a man's voice said almost directly into his ear: 'There's only one distortion in his brain profile that doesn't resolve. But there's no power connection to that. So he can't use that against us in any way that we can anticipate. But now what do we do?'

It was a question that was surely as applicable to Gosseyn himself as it was to the speaker. The time had clearly come for another cortical-thalamic pause.

He noticed that this time he was more hopeful. True, there was silence again, and the darkness remained as black as ever. Also, he was still lying on the couch; and the feel of his naked body, with its numerous attachments, was still there, exactly the same.

But as Gosseyn mentally replayed the words he had heard, their implication was that he was being closely observed by someone who spoke the English language of Earth.

He visualized the exterior condition in its drabbest form, taking into account what had been said: . . . I'm guessing that I'm inside a metal box, roughly the shape of a coffin. The box is resting on a solid table in a laboratory. And electronic devices are peering at me after the manner of X-ray machines or certain types of particle initiators. Whoever is doing the looking, doesn't know that I am Gilbert Gosseyn, because that brief, spoken analysis was impersonal; and although he demonstrated exceptional refinement of understanding – and apparently noticed the extra-brain inside my head – the observer showed no awareness of identity . . .

Accordingly, this was a stranger, and not connected in any knowledgeable way with what Gilbert Gosseyn had been doing out there in the exterior universe.

Presumably, there would presently be more observations made; and the prisoner's best purpose was: wait at least a little longer in the hope of obtaining some kind of meaningful information. He really ought to know what had happened, and what was happening.

He had not long to wait. A somewhat deeper, more baritone-ish voice said, also in English: 'Tell me the exact circumstances whereby you took this person aboard.'

'Sir,' was the courteous reply, 'we detected a capsule floating in space. Our spy rays observed that there was a male human being inside, who seemed to be either sleeping or unconscious. However, now that we have him aboard, closer observation has determined that he was in a special state of suspended animation, whereby the brain was receptive to a variety of incoming signals. What those signals are is not wholly clear to us. But he seems to be a recipient of all the thoughts of an Alter-Ego, who is actively pursuing some life situation while in a state of normal activity many light-years distant.'

Another pause. Then the second voice said, 'Perhaps he needs to be placed under stress. So let's leave him isolated, as he is – and let him be aware.'

'Of what?'

'We'll consult with the biology department.'

A new voice, quiet, determined, holding in its tone a quality of higher command, said, 'I have been monitoring this experiment. And it is not on such a cautious basis that a decision can be made. Our problem is severe. We don't know where we are, we don't know how we got here. Bring him out of that capsule. It may have equipment that could operate in his favor in a crisis. So let's get him away from his one possible assistance area.'

To Gilbert Gosseyn, it was a false-to-facts evaluation. Surely the one thing he needed, most of all, was to get out of his tight, little prison. Presumably, then, he would be able to see what his captors looked like; and maybe he might even find out who they were.

There were other vague thoughts operating in the back of his mind: among them, the beginning of an analysis of the words that had now given him a picture of where these people had found him – in a capsule floating in space. The location raised as many questions as it answered – but better not to think of that now.

Because he had a feeling of movement. The movement seemed to be in the direction that his head was pointed. Gosseyn reached up tentatively to check his impression. Moments after he had touched the cushiony stuff above him, there was no question of it: the 'ceiling' was moving past him towards his feet; moving very slowly.

The double awareness brought a mental picture of a container with a sliding bed in it. Interesting, and logical, that people who could 'see' inside a human brain, were able with their instruments to observe the mechanism by which the capsule was put together, and were in the process of unlocking it.

Gosseyn anticipated that, any instant now, the head end of the capsule would fold back, or release, and light from the room would glare into his eyes. In a kind of way, then, he braced himself for the shock of the brightness.

What actually happened: the movement under him ceased. A sudden freshness touched his cheeks. It was another level of perception, or maybe several levels. More air around him, and a tiny change in temperature: cooler.

Which suggested that his head and body had emerged into a room that was as dark as his prison had been.

. . . They're really taking no chances!

What was doubly interesting was that, except for the flexible rubber devices attached to his body, presumably he could now get up.

But he didn't.

The memory of what he had heard held him back from any sudden movement. His memory of the background of the Gilbert Gosseyns — it seemed to him — was relevant to the picture evoked of a man's body found floating inside a capsule. It seemed to mean that he was now in a spaceship. Those on the spacecraft has picked up the capsule, and had taken it aboard.

The fantastic implication was: . . . I must be another Gilbert Gosseyn body, somehow awakened before the previous one died.

As he recalled it, Gosseyn One had arrived in the city of the Games Machine, on Earth, with a false memory of where he had come from. Then, after he was killed by an agent of the interstellar invasion force there on earth, suddenly he was on Venus, believing himself to be the same Gosseyn. That second Gosseyn had proceeded to defeat the invasion forces, and had subsequently gone to Gorgzid, the home planet of the invaders.

That Gosseyn Number Two was still out there in far distant space, and was, in fact, the Alter Ego referred to by the third voice. And at this moment — if there could be a similar moment so far away — that Number Two was recovering from an attempt by a group to 'jump' to another galaxy, from which (they believed) the human race had come tens of thousands or a million years before.

Gosseyn Three, lying there in the pitch darkness of a location aboard what he believed was a spaceship, paused in his recollection of the past history of the Gilbert Gosseyn bodies, and, addressing that distant Gosseyn Alter Ego, said mentally, 'Have I got that correct, Gosseyn Two?'

The reply — it must have been a reply, and not just a thought of his own, because of what it said — came instantly:

'We could argue the number. My understanding was that the next group of Gosseyn bodies was eighteen years old. You seem to belong to my generation. Which makes you Number Three of those who actually emerged from their state of suspended animation and became consciously aware.'

'All right, I'm Three and you're Two. Well, Two, my question is, do you think I can handle this situation, even though I'm newly awakened?'

'You've got all the stuff I have,' came the remote reply, 'and of course you have me monitoring what's going on.'

'I have an impression you're far away, and can't be too helpful.'

'As soon as you're able, get a twenty-decimal mental picture of some floor location; and in an emergency — who knows?'

'Do you think it would be wise for both of us to be in a place where we could get killed?'

'It really wouldn't be wise.'

'Why do you think they're keeping me in a situation where I can't see anything?'

The faraway reply came at once: 'Two possibilities. First, they're just being careful. Second, their set-up is an autocracy. In such a situation, all lesser persons have to protect themselves from subsequent criticism by appearing to take no chances. That third voice sounded strong, and maybe he, also, wishes to point out later that he proceeded step by step. On that basis, you'll presently hear from Voice Number Four with even greater authority, taking *his* precautions.'

'What are you going to do?'

'We intended to organize a second jump after the first one apparently failed. But what has happened to you creates a confusion. And we now intend to delay until your situation clarifies.'

Gosseyn Three, lying there in the darkness, was silent, noting the fleeting thoughts he had. 'Of course,' he said, 'the simplest solution could be for me to just join you out there, and try to help you —'

His thoughts stopped. Because he was getting a no. 'Okay,' he acknowledged, 'I get the reasoning. Someone conscious has to stay here. And we don't know how many sleeping Gosseyns remain at our age level, and can't be absolutely sure that there is an age eighteen group.'

He broke off, 'Anyway, I'd better concentrate on this situation. It has a powerful look to it.'

'It sure does,' came the thought from that far, faraway Gosseyn Two, 'Good luck.'

Chapter Two

So here he was — so he believed — in a room, now; no longer inside the capsule.

Emotionally, he felt more secure. The rubber attachments were explained: long ago, a number of Gosseyn bodies had been put in various hiding places. And each one, apparently, had his turn at awakening, following the death of the Gosseyn whose turn had come earlier.

Except, of course, he himself — Gosseyn Three — had awakened while Gosseyn Two was still alive. Which explained why the rubber attachments were still in place. They probably constituted an intricate system for providing sustenance, and draining body wastes, and were designed to keep each body alive while it was still in a state of suspended animation.

Except, naturally that wouldn't apply any more. Not now that he was no longer in the capsule and, so far as he could determine, in a large room.

. . . Here on this sliding bed, my body is still attached to all those rubber connectors. But the connectors themselves must have let go of whatever tanks and machines they were fastened to inside the capsule. Let go in some automatic fashion when I was moved out here —

And, somehow, through it all, he had done his breathing without any tubes. That was true both there and here.

. . . So why not disconnect this junk, and see if I can get up.

Meaning, among many other realities, could a body that had not moved, or exercised, during its entire existence, actually function muscularly? Though, come to think of it, he had moved his arms. Had pushed against the ceiling. Had probed into the various reaches of his little home.

But, surely, disconnecting would put him in a better position to act. No use just lying here. Time to force a few issues, and find out how his captors responded.

It was a do-something-himself purpose at last. Firmly, Gosseyn moved both hands down to the same location: his stomach. The biggest tube was there.

With the fingers of one hand he grasped the flesh at the point where the tube was attached. With his other hand he grasped the tube. And he was about to tug with determination – when the lights went on.

Simultaneously two pairs of hands grabbed him.

'I think *we* had better disconnect the survival equipment.'

It was the voice that he had named Voice Number Two. The identification of the speaker was somewhere in the back of Gosseyn's mind. The front part of his brain was occupied with the sudden flood of illumination. The glare was briefly too much for Gosseyn's vision centers.

He had a score of fleeting impressions, nonetheless. The room itself seemed to glitter. The two men were medium-sized individuals in white – or so it seemed in those moments of utter dazzlement. The walls seemed to be darker, but did gleam, somehow; however, they seemed far away. Vaguely, through all the confusion, he was aware that he had let go of the rubber connective to his stomach area.

His captors must have accepted that as a victory for their purpose, whatever it was. Because they stepped back, and away from him. And he was vaguely aware of them standing there, and watching him.

Gosseyn stayed where he was, slitting his eyes against the glare of light. And, swiftly now, adjusting to a realization that there was a source of intense brightness directly above him. Which had undoubtedly caused most of his initial vision difficulty.

Moments after that discovery, since there seemed to be no point in pretending, he turned his head. Gazed directly at the two men. And said, 'I am no danger to you, gentlemen. So, tell me! What is your problem?'

It was his first attempt to obtain information. Which was, it seemed to him, the only purpose he could have at this stage, in his condition.

There was no reply. But that was not a total nothingness. Simply observing them provided an opportunity for observation, and for additional analysis of his situation.

What he was looking at, lying there with his head turned, was a large, bright room with machinery in it, and, directly facing him, a wall with row on row of built-in instrumentation. That was what had gleamed.

Interesting, also, in terms of information, that the two men were as white as he was. But their faces were, somehow subtly, not the West European-American of Earth, as the Gosseyn memory recalled them. And their clothes were absolutely ridiculous: tight-fitting, metallic looking shirts that came up to a tight fit at the neck. Puffy white pants that extended down to the knees, and, below that, white stockings were drawn tightly over lower legs that seemed to be a little on the short side.

In addition each man wore a cap over yellow-gold hair. It was a bulky head covering. What gave the cap its enlarged appearance was that an intricate instrument was mounted on top of it. Or in it; the cloth and the metal seemed to be interwoven.

The arms of each man seemed to be of normal length and shape; but they were also covered by what seemed to be the same material as the stockings. The white cloth ended at the wrists. The hands and fingers were out in the open, and apparently ready to manipulate whatever was required of them.

Even as he swiftly sized up, so to speak, the two human beings who, for want of a better identification, he silently named Voice One and Voice Two, Gosseyn found himself remembering what Voice Three had said about not knowing 'where we are or how we got here'. And he spoke again:

'Perhaps, I can help you find out what you want to know.'

Silence. Not even an attempt to reply. The men simply stood there gazing at him. Gosseyn found himself remembering what his Alter Ego had tentatively analyzed about these people: that they were not citizens of a democracy.

The implication here and now: these poor lackeys were

waiting for orders from a higher-up. Maybe from Voice Three, or higher still.

In a way, then, the analysis proved to be correct. From a point in the ceiling, an entirely different voice said grimly: 'The prisoner is our only contact with what happened to us. So push at him to find out what he knows. And don't be so gentle, or slow!'

Gosseyn had time to name him Voice Four. At which moment Voice Two stirred. And said courteously, 'Sir, shall we disconnect the prisoner from his life support system?'

The reply was absolutely, wonderfully devious. Voice Four said, 'Of course. But don't make any mistakes.'

Those words almost distracted Gosseyn. Because the meaning seemed to be a total — but total — validation of his Alter Ego's evaluation of the political system of these people.

Somehow, in spite of that marvellous meaning, Gosseyn managed to notice a phenomenon: in speaking as he did, the mouth of Voice Two had parted; and he undoubtedly said something. But it wasn't from his mouth that the English words were spoken. *They* came from the instrument in the cap at the top of the man's head.

Presumably, Gosseyn could have attempted an evaluation of the nature of a science that had taken a language out of his brain — or was taking it moment by moment. But the fact of such a system, and a fleeting awareness of its reality, was all that he had time for.

What the fleeting awareness told him was that here, apparently, was a computer-level explanation for what, in a universe of millions of languages, had briefly seemed to imply that here, indeed, were special people. There was no time, then, for analysis of how such a machine operated. Because, even as that much simpler reality — of the existence of a mechanical method of speaking another language — penetrated . . . Gosseyn saw that Voice One was approaching him.

The man had a faint smile on his somewhat square face. It was the kind of smile that his shared memory of the experiences of Gosseyn One and Two on Earth would describe as being satiric. As the man paused, and stared down at Gosseyn, his eyes, seen close up, were dark gray in color. And the smile gave them what would, on Earth, have been considered a sly, knowing look.

His manner did not appear threatening. And, actually, for a man lying on his back there seemed to be no response that could be meaningful quickly enough. Except just wait for, at least, the other man's first move.

The 'move' was, as it turned out, more words. The voice box from Voice One's cap said, 'As you may have heard, our instructions are to remove all this!' His hand and arm came up: the hand and one finger indicated the rubber tubing. Voice One finished, 'And we are also instructed to remove it rapidly, as you heard.'

There still seemed no need for a response on any level. But Gosseyn was vaguely unhappy with himself, suddenly. The man's voice had a one-up tone in it.

. . . Am I missing something? Or rather — Gosseyn silently corrected himself — have I already missed it?

Voice One was continuing with the same faint, knowing smile: 'I wish to reassure you that the speed at which these devices are going to be removed will not in any way discommode you, because' — triumphant tone — 'they all disconnected automatically on a lower level when you were removed from the capsule.'

The reaction seemed excessive; and — it occurred to Gosseyn — not necessarily a precise truth. Some of the rubber tubes might be connected through his skin to internal organs, or blood vessels, or nerves; and should not be wrenched loose.

Nevertheless, he lay silent as the hands and fingers of Voice One touched his skin. And pulled. And tugged. And wiggled. Always the object of the action was one of the tubes, as they were removed, one by one. There was no pain at all, which was interesting, and relieving; but also he was able to have a thought or two about his situation. The result: a double purpose.

And so presently, as Voice One, still smiling slyly, stepped back, Gosseyn sat up. Twisted his body. Swung his feet over the edge. And sat there, still naked, facing his captors.

Because of his purpose, it was not a time, if he could help it, for more conversation. Thus, even as he came to his feet, and as he straightened, he was turning slightly. And looking.

What his eyes sought, then, was a view of the capsule from which his 'bed' had been ejected. Exactly what he expected in that purposeful action of looking was not obvious to his inner self. And so, several seconds went by before the huge thing that was there registered.

His first impression was that he was looking at a special wall with an unusual door that seemed to lead into a darkened area. And it took several seconds for his mind to adjust to the reality that the darkened area was the inside of the capsule.

. . . A long, big, rectangular object with – he noted – a metal casing. Seeing the twenty foot high, and – he estimated – forty foot long container, was instantly reassuring. Because one of his mental hang-ups had been: even if there was equipment for re-processing the wastes of a living creature, where was the storage space for all the liquid that would be needed for even one human-sized body?

In a way, it still didn't look big enough. But maybe – he analyzed – that was the best the Games Machine on Earth had been able to do before it was destroyed.

As he turned once more to face the men in the laboratory, it seemed as if part two of his purpose should not be delayed. And so, remembering that Gosseyn Two . . . out there . . . had offered help in an emergency, the third Gosseyn decided to take the time for the precaution that would make that possible.

So he looked down, now, at the floor, slightly off to one side – where there was a clear space – and mentally 'photographed' it in the twenty-decimal fashion.

Without pausing to see what his captors were doing, he half-turned towards the 'bed' section. Looked down at it. And in the same way made a detailed picture in his mind that constituted twenty-decimal duplication.

Since all his actions had taken place within the time of one minute, it was obvious to Gosseyn that what he had done was not really well considered. But the reality – so it seemed – was that here in this capsule and its ancillaries was his home territory. And it could be that there were things here that would later be useful, even vital, to his survival.

His defensive acts completed, he glanced now, finally, towards Voice One and, beyond, Voice Two. As he did so, there was an interruption: 'Your excellency' – it was Voice Three, speaking from the ceiling – 'may I say something urgent?'

There was a pause. Then, also from the ceiling: 'For what purpose?' Voice Four spoke in an even tone.

'Sir, the prisoner's brain manifested an unusual configuration of energy flows, according to our instruments.'

'You mean – just now?'

'Yes, excellency.'

Pause. Then: 'Well, prisoner, what did you do?' Voice Four spoke in a demanding, sharp tone.

To Gosseyn it was one of those special moments when the science of General Semantics was needed in its drabbest fashion.

Accordingly, he said, 'Sir, as I climbed off the couch on which, as you know, I had been at rest for an indeterminate time, and to which I had been attached until I was released a very short time ago, my first interest was in the craft that, according to the words spoken by your aides during the past many minutes, has been a transport for my body. I had, and have, no recollection of ever having seen this craft, which the words I overheard described as a capsule found floating in space. So I gazed at it out of genuine curiosity. Then I turned my attention to the couch itself. And that's it, sir. In both instances, I was extremely interested. Perhaps this registered on your dials in some excessive way.'

Even as he was speaking the elaborately evasive explanation, Gosseyn found himself progressively unhappy with the necessity for doing so. Although the long-winded explanation-type-of-thing was, in a negative fashion, within the frame of General Semantics, and definitely a technique, a more basic reality of the human nervous system was that lying, or evasiveness, were not good for the individual. Worse, he had the unpleasant feeling that he was only at the beginning of a period where evasive answers would be required for his survival.

There was silence after he had spoken. He could see that

Voice One and Voice Two were standing very quietly. And it seemed advisable for him to imitate them while 'his excellency' considered the over-verbal reply the 'prisoner' had given.

It was not too difficult to guess what had happened. Apparently, their instruments had reacted in some way to the brain processes with which he had achieved his two actions of mentally photographing with twenty-decimal accuracy the two locations in the room, that he had selected as being most necessary for him in the event that there were further developments at some future time. And that act of 'photography' was not a phemonenon that he cared to describe to his captors.

It was more than that. He realized he was startled in a complex way by the fact that they had, twice now, been able to detect his extra-brain in action — the first time when he communicated with Gosseyn Two.

The feeling of disconcertment had in it a strong implication of defilement . . . his greatness being observed by instruments. Somehow the extra-brain inter-connection with a basic reality of the universe seemed abruptly to be a more prosaic phenomenon . . . if it could be examined.

In action, what he could do transcended the known inter-galactic vastness; yet, obviously, there were energy flows involved.

What was still missing was the nature of those flows . . . One of these days, he thought . . . It was a vague beginning of a purpose: to discover the underlying dynamics. But even as he had that tiny, initial consideration, the expected interruption came.

Abruptly Voice Four spoke in the tone of a commander giving an order: 'Remove this person from this room, and from all contact with this area. Do not bring him back here for any reason without the consent of top authority!'

The removal that followed had only one delay in it. Voice Two reached to a wall, and grabbed what looked like a gray uniform. The coat part was flung at Gosseyn; and, as he caught it, the two men jumped forward, and slipped what seemed to be pajama bottoms over his lower legs.

Realizing that he was being given clothes, and that super-speed was demanded by Voice Four, Gosseyn hastily put on the 'coat'. And then, literally, slid down into the legs of the 'pants'.

As he adjusted them over his waist, the two men jammed something onto and around his feet, one man to a foot. Gosseyn had no time to examine what the 'shoes' were like, or even to glance down at them. But they felt as if they were made of a thin, stretching rubber; and they tightened automatically over the foot and heel, and, in a sense, clamped into position.

By the time that awareness was with him. Gosseyn was being led rapidly – and unresisting – towards a door in one corner, and through that door into a narrow hallway.

Clearly, the next stage of whatever was to happen, was somewhere ahead.

Chapter Three

Corridors   Gosscyn told himself – do not go on forever. And, since he still believed that he was on a spaceship, he felt entitled to anticipate that his two guards and he would presently arrive in another room. He presumed, further, that it would not simply be a residential room of the type found on a planet, where people lived in apartments and houses. For a location inside a spaceship – particularly, as he had reason to believe, a space warship – he expected to be another place where machinery was kept.

The first signal that, perhaps, the journey through the dimly-lit metal hallway was about to end, was that Voice One and Voice Two slackened their rapid walking. And their gripping fingers on his arms slowed his walk, also. Naturally he adjusted to the easier pace immediately. And, when moments later, they stopped before a barrier, he was not surprised when a hand reached past him, and touched something in the wall.

There was a click. And then the wall moved, and became a sliding door. There was brightness beyond. Gosseyn needed no urging. Even as they pushed him, he stepped forward willingly. And there it was: a room.

It was a large room, with walls and ceilings of what seemed to be a glassy substance. The glass was opaque. The walls were light blue in color, and the ceiling a darker shade of blue. The floor that spread a good hundred feet in front of Gosseyn looked different.

A hundred long, and about seventy wide, of emptiness. No machinery was visible. No tables. No chairs. No equipment. The floor seemed to be made of some non-glassy material, but was vaguely bluish in color and was decorated by an unusually intricate and repetitive design.

The deserted condition of what he had been brought to evoked a feeling of surprise. But there seemed to be nothing to do but await further communication.

Once more, Gosseyn waited. His captors had removed their hands from him. And so, tentatively and slowly, Gosseyn took several steps forward, thereby entering the room. No attempt was made to stop him. In fact, he was aware that Voice One and Voice Two had followed him, and were still on either side of him, as close as before.

It was Gosseyn who, after going forward half a dozen feet, came to a stop. He stood there. And it seemed to him that there was still no purpose he could have in this situation, except a sort of re-affirmation of future purpose: keep finding out, if possible, what this big ship was and where it has come from. Provide only minimum clues about himself. Do nothing dramatic, or revealing, except in an emergency. But he didn't know at the moment what he meant by an emergency.

With those limitations in mind, he parted his lips, intending to test if there were any communication outlets in the glassy stuff on either side or above.

And he actually, then, had time to say, 'My impression is that I am being badly treated for no good reason. I should not be regarded as a pris —'

That was as far as he got. From the glassy ceiling Voice Four interrupted, coldly: 'You will presently receive the exact treatment that you deserve. In our predicament, we are entitled to be intensely suspicious when, after being precipitated to an unknown area of space, we find a capsule in that new location with you in it. And the fact that, on being awakened, you were immediately in communication with some distant Alter Ego makes you very suspect, indeed. Accordingly —'

Pause, then: 'Accordingly, we have brought you to this room, which we normally use for lectures, to be interviewed in the presence of our top specialists, who will determine your fate in not too many minutes.'

Almost without pause, Four added commandingly to what

29

were evidently subordinates, 'Take him to the podium!'

That last part, at least — it seemed to Gosseyn — had very little, or no reality. As he was led — he moved willingly, as before — across the intricately designed floor of that empty, empty 'lecture' room, no podium was visible.

Except that when his guards and he were halfway to the far end of the room — where they seemed to be heading — the floor there suddenly moved.

Lifted. Silently raised itself about two feet.

Simultaneously a complex of movements began on the raised portion. Parts of the 'podium' floor folded upward. Suddenly there was a table taking shape, and chairs behind it. They faced towards the length of the room.

Several smaller movements between the platform and the floor produced a set of small steps.

Moments later his guards and he came to the steps. And, since they seemed to be a destination, Gosseyn climbed them without a word. He thereupon also presumed his next move: without looking back, or awaiting instruction, he walked around the table, and sat down in the middle chair.

. . . Just in time to see the hundred feet of floor, over which he had just been escorted . . . start moving. Up.

It was no longer a complete surprise. As he gazed, interested, the intricate floor design was wordlessly explained. Each of the repetitive decorations, it quickly developed, was a folded-down chair. Which now folded up. And clicked into place.

Within a minute several hundred seats in the time-honoured rows of auditoriums, theaters, and lecture rooms, were waiting out there in front of him for —

Click! click! click!

In three separate locations — back, middle and front — of both of the side walls a wall section slid back. Through the six doorways, so swiftly created, trooped long lines of men. They were definitely all males, but differently arrayed than Voice One and Voice Two. In face and body they resembled his two guards. But their clothing was not puffed out. Was more streamlined, and uniformly gray.

And that, of course, was the clue: these were uniforms.

Those who wore them must be military personnel.

Gosseyn held himself, unhappily, in his chair, as the long lines of 'top specialists' — he recalled the status as named by Voice Four — walked in through the six doors. Seemed to know where they were supposed to sit. And virtually, within a minute, were sitting there.

Staring at him.

. . . .To be in a lecture room, sitting down at a table on the podium facing an audience: it was an Earth stereotype for professors and other lecturers.

So it required a conscious mental effort on Gosseyn's part to dismiss those automatic memory associations. It was not that the recollections of the stereotype took over his awareness; but they were there intruding, and interfering just enough to divert his attention from what, at another level of awareness, he believed was the hour of decision.

Voice Four had taken the big step. Thus, in a single action, the man was warding off responsibility for anything that might now occur, or be done.

In an autocracy, what Voice Four had done had to be close to the ultimate defense.

. . . Can I have any meaningful approach to what is about to happen? It was Gosseyn's silent question to himself.

Before he could analyze what such an approach might be there was a sound to his right of a chair scraping. As Gosseyn turned to look he saw that a large man, also in a gray uniform, was in the act of sitting down. At the moment — in that first look — there was no indication of where the new arrival had come from. Undoubtedly, another sliding door.

The big man had a square face, and a big, bushy head of brown hair sticking out from under the complicated head covering *he* wore. He must have been aware of Gosseyn's glance. But he did not turn his head to acknowledge the look or the presence.

. . . Making sure, thought Gosseyn, cynical again, that no one, afterward, could accuse him in any way of treating the prisoner as a fellow human being.

The newcomer was clearly a key figure. For he raised his right hand and arm stiffly in front of him. Down there in the audience there was surprisingly little shuffling, or sound. But if there had been, the authoritatively raised arm was clearly intended to stifle it.

After waiting several moments, apparently to make sure he had everyone's attention, the big man parted his lips, and said in English: 'In the name of his Divine Majesty, I call this meeting to order.'

For Gosseyn it was a brief period of confusion. Because, English − spoken directly. At once his earlier analysis of the source of the spoken English tongue (his belief that it came from the headgear, as a translation) was made meaningless.

That was only his first reaction and awareness. The second followed at the speed of thought. Because every word his seat mate had spoken was loud, obviously intended for the audience to hear. But the voice that spoke the words was that of Voice Four.

So . . . no question; the analysis was off somewhere to one side of his thought: Voice Four was a somebody in the hierarchy that was confronting him in this determined fashion.

But, of course, the biggest revelation were the words: 'In the name of his Divine Majesty . . .' There, finally, was the ultimate authority in this fantastic situation into which the third living Gilbert Gosseyn had been awakened. And, since everybody was being so careful, it was evident that 'his Majesty' operated in the grimmer regions of penalties and autocratic rule.

The tumble of thoughts in Gosseyn's brain came to a pause. Because, suddenly, more was happening: out there on the floor a rhythmic action. Every man in the audience leaped − virtually leaped − to his feet. Saluted. And sat down again.

Then there was complete quiet.

The speed of the entire sequence, from the moment the revealing words were vibrantly spoken to the final silence, left the one neutral listener essentially blank.

Not totally blank, of course. The meaning of 'Divine Majesty' kept stirring associations. And there remained the fantastic fact that English was being spoken and understood by everyone. Yet, already, it was very apparent at this stage that any thought he could have on what had happened would be mere speculation. And he had — it seemed to Gosseyn — already done enough of that.

Time, therefore, for his own verbal approach to these people . . . The first words he spoke, after he had had that decisive thought, were easy. Because: when in doubt throw the onus of — whatever (in this case, answers) — upon the other party.

What he said was, 'I don't understand what your predicament is. Earlier I heard the statement that you people don't know where you are. But the question to that has to be: in relation to what? Where are you from? And who are you?'

A pause. In speaking, he had turned to face the big man, presuming that, since the two of them were on the podium, any question and answer cycle would be between himself and Voice Four.

There was a pause. A pair of orange-yellowish eyes stared into his — color unknown; unless all the Gosseyn eyes were the same, in which case steely-gray was what Voice Four was seeing.

It was the orange-yellow gaze that narrowed abruptly. Whereupon the hard, accustomed-to-command voice said, 'We'll do the questioning. What is your name?'

Gosseyn did not argue. It seemed to him that only the truth would evoke from these people the information that he wanted.

'My name is Gilbert Gosseyn,' he said.

'Where are you from?'

'Essentially,' said Gosseyn, 'I am a human being from a sun called Sol, and from a planet, Earth, in that sun's system.'

There seemed no point in volunteering that Gosseyn One and Gosseyn Two believed that Mankind of Earth apparently had come long ago from another galaxy.

'What were you doing in a state of suspended animation in a space capsule?'

Gosseyn took time for a deep breath. Undoubtedly this was the big question. But since they already had significant data, Gosseyn said in the same even voice, 'I am a duplicate body scheduled to awaken if my Alter Ego is killed.'

'Has he been killed?'

Gosseyn did not hesitate. 'As you should know only too well, I was awakened by the equipment of your ship. So now there are two of us; but we are far apart.'

'Is this a common technique for personality survival among the human beings who live on the planet Earth?'

'No, it is unique to myself and my predecessors.'

'Do you have any explanation for your special situation?'

'Not really. A few speculations on the part of my predecessor that would take a while to tell'

'Very well.' The face staring at him was suddenly grim. 'How would you explain the coincidence of 178,000 warships of the Dzan empire suddenly, without warning, finding themselves in an unknown part of space, and in that space is a capsule with you in it in this unawakened state?'

After a period of blankness, Gosseyn made the cortical-thalamic pause. He was thinking: I asked for it. It was information I wanted . . . And the trouble was that he had got more than he bargained for. He was aware of a vague analytical function in his mind adding up figures, among other items, including the possibility that on each of those warships were thousands of fighting men.

It was an event in space-time so colossal that, finally, it seemed to him only General Semantics could offer a conditional answer. With that thought he said, carefully, 'There is a possibility that at base the universe is a seeming, not a being; and that if, by any means, that seemingness is triggered, the nothingness momentarily asserts. During such a split-instant distance has no meaning.'

It did not seem advisable to reveal that this was the frame within which — it was believed — the extra-brain of the Gilbert Gosseyns operated during twenty-decimal similarity travel.

Even as Gosseyn had the cautionary thought his eyes were watching the face of Four, as that face reflected the big man's reaction. In that face Gosseyn could almost see the man evaluate the fantastic meaning. Consider each datum. Arrive, finally, at the enigma.

'Yes' — the tone was argumentative though not angry — 'but what would be the connecting factor between that point in space where we were engaged in a major battle with the fleet of our mortal enemy, and this area in space where you were in that capsule?'

No question — thought Gosseyn after a pause . . . I'm getting more information than I bargained for. Because, battle. 178,000 Dzan battleships against a 'mortal' enemy. The meaning was 'major' on a level beyond the grasp of the human mind. It was an event in space-time overshadowing even the great battle of the Sixth Decant between the colossal forces of Enro the Red and the League; which Gosseyn Two had managed to bring to a halt in his defeat of the Follower.

The implications brought a thought of equal vast meaning; and the words came almost automatically: 'What do you think happened to your enemy at that moment? Is it possible that you were lucky enough to leave him and his fleet . . . back there?'

'Your concept of what is lucky,' came the immediate cold reply, 'is not ours. Our disappearance from that battle means that our vast civilization . . . back there . . . now lies at the mercy of a hostile non-human culture. And it is our belief that you are in some way responsible for this disaster. So —'

As Voice Four paused, threateningly, there was an interruption. A young boy's high, treble voice yelled from a source in the ceiling:

'Bring him up here! I want to see him! I'll find out what happened! I'll handle him!'

Complete surprise. And amazing what happened then. Out on the floor everybody stood up, and saluted. And remained standing. From beside Gosseyn, a suddenly breathless Voice Four said urgently, 'Yes, your Majesty! At once, your Majesty!'

Unexpected development! . . . A boy king, with total power —

But Gosseyn did have a thought: What kind of power?

Chapter Four

It was a golden room. That was Gosseyn's first impression:
decoration emphasizing the color of golden yellow. Plush gold
floors, and gold-colored hangings on the walls. The walls
themselves, where they showed through here and there, seemed
to be silver gray.

He had a vague awareness of other colors, used as contrast.
But there was no time to notice such additional details. Because,
also, at the moment he was led into the room, he saw that at one
end of the room was a small dais, and on it was a large gold-
colored chair.

In that chair sat the boy-emperor.

Several dozen men in gleaming clothes were standing off to
one side. And what made things difficult for Gosseyn as he
entered was that the door he came through was directly across
from this group of . . . courtiers?

So that he actually noticed them first. Whereupon, he had to
turn his head to his right to see the small boy in the silver shining
suit who sat on the golden throne chair.

It was obvious that the boy had already seen him and his
escort. Because by the time Gosseyn became aware of him the
boy's hand and arm were already raised. Instants later he spoke
in the same boyish voice that Gosseyn had already heard, and
with the same anger in it.

'We've been waiting!' the high-pitched treble voice said.
'What kept you? Where have you been?'

Four had stopped respectfully. His face, seen from the
side, was tense with awareness of the unreasonable impatience
in the question, and of the impossibility of explaining to a
boy that it required time to cover distances. 'We ran

all the way, your Majesty,' said Four.

Four added quickly, 'After we got the prisoner started, that is. He resisted.'

It took several moments for Gosseyn to comprehend the perfection of that accusation. By speaking those final words Four had skilfully absolved himself of blame. And had simultaneously placed the onus upon the one person who could probably not defend himself from the lie. And what was even more important, it was equally probable that, being already a prisoner, he was in no more danger than he had been anyway.

The truth was that, back in the lecture room, as Four grabbed at his arm, Gosseyn had got the idea at once that there must be no delay. So, as he was shoved through the door at the rear of the podium, he willingly broke into a loping run.

The brief memory of those events was interrupted. 'Bring him over here in front of me!' the yelling voice commanded. 'I'll show him!'

This time they merely walked. But another awareness was in Gosseyn's brain. His extra-brain was in a state of stimulation. It was receiving an energy flow. Different. No such sensation had ever been perceived by the earlier Gosseyns, whose memory he shared.

It changed his purpose. He had intended to be neutral. Intended to await events. To suspend judgment and delay any decision for action of his own until he found out what made this boy dangerous to adults.

After all, human history on earth had numerous records of boys becoming heirs to thrones, and of grown-ups dealing skilfully with all the consequent problems.

This was different.

And, since he didn't know exactly what the difference was, Gosseyn initiated the extra-brain mechanism for total awareness of the boy emperor's body. It was a complete mental photograph of every molecule, atom, electron and particle.

The boy was speaking. 'We're going to get your secrets out of you. Every bit of information. How you did this to our ship. So start talking. And just so you know that I mean business I'll burn you a little bit.'

Even afterwards Gosseyn could not be quite sure what

37

happened then. A fleeting awareness was there — later — that energy was building up in a metal rod in the throne chair above the boy's head, and that the energy came from the boy.

It was too fast for analysis. And his response, having been pre-set, was at a speed too great for visual, or auditory, or analytical awareness.

In that split instant his extra-brain similarized the body of the boy emperor onto the couch of the capsule on which, earlier, his own body had lain.

It was one of the two areas of the ship that he had 'photographed' for future similarization escape purposes. And he chose it for the boy because it was a cushion, or mattress. And it would be more comfortable to arrive there than on the floor.

During the next few moments, inside the throne room, there took place a series of events.

The energized rod on the throne chair actually lit up, and a small flame leaped from it. The flame hit the ceiling with a sputtering sound.

Beside Gosseyn, Four made a startled sound. And to his left, and behind, there was a collective gasp that could only have come from the courtiers.

In front of all of them the throne chair was visibly unoccupied. The boy-emperor had disappeared.

At least a dozen seconds went by.

It was a distinct period of time. Each passing instant seemed almost palpable because there was, almost literally, no sound or movement. Yet he knew, of course, that there were other people in the room. And, although the term had no meaning in any extended sense, the *feeling* Gosseyn deduced as existing inside the skins of the young emperor's retainers and followers, correlated with some variation of . . . dreadful pause!

Silence ended abruptly. Several people gasped.

For Gosseyn it had been a valuable few seconds. During that pause he had time to realize that he had better decide how he could guide these people to an awareness of what had happened — without being blamed.

It was purpose, but without a single thought, yet, of what his explanation might be.

At the moment all he had was a limited recollection of what

38

had happened. Standing there, he took the time to try to recall the details.

His extra-brain had detected a particle flow in those fractional instants when the flow began . . . before it gained the full force it would have a few millionths of a second later. Unexpected, definitely. But fortunately he had pre-set a twenty-decimal similarity as he realized how dangerous the imperial boy was.

All of those particles were diverted to the energy rod behind the boy. And the resultant momentary energy shine had actually made a crackling, hissing sound.

The unexpected, incredible reality was that here, in the boy, was something of the same order of magnitude as the Gilbert Gosseyn extra-brain. The young emperor had an equivalent equipment inside his head of an additional portion of brain matter. A special mass of cells that was not possessed by normal human beings.

Unfortunately, it was not merely a defensive mechanism. It operated by direct control of energy, which could be guided to a target. The boy's stated intent had been to 'burn' Gosseyn 'a little bit'. The limitation implied some kind of moral consideration. Which further suggested that there had been an attempt somewhere in the boy's early training to install restraint.

Clearly this child did not automatically kill those who offended. He merely damaged them, and thus frightened them. It was all-powerful in its way; but not as totally mad as it had seemed to begin with.

The implication: something could still be done.

It was high speed evaluation . . . that completed as Gosseyn grew aware that others were recovering from *their* shock.

Beside him Four was straightening, turning. And Gosseyn, relieved, turned with him. In time to see Four bow in the direction of the courtiers, some of whom Gosseyn now, belatedly, observed — were in uniform.

'Draydart Duart,' said Four, 'will you take charge?'

There was a pause. And, evidently, everyone but Gosseyn knew who was being addressed. For, when movement came, it was one of the uniformed men who stepped out of the group, and walked towards where Four and Gosseyn waited. The other courtiers remained where they had been at the moment of

Gosseyn's entrance, and since.

The man who came forward wore a reddish uniform. The upper part of the uniform sparkled with glinting metal shapes that, on Earth, Gosseyn would have taken for granted were decorations. On that same Earth the man who wore the uniform would have been taken for age forty or so.

And, since Four was deferring to him, he evidently represented high position indeed.

Gosseyn vaguely expected that the officer and Four would have a discussion. But, as he came up, it was Gosseyn that the military man addressed. His voice held an unexpected beseeching note in it, as he said, 'He's still alive?'

Being addressed directly, being held responsible — automatically — gave Gosseyn an opportunity to present the self-protective thought he had had.

Gosseyn said, 'This seems to be a special area of space for which you people have a strong affinity. I had a fleeting impression as the emperor disappeared that something inside the capsule, where I was found, was somehow triggered by the emperor's special brain control of energy.

'So now,' he continued his lie, as he began to expand his explanation, 'we may have our first clue as to how you got here from where you were originally. Is it possible that his Majesty was engaged in some penalizing act at the instant before the Great Transition took place?'

He concluded, 'I think you'd better send a guard of honor to the laboratory where you have the space capsule. My guess is that the boy . . . uh . . . his Majesty is inside it.'

'B-b-but,' sputtered the officer, 'we thought it might be dangerous to keep aboard. So' — his face was gray — 'we launched it the moment that you left the laboratory.'

It was the second big moment of shock.

How fast can people react? Twice? Observation by way of General Semantics established that a thalamic response could be virtually instantaneous. . . The muscles twist away from a threat. The body jerks and pulses. The voice may even utter sounds, or words. . .

How sensible were such responses? That, of course, depended

40

on how much cortical activity was incorporated into those early responses.

As far as Gosseyn could determine, very little of the cortex was involved in what he observed during those first moments after the military man uttered his fateful words. A dozen voices yelled almost simultaneously. There were sounds of people milling about. Several persons actually ran past where Gosseyn stood. If their direction showed purpose, then they seemed to be heading toward the throne chair. But, in fact, those particular movements ceased before the movers got to the throne. They stopped running, and did additional milling around.

It had the total thalamic look. But another possibility had occurred to Gosseyn. These were experienced toadies. Here were men so accustomed to being two-faced that, obviously, they would only feel relief if the imperial boy was completely and forever out of the way. Yet . . .

Equally obviously, if the emperor was still recoverable, then each man had to establish for the benefit of onlookers that he had manifested sincere concern. Probably of equal importance for the future of these courtiers, whatever developed, there would be another heir, who would later judge these intimates. And the usual tattlers would be busy reporting on the unwary.

For Gosseyn, who had his own problems, the detailed reactions of particular persons didn't matter. It seemed real to him that his own future would be more secure if the boy was still alive. So he followed a simple rule: the observation of the earlier Gosseyns was that in a crisis the military took over. So — very simply — he kept his attention on the officer who had questioned him: Draydart Duart, whose rank was surely some variation of Top Commander.

As he anticipated, the Draydart recovered quickly from his own initial shock. Whereupon he turned abruptly, and walked to a section of the wall near the throne chair. Having arrived there, he pushed aside the drapery. Touched something on the wall itself. And began to talk.

The precision reaction must have been noticed by others. Because, progressively, silence settled over the room. The elegantly dressed gentlemen-in-waiting ceased their milling and verbalizing at each other.

And so the Draydart's voice was suddenly audible as he, evidently, concluded his commands: 'Act at once! And be very careful!'

With those final admonitions the officer allowed the draperies to fall back into place. And he turned; and that lean, fortyish face and body headed towards where Gosseyn waited with Four. As he came up, he seemed to address them both, as he said:

'Naturally our instruments kept track of the capsule. It has now been located, and is in the process of being brought aboard once more.'

He added, 'A special team of scientists will open it, and escort the emperor to wherever seems best for him.'

He concluded, speaking now directly to Gosseyn, 'I'm not sure whether we should have you here when the emperor returns.'

It was interesting to Gosseyn that the Draydart could talk as if concern for the boy, and where he should be taken when he was rescued, should be what was 'best for him'; yet in the final comment take it for granted that the destination was automatic return to the throne room.

Presumably all that would be resolved at the moment of rescue. But actually there was a simple solution to Gosseyn's own situation. 'Why don't you,' he said, 'when the time comes, ask his Majesty whether he wants me present?'

There was a pause. He was looking at the officer's face; and there was visibly an adjustment of thought taking place. In seizing control as he had, the Draydart had manifested total military ascendancy over civilians. Automatically that attitude had placed the boy, mentally, in a victim category, to be moved and maneuvered for his own good according to the Draydart's best judgment. Just as the emperor would be not asked if he wished to be rescued, so in the first moments afterwards he would be treated within the frame of rules and regulations.

The pause ended. 'Of course,' acknowledged the super-commander.

It took a while; about twenty minutes. During that time everyone stood, strangely silent, waiting. People seemed to be gazing, not at each other, but off somewhere.

Abruptly there came the boyish voice again, from another

42

hidden ceiling speaker: 'Yes, I want that so-and-so to be present. Don't let him get away!'

Gosseyn decided to assume that the so-and-so referred to was himself. It seemed to him that the emperor's tone as he spoke the words didn't sound very favorable.

As he had that thought, a man's voice said from the ceiling: 'Draydart Duart, check − ' The word that followed was unknown to Gosseyn; it sounded like 'rutule'.

What happened: the officer reached quickly to one of the decorations on the left shoulder of his uniform. The small, shiny object that he grasped was something on a chain. The Draydart simply lifted the thing to his left ear. And he seemed to be listening. After only a few seconds he allowed the small, silvery decoration to drop back in place.

As he did so, he turned to the group of courtiers, and said, 'We're to adjourn to the − ' Once again it was a word unknown to Gosseyn. This one sounded like 'braid'.

But the basic meaning was obvious. The next interview would be in another room.

Presumably it was intended to be a location where the prisoner − Gilbert Gosseyn − would be confronted by more defense systems. Gosseyn, recalling how the activity of his extra-brain had already been registered on their instruments twice, had the unhappy feeling that new, protective devices would be available to defend the emperor against anything he might do in that area.

Since, in all this, his overall purpose was to defend himself and, possibly, gain more information, it seemed obvious that the moment when he would have to make some final decision was upon him.

Chapter Five

Since he had no ulterior motives in connection with 'his Majesty', Gosseyn decided there was no value in making a twenty-decimal mental photograph of any portion of the throne room.

The truth was, if for any reason he ever returned to such a significant area, it would look suspicious to everyone; and no excuse would thereafter be acceptable to the young emperor's henchmen. As of now they felt he could be of use to them in finding out what had caused their fleet to move to an unknown part of space: unknown to them, and, actually, unknown to him. So he had things to learn, also.

The immediate information available was minor. But nonetheless Gosseyn took careful note that he was led from that very throne room along a corridor to an elevator area – there were half a dozen elevators in a row. One of these took him up – he estimated – the equivalent of eight floor levels. Then he was led along another corridor, this one lined with guards in gray uniforms, each of whom drew himself stiffly erect, and made a hand motion, as the Draydart walked by.

The hand motion consisted of each guard placing the right palm on the middle of the chest. Presumably it was a lower status military salute.

The room they came to, presently, seemed to be more of a social reception area. There were settees and large chairs and tables; and the large group of courtiers, who had crowded into adjoining elevators, and had walked behind Gosseyn and his two guides – Four and the military chieftain – took up standing positions near one or another of the seats.

There seemed to be several other entrances to the big room.

From where he had stopped beside the Draydart Gosseyn could see, off to one side, part of an alcove that undoubtedly led somewhere. And there were three draped doors, one on each wall. That was in addition to the one through which he had arrived.

So here he was, standing with the others . . . waiting. Gosseyn felt no particular need to pre-plan his response to the second interview. But he felt vaguely unhappy because — what a waste of time! All these men and himself, obviously involved, he in his fashion, they in theirs, in a colossal event, but waiting now for a boy king who could be counted on to cause more problems.

Instants after he had that negative reaction, the boy came at a rapid walk in through the alcove. Surprisingly, moments after entering, the child-emperor came to a teetering halt. And then, as if it were a last moment decision, he walked forward to within a dozen feet of Gosseyn.

In its way, in view of what had happened, it was a brave action. And his bright eyes were equally brave as he stared at the prisoner. Abruptly his face twisted.

'What did you do? What did you do to me?'

It was attack. The voice was high-pitched, outraged, brave. And Gosseyn's first reaction was: okay, here we go again! Yet, after a moment, he sensed a different level of courage; and, at once, the situation seemed less threatening than . . . earlier . . . in the throne room.

— As if this boy-emperor's brief sojourn inside the blackness of the capsule had triggered, for the first time in years . . . caution.

'Your majesty' — Gosseyn spoke quietly — 'my suggestion is that, until your scientists find out how your special control of energy operates in this area of space, you use that extra part of your brain only when it is absolutely necessary.'

Surprisingly, the boy was silent. Did it mean that he was having a rational thought?

The answer to that question, Gosseyn realized grimly, was compounded by several negative aspects. The human cortex, where the ability to reason was believed to reside — and he accepted that it did — normally required until about the age of eighteen and a half, Earth time, to become physically fully developed.

Alas, the imperial boy was visibly about age twelve or thirteen. Five or more long Earth years would have to pass before he could have the necessary brain equipment. And yet, though boys of twelve were impulsive, they could learn. They could grasp ideas. They could learn, particularly, to practise restraint.

Maybe right now this boy was getting his first real lesson in self-control.

Gosseyn sighed inwardly, vaguely hopeful, as those thoughts flashed through his mind. Because, recalling the scared courtiers, the subservient military personnel, and, in fact, everybody he had met so far, it was about time.

During those moments of Gosseyn's private thoughts, the boy continued to stand. His face remained slightly twisted.

And there was no question: something was about to happen.

Was there anything Gilbert Gosseyn Three could do to channel in some acceptable fashion the strange combination of courage and incomplete brainpower that confronted him in the person of this youngster who, by inheritance, had the right to command the military crew on this warship?

Standing there, Gosseyn realized what was the real cause of his uncertainty: he had no personal life experience to help him determine what a twelve-year-old might do.

Neither he nor the earlier Gosseyns had any recollection of ever having been a boy. True, those predecessors, having been both on Earth and on other human-occupied planets, had watched children in various circumstances; and the memory of that was now in the mind of Gosseyn Three.

But what they had observed seemed to be mostly children at play. Children competing in games of sport. That was the basic awareness now. Competition within the frame of games of all kinds.

That had to be it. Hey!

In its way it had been a lightning swift mental survey of the situation. And so, abruptly, not waiting for that incomplete brain to arrive at some wrong conclusion, and, in fact, abandoning the courtesy that was due this superboy, Gosseyn spoke without waiting for permission.

He said, 'I'll bet I can hold my breath longer than you can.'

There was a distinct silence in the room. Gosseyn Three had time to be aware of adult retainers in uniform and other formal attire, stiffening, and looking – yes – startled.

Then: 'I'll bet you can't,' said the boy-emperor.

Whereupon, without waiting, he gulped in a large mouthful of air. His lungs expanded. His cheeks puffed out.

And, Gosseyn Three, responding immediately, did the same thing.

There they stood. And at first the man was thinking: well, that's one minute or so I've gained before – what?

Presumably for about sixty seconds he had headed off a contest with more serious implications: the Gosseyn extra-brain contesting again with what was, apparently, some equivalent brain power possessed by a few people (families) from wherever these people had come; one of the possessors being the boy.

With each passing second, Gosseyn became more vividly aware of how idiotic this little contest must seem to the onlooker. And yet, of course, since their emperor was involved, no one dared react adversely.

There each person stood, frozen, like the two contestants. Of the thirty or so men, not counting the guards in the background, only three – though they also did not move – seemed to be sizing up the situation speculatively.

Gosseyn could see the Draydart and Four, and a third man to one side, all three with their faces reflecting inner scheming. Seeing him looking at them, their eyes shifted. And then the third man turned back, and, deliberately seeking eye contact with Gosseyn, moved his lips, and framed the words: 'Let the emperor win.'

That was a problem which Gosseyn had already started considering. What would be best for dealing with the boy? A swift glance at the young emperor showed that his eyes were bulging, his face looking strained.

It was the moment for decision. With a gasp, Gosseyn exploded his own breath in the room. And bare instants later the boy did the same. But he yelled delightedly, 'I won! I won!'

Gosseyn, having a fully developed cortex – at least so he had reason to believe – had already had a series of second thoughts.

Accordingly, he gulped a few mouthfuls of air, smiled his acceptance of defeat, and said, 'It's the power of being young. But I'll bet there are games I can beat you at.'

The good-looking child face still needed a few more quick breaths. But it was already lighting up.

'I'll bet you can't beat me at scroob,' said the twelve-year-old finally. 'My mother doesn't want to play with me anymore because I'm too good for her.'

Gosseyn said, 'I'd have to see what kind of game it is before I argue with you. But maybe we can try a game after I've been assigned living quarters and have had a chance to eat some food.' He added, 'After all, it's time that a decision be made that I should be treated like a guest and not a prisoner; since I assure you I am quite willing to help your scientists in any way that I can.'

It was the only way he could think of to postpone an immediate challenge. And obviously, if he could win the kind of reprieve he requested, it was the best.

He was glad, then, to see that everybody looked relieved, as the boy said, 'Okay, later.'

The young emperor thereupon turned to the man who had, in effect, whispered to Gosseyn to 'let the emperor win', and said in his boyish voice, but firmly, 'Breemeg, find him living quarters in the – ' it was one more new word; it sounded like '. . . palomar. And then,' the boy continued, 'after he's eaten, bring him to the . . . Place.'

That was the way that final word seemed to be pronounced: the Place.

The courtier, Breemeg, was bowing. 'Very well, your Majesty, it shall be done immediately.'

The young emperor was turning away. 'That's where I'll be, myself.'

Gosseyn stood quietly with the others, as the boy walked off into the alcove, and out of sight.

Chapter Six

The journey to . . . Palomar . . . started out on the double. As if his guide, the sauve courtier, Breemeg, realized — as had the other guides before him — that this interlude had better be brief.

As he sped along another lengthy corridor at his fastest stride short of running, Gosseyn nevertheless took the time to glance at his companion. Breemeg's profile, earnest, intent, had the same pointed, slightly oversized nose that he had noticed in the others. The skin coloring was the same white as Earth whites, but something was subtly different; maybe it was too white, virtually bloodless. The mop of golden hair on top of the head seemed to be a physical quality common to one of the human types among these people, the other being the brown hair of Four.

Right now Breemeg's was a face with a clenched jaw and eyes narrowed, as if some unpleasant thought was working through the man's mind.

Since Gosseyn could not know what these thoughts were until they were expressed, he took the rest of the brief journey in his stride, so to speak. And he was not surprised when, presently, Breemeg and he went through a door into — it had to be —

Palomar!

His first impression: an indoor garden. Small trees. Shrubs. Some equivalent of grass. Presumably — that was the immediate thought — a large greenhouse aboard this huge vessel.

He had other fleeting awarenesses — of distinctly higher ceilings, of half-hidden doorways, dozens of them, partly visible through the shrubbery. The doors were at the far end of the garden. In between, mostly to his left — he had glimpses only — was the glint of water.

A pool? He couldn't be sure. Because, at virtually the exact moment that he and his guide stepped across the threshold of the double door that Breemeg had opened, and stepped onto the garden walk, the man said:

'Well, Mr Gosseyn, now you know the problem of the adults aboard this command vessel of the Dzan fleet. We have to spend our waking hours in sickening, miserable, outrageous subservience to a mad boy who has a special brain control of live energy.'

Unexpected remark, yes. But at some level, not totally. The earlier Gosseyns had met and observed toadies. So, now, silently, as he heard those bitter words, Gosseyn shook his head unhappily. His thought: . . . I'm about to hear an attempt to involve me in the secret politics of a resistance group. And of course the answer to that from a General Semanticist had to be — what?

Obviously, something related to survival.

He thought: . . . I'm on this ship, still — I decided to stay — not because I intended to take sides, or make special friends, but to find out what happened to cause these people to arrive in the vicinity of the space capsule where I was waiting in a very special state of suspended animation.

That had to continue to be more important to him than any problem that the Dzan lesser nobility had with their monarchy. Except —

Well to remember that the captured inhabitant of the capsule — Gilbert Gosseyn — had now been given secret information: someone or group hated the imperial power so viciously that, presumably, they were revealing that hatred with the intention of using the new arrival against the young emperor.

And, if it turned out that he did not consciously intend to involve himself, then what would the plotters do?

Would they feel that they had to silence him?

That was likely, but least likely. Because, if they were capable of murder, then it would be simpler to murder the boy and throw the blame on this strange, mysterious individual who had been brought aboard against the advice of, uh, the plotters. That could be the ploy.

Gosseyn realized that he was smiling grimly. The fact was, he thought, it would take a while for this situation to develop. And so his preliminary response had to be . . . questions.

The first question he asked seemed to be far from his basic purpose in the interrogation sequence. But it had its own significance. He asked: 'The young emperor's father — what happened to him?'

They were almost at one of the doors by the time Gosseyn spoke that warding-off sentence. The words seemed to have an impact, because Breemeg stopped. Simultaneously, he reached over and placed a restraining hand on Gosseyn's arm.

Gosseyn accepted the touch as a signal to halt. And so, he stopped also. Slowly, then, he turned to face the other man. And added to what he had already said, 'I presume the boy inherited his position from a deceased parent.'

He was looking at Breemeg's face as he spoke. And so he saw the thin lips tighten, and become thinner, if that were possible. And then that lip action reversed. The face twisted into a snarl, with the lips drawn back, as Breemeg said harshly, 'That S.O.B.!'

It was a reply that left no doubt: the unexpected revelation of this man's feelings would have to be dealt with — from now on.

Gosseyn stood silently, and waited for clarifying words that might explain the strong feelings against the missing father of the emperor. Without such additional information, it was not easy to bridge the gap between this hate-filled individual and the suave, alert courtier who had had the good sense to urge that Gosseyn let the emperor win the breath-holding contest.

And, of course, it would be equally difficult to determine what approach, deriving from General Semantics, could be used to deal with the problem. Solutions required that the person doing the solving should understand the situation.

The moments went by; and Breemeg stood there, staring. And so it seemed to Gosseyn that it was time for a practical purpose, having nothing to do with the emotional reality that held the other man rigid.

What he said had its own simpler reality: 'How long have I got before I'm due at the Place?'

'Uhhh!' said Breemeg.

If it were possible, the man's face actually seemed to turn whiter. It was as if he was coming up out of some enormous inner depth, and back to the world around him. Abruptly, his fingers on Gosseyn's wrist tightened. And tugged.

The direction of the tug was toward the door in front of them. And, suddenly — just like that — the suaveness was back.

It was the courtier who said quietly, 'We'd better get you inside, and provide you with food. His Majesty doesn't like to be kept waiting — as you should know.'

It was purpose again, which would lead to more information. Moments later the door was opened by Breemeg's free arm and hand reaching toward some equivalent of a latch, or automatic lock.

The door swung inward. As it did so Gosseyn had a quick view of a carpeted floor, a green colored settee and large green chair, with some tables off to one side. And then, from that area — where the tables were — the voice of Voice Two said: 'Come in, come in, Mr Gosseyn, we've got everything ready for you.'

In a way it was a surprise to hear that familiar voice, though not a disturbing surprise. But, as Gosseyn walked across the threshold and so into the outer room, he had already savored Voice Two's use of the word, 'we'. Thus as, first, he saw Voice Two, and then through a doorway that led to another, smaller room, Voice One, he deduced that he was to be kept in contact with a small number of individuals, particularly persons who were already acquainted with his background.

So he said, 'Hello!' to Two, and waved vaguely at One. Throughout the brief interchange he was aware of Breemeg behind him. And so it was not unexpected when the courtier said, in a tone of a superior talking to a subordinate:

'Mr Onda, what have you prepared for our guest?'

. . . So he was about to learn names. Or — as it turned out — only one name. But even that was welcome.

Voice Two — Onda — said in a tone that accepted the subservient role, 'Sir, we have chemically tested the fluids that were used in the capsule to feed our, uh, guest. And we have prepared a soup mixture combining some of the food elements we found.'

He was the larger of the two men, except for his head, which was long, whereas Voice One had a square-built face. Onda was the older of the two men. He spoke now almost apologetically, 'It will require a few hours to prepare a more substantial meal.'

Breemeg acknowledged the explanation with a curt nod that somehow conveyed imperious acceptance. Whereupon, he took Gosseyn by the arm. 'Let me show you your quarters,' he said.

It was the first actual verbal confirmation that he had, indeed, arrived at the first of his destinations. And that here, presumably, he would be staying while he was aboard ship. Gosseyn decided not to consider at that moment how long he would stay aboard. That decision should be discussed with his faraway Alter Ego.

What followed was a quick tour to, first, a bedroom, with an adjoining bath, then to a small combination study and dining room — at least that was his silent description of the place: what made it a study was that something resembling a TV screen and other electronic equipment was either on one wall, or extended from it; and there was a chair and a desk; and at one end a glossy table that could have been a dining table. A number of chairs were spaced at intervals.

He presumed it was normal that his identifications reflected Earth ideas on such matters; but then so did the apartment, with its resemblance to living quarters all over the solar system for human occupation. The similarity extended to the fourth room, which had the look of a kitchen, complete with something that looked like a cooking surface; and a small table, with a chair in front of it, where Voice One had already set up a steaming bowl of greenish-brown soup.

There were other objects, including shelving, and drawers. But the purpose of the soup was so obvious that, as Onda indicated for him to sit down in the chair in front of the bowl, he did so automatically, and definitely expected no unpleasant surprises.

So that the words that were spoken next came as a distinct shock.

It was a question, spoken by Onda: 'Perhaps, Mr Breemeg, before we proceed, you are now able to make a comment about the defect we mentioned earlier, in relation to Mr Gosseyn.'

The courtier, who had been standing off to one side, came

forward. 'The broken connection?' he asked.

'Yes, sir.'

Pause.

'General Semantics,' thought Gosseyn, ruefully, 'where are you when I need you?'

His feeling: this ship and its people continued to confront him with unanticipated situations. . . . Defect! Broken connection! – there were vague, unpleasant implications; and nothing to do but wait and find out what they were.

He saw that Breemeg had walked to the opposite side of the table, and was gazing at him. Breemeg said, 'In your opinion, are you in good health? Do you have any awareness of a weakness, or of anything missing? How are you reacting physically to so much activity after years of being in a state of suspended animation?'

On the surface it seemed to be a reasonable question; and Gosseyn was aware of himself relaxing. Reasonable – he thought – except for the negative meaning of 'defunct' and 'broken connection'.

Thinking of that, he said tentatively, 'I seem to be in good physical condition. Why do you ask?'

Breemeg nodded toward Onda. 'You tell him.'

The larger of the two scientists – which was what Gosseyn presumed they were – also did a nodding motion with that long head of his, saying, 'One of the connections from your life support system inside the capsule was broken. Examination of the two broken ends, one of which was connected to a nerve end in your neck, would indicate that the break occurred long ago.'

'So –' he shrugged – 'something that someone believed was needed to keep you in good condition in that confined area, has been missing for years.'

He broke off: 'You haven't noticed anything?'

Gosseyn had already done a swift, mental survey of his actions since awakening; and so General Semantics did something for him, now, when the direct question was asked: he had no need to re-examine what had already been evaluated. He simply shook his head. 'I feel alert and strong.'

'Well,' said Onda, in a doubtful tone, 'it's hard to believe that the builders of such equipment would include anything that wasn't vital to the life process. So — ' he straightened his thick body — 'our advice to you is, if you notice anything at all, report it at once, and maybe we can still do something to rectify the missing element.'

Gosseyn nodded. 'It is in my interest to do so.'

'Something electrical involved.' Voice One spoke for the first time from where he stood in the doorway. 'A neural stimulant of some kind.'

Gosseyn saw that Breemeg was getting restless; and since he had already noticed that there was a half-inch wide, ten-inch long, plastic straw lying beside his soup bowl, he now picked it up.

What he was presently sucking up through the straw had some of the flavor of what the earlier Gosseyns might have labeled dishwater, and a vague taste of sweetness, resembling orange juice, and an impression of fatty material in small quantities.

It turned out that his stomach was able to hold down the entire liquid mixture. At which point, as he virtually drained the bowl, he looked up and saw Breemeg was motioning to him.

The man said, 'All right, Mr Gosseyn, let's go . . .'

The Place was another garden-like approach to a somewhat more ornate door. But the emperor himself answered the bell, or whatever signal was triggered when Breemeg touched something at one side.

Gosseyn was aware of the courtier swallowing, literally — his throat moved in the gulping movement. But before the man could recover his official aplomb, the boy said dismissingly, 'You may leave, Breemeg. I'll take over our guest, thank you.'

He thereupon beckoned Gosseyn with a hand gesture. Moments after that, it was over; Breemeg, with the door closed in his face, was presumably either seething outside, or relieved to be able to depart . . .

Chapter Seven

Dutifully — in at least one meaning of the word — Gosseyn followed the boy-emperor across a large, tastefully decorated room. But noticed that here, also, as in his Palomar apartment, the elegance, which was here much greater, was nevertheless modified by the requirements of space flight.

The settees, and chairs, and tables, were built-in: everything was locked in position. And, through the carpet under his feet, he could feel the no-give metallic floor below.

He was surprised that the boy seemed to be alone. There were no visible servants, no sign of the mother, and no guards. There were several closed doors; but not a sound was audible from the rooms they presumably led into.

. . . Himself and the young emperor heading in a specific direction toward what seemed to be a decorated wall. He was not surprised when the decoration turned out to be the field of play of the game, scroob.

What am I doing here? he wondered, ruefully.

But, of course, he knew. He had saved himself from a confrontation with a mad boy by, personally, introducing the game element. And so, that same boy was now eager to introduce him to a shining surface on the wall, whereby, when you pressed a small decoration, that part of the surface changed color. They were most of the colors that he knew; and the idea was that if you could be the first to line up one color the length of that surface either up, or sideways, then you were the winner.

When a game was won the pattern was restored for a new game by pushing a decoration that was off to one side: a control button whereby a computer promptly set up a new, hidden, winning line and winning color.

There were supposed to be clues, as the young emperor explained it, in the color sequence, that turned on whenever a decoration changed color. If you were smart you could eventually read the clues, and decide which color would be the next winner, and which direction would win.

Gosseyn was smart, and, after he lost three games to a delighted young winner, he saw how he could win the fourth game. After a momentary hesitation, he, in fact, decided to win it.

The boy's reaction to the victory of his opponent was . . . he whirled. He ran across the wide part of the floor, dodging tables and chairs. Moments later he was pounding on a beautiful blue door in one corner, and yelling: 'Mother, Mother, he beat me at scroob!'

There was a pause. And then the door opened; and a young woman emerged. Or, at least, Gosseyn assumed that the blonde individual, who was dressed in a man-like uniform, with trousers, but with only a colored shirt over the upper part of the body, and no jacket . . . that this fine-faced individual was, in fact, the mother, so urgently summoned moments before.

And, indeed, when she spoke it was a woman's musical voice. What she said, was, 'Sir, Enin told me about you. He doesn't seem to remember your name clearly.'

Gosseyn pronounced it for her, and added, 'I think I can show the emperor what the clues are that lead to the winning condition.'

He continued, 'He knows some of them, but there are a few special signals.'

As he made the explanation, he was noticing her slim form, and her even-featured, distinctive face. And his judgment was that the emperor's mother could be a real beauty, properly arrayed in silks, or in dresses, generally.

He also noticed the name she had called her son: Enin . . . I'm really getting fast information on this big ship, and from top echelon people —

It could be that that had to continue to be his purpose: learn, find out, get details.

The woman was speaking again: 'No more games right now, Enin. It's time for your lessons. Off you go, dear.'

She leaned over, and kissed him on the right cheek. 'Leave Mr Gosseyn here. I'd like to speak to him.'

'All right, Mother.' The boy's voice sounded subdued. He thereupon turned to Gosseyn, and said in an almost beseeching tone: 'You're not going to be a problem of any kind, are you, Mr Gosseyn?'

Gosseyn shook his head, smilingly. 'I'm your friend and fellow game player from now on.'

The small face lit up. 'Oh, boy! We're going to have a great time.' He turned happily to the woman, and said, 'You treat him right, Mother.'

The woman nodded. 'I'll treat him just like I did your father.'

'Oh, my gosh!' The boy trembled. The blue eyes widened. 'You mean — maybe you and Mr Gosseyn will go into your bedroom, and lock the door, and won't come out for an hour, the way you and Dad used to do?'

Before she could answer, he turned to Gosseyn. 'Sir, if she takes you into her room, will you tell me afterwards what the conversation was?'

'Only with your mother's permission,' Gosseyn replied, 'will I ever reveal anything about a private conversation.'

'Oh, damn!'

'That,' continued Gosseyn, 'applies also to anything you and I discuss in private. And, as one example, I won't tell anyone that I beat you at one game of scroob — without your permission.'

'Oh!' Pause. The face looked acceptant. Then: 'I guess that makes sense.'

The mother was taking her son by the hand. 'All right, darling, off you go.' Whereupon, she led him to a brown door at the far right, opened it, and called out to someone who was evidently there: 'Your pupil has arrived. Time for lessons.'

It was a little difficult for Gosseyn to visualize the teacher's reaction to those words. Whoever it was might not be any more happy about this pupil than, for example, Breemeg and his fellow courtiers. Unless —

Could it be that here in the Place, it was a normal family life that the boy-emperor lived? Here, with his mother as an accepted and beloved guide.

But as for himself, and his progress toward anything that mattered – he could see nothing . . . I'm being shunted around from one minor situation to another. Basically, it was a zero situation.

Standing there, he couldn't even imagine anything that he could do. He was a prematurely awakened, duplicate Gilbert Gosseyn. It still seemed true that there must be a significant reason for his being discovered by the Dzan. But it was also likely that Gosseyn Two could handle all necessary investigations relating to the arrival of these people in this area of space.

Unfortunately, now that he was conscious, the idea of deliberately returning to the space capsule – which was certainly one of the options – was not something he cared to contemplate.

So here he was, an unneeded Gosseyn, who presumably – if he could help it – would be around for a while. But he had better leave the serious business to his predecessor.

'. . . How about that, Gosseyn Two?'

The reply, as it came into his mind, seemed to have a smile associated with it: 'My other self, you are in the center of the biggest event in the space-time of this galaxy; and I'm way out here with a few important friends, watching from a distance. I should tell you that Enro seems to be the most disturbed by what has happened, and would like to use our transport method, personally, to come over there, and talk to these people. So far I have resisted the idea; but even Crang would like to visit you on the command ship. Perhaps, now that you are on friendly terms with both the emperor and his mother, something could be arranged.'

Gosseyn Three replied mentally, 'For all I know, they would be interested in having visitors. But maybe not right now.'

Gosseyn Two's reply was: 'It isn't settled in our minds here that it would be a good idea at all. So we'll discuss it later.'

Gosseyn Three did not pursue the matter. It had been a swift mental conversation. But even as it was, the woman had had time to close the classroom door, had turned, and started in his direction.

It seemed to be a perfectly normal moment in time and space. As Gosseyn watched her coming towards him, he had a simple, unsophisticated thought; and so he said, apologetically, 'Madam, I imagine I should now have someone take me back to my assigned apartment until your son has further need of me.'

The young woman had paused while he was speaking. And now she stood gazing at him with an odd expression on her face. The expression included a hint of a smile. Then:

'That will be in a little over an hour,' she said. And added, 'The lesson, I mean.'

She was the Greatest Lady of this realm; and so the naming of the time lapse had no significance for Gosseyn; made no personal connection. What did strike him once more was the perfect use of English. But even that mystery was something he had no intention of discussing with her. That was for scientists to deal with. Later.

Again, considering all that he had heard, he deduced that the boy's father had somehow died in his late twenties or early thirties. The age, of course, was an Earth comparison. But, presumably, imperial widows of Dzan did not succeed their husbands in power and position.

And that fleeting thought, also, ran its rapid, unsuspecting course.

The . . . unexpected . . . came instants later, as the young woman said, earnestly, 'You're the first man to whom Enin has responded as a boy might to a father. And I'm wondering, now that I've seen you, if you would marry me, and try to do for him what no one else apparently can do?'

A faraway thought floated into Gosseyn's mind. It was a thought he had had before, but it came now with a special impact: at this moment, I am utterly surprised. I feel as if I have been taken off guard the way no one with General Semantics training ever should be.

The reality was that he was not prepared for such a proposal.

. . . Would a refusal or even hesitation in answering be regarded as a mortal insult? There was, of course, a type of man who would instantly accept all the opportunities of this situation. But men trained in the General Semantics orientation were not such a type.

Aloud, he offered the first barrier: 'Your Majesty, the honor which you offer me may not be a wise action on your part. It is

60

possible we should discuss what might be the repercussion of such a marriage for you and your son.'

The young woman smiled. There was no sign that she realized that she had, in effect, been rejected. She said, 'That's a very thoughtful remark. But it does not take into account that it is now two years since my husband and lover was killed. Therefore, before we have any discussion about the long-term situation, I wish you to come into my bedchamber, which, as you know' — she nodded toward the blue door on her left — 'adjoins this sitting room.'

She went on earnestly, 'I need very badly to be made love to by the first man I've met since his death who has instantly and automatically aroused in me feelings of desire. Come!'

She had paused about eight feet from him. Now, she walked over and put her hand on his arm. As Gosseyn unresistingly allowed himself to be led in the indicated direction, there were more of those fleeting thoughts.

. . . The problem of the man-woman relationship was not obviously the subject of General Semantics discussion. Men had from time immemorial on earth had a strong need for sexual release. Presumably this could be, and in some instances was, satisfied by many women. But mostly the individual male found himself attracted specifically to a female of his own age, or younger, who, according to psychological theory, reminded him at some deep level of his being, of his mother. So, essentially, a young woman who elicited a love response brought about a fixation in him. And she had to do numerous unmother-like things before the feeling of need diminished. There were, of course, many instances whereby presently some other woman reminded him even more strongly of his mother. And so, in due course, he was over there.

The Gosseyn bodies had never had a mother in this galaxy. No doubt, a million or more years ago, before the Great Migration, a child had been born in the traditional fashion. And it could even be that that child's early relationship with that long, long, long ago mother still permeated his subconscious memories. But it would be a little difficult to determine which of his feelings related to an ancient mother, and which were the product of his acceptance that a man should eventually have a relationship with a woman.

Incredibly, his first opportunity to have such a relationship already had hold of his arm. And, as he went with her, he could see once again that she had unusually good features, and a splendid female body. At the very instant that he noticed that — again — she made a remarkable statement. She said: 'You remind me of my father. So I feel completely confident that I have found the man most suitable, not only for Enin, but for me.'

Moments after that they were through the open door, and she was pushing it shut bchind her.

Gosseyn heard the click of a lock catching.

Chapter Eight

It was surely — Gosseyn Three thought ruefully — not one of the great moments of history.

. . . A superman — in its way that was a proper description for the Gilbert Gosseyns of this universe — was being pressured by a human-type female to participate in what appeared to be a normal sex act. The superman was resisting the opportunity; and yet he was a single man with no previous commitment to any other woman. At least equally significant, neither of his predecessors, who also had no known commitments — according to his joint memory with them — had to date had an intimate relationship with a woman.

Only two living women had had an opportunity to participate in such a relationship with a Gosseyn: Leej, and the former Patricia Hardie. So, perhaps the latter could offer an explanation as to why nothing had happened the night that she had spent in the same bedroom as Gilbert Gosseyn One.

With these numerous, sketchy considerations motivating him as the bedroom door closed behind him, Gilbert Gosseyn Three spoke mentally to his Alter Ego, far away in space:

'Can you ask the lady for an explanation, Mr Gosseyn Two?'

He realized that he was hoping for some bits of data that would help him to deal with this situation. And already there was a second awareness in him: that anything intimate he did with anyone would automatically be registered in the mind of Gosseyn Two.

It seemed to be an additional barrier to special actions of any kind, requiring something to be agreed upon on the basis of . . . I'll-look-the-other-way-if-you-will . . . sort of thing.

He was aware that, as he had these new thoughts, Gosseyn

Two was questioning the former Patricia Hardie.

There was a pause. Then the young woman's 'voice' spoke through the brain of that faraway Gosseyn Two. The 'tone' seemed faintly amused, as if it were a subject about which she hadn't previously had any thought; but if she had it would have been funny.

She said: 'If you will consult the joint Gosseyn memory, you will recall that we were all in quite a tense situation; and that I was, unknown to the other involved persons, the sister of Enro — with all of those automatic restrictions on my behaviour. And, besides, I had already met Eldred; and my fascination with the philosophy of General Semantics made him a very special person for me. Also, I should mention that Gilbert Gosseyn One seemed very much a protective type of individual to me, someone upon whom I could depend.'

She added, 'Now that we have a Gosseyn Two and a Gosseyn Three, both alive at the same time, we can realize that the first Gosseyn was, in fact, a different living being; and that subsequent Gosseyn duplicate bodies having his memories is certainly interesting, and even fascinating. But you can deduce that, taking into account all the factors I have mentioned, that night he and I spent together we were not likely to engage in an intimate personal relationship.'

She seemed to be smiling again, as she concluded: 'Somehow, I cannot bring myself to feel horribly sorry for you in your predicament. But I do have the thought that if Gosseyn One's reason for not trying to take advantage of the situation had to do with General Semantics, then we have another worthwhile moral consideration operating in the world. As you know, there are many good men in the universe, who have their own fine morality to restrain them from criminal and unkind actions; and I approve that this is so.'

The analysis by the former Patricia Hardie was somewhat long, but essentially convincing — so it seemed to Gosseyn Three. Equally important, the time involved for her to voice it appeared to be exactly what he needed to have a moral consideration of his own.

'Of course,' he thought then, 'what else?'

It seemed to be a cortical decision that he had come to. And so, there he stood near the entrance of what, even by fleeting first glance, was unmistakably a luxurious bedroom − stood and shook his head gently at the woman, who had half-turned and was looking back at him.

'My philosophy, and also my sense of protectiveness for you' − those were his rejecting words − 'do not allow me to take advantage of your good feelings for me.'

In a way it was a little late. The woman had already removed the strange unwomanly shirt, exposing some kind of filmy undergarment and the upper halves of two bare breasts. This became even more evident, and intimate, as, after he spoke, she turned all the way round and stood facing him. It was difficult to decide from her facial expression, and slightly bent forward body position, if she was in a state of shock.

'Your philosophy?' she echoed finally. 'You mean − a religion?'

'General Semantics, it's called,' said Gosseyn as blandly as he could.

'And' − she had straightened − 'it forbids sex between a woman and a man without marriage?'

Since General Semantics did not expressly forbid sex in any situation, Gosseyn Three had the wry awareness that his reasoning was being challenged at a rather high speed.

But he remained calm. He said:

'A General Semanticist, madam, is trained to take into consideration more of the realities of a situation than a person without such training.'

He continued: 'I have to admit that I have not available inside me at this moment a clear picture of all the factors that a woman General Semanticist might take into account in dealing with the instinctual behavior of herself as a devoted mother and former empress, who is also a widow. But, fortunately, we have more obvious reasons for not acting hastily in this situation.'

The woman had been staring at him, as he spoke the analysis. Now, she shook her head in what seemed to be a chiding manner.

'Was that,' she asked, 'a typical, long-winded sample of your day-to-day conversation as a General' − she hesitated − 'Semanticist?'

Gosseyn glanced mentally back over his analysis; and it was surely the most involved statement that had recently been spoken by any of the Gosseyns.

Nonetheless, he braced himself, and said, 'Madam, I want you to picture the situation that exists here. A short time ago, a stranger — myself — was brought aboard this vessel. Within an hour after he is awakened by ship scientists, the emperor's mother announces she will marry this stranger. The outward appearance is — would be — that I have used a malign mental power of some kind to influence the emperor's mother. Once such a thought was presented to the officers of this great ship, they would come charging to your defense. Nothing would dissuade them from taking whatever action they deemed necessary.'

He was aware that as he spoke there was a progressive change of expression in the woman's face and eyes: it seemed to be acceptance of his reasoning.

Indeed, moments later she began to nod. And then she said, 'I can see a speedy marriage would be unwise. But a very private liaison, with the understanding between you and me that the end-result would be marriage, should surely satisfy all your religious scruples.'

Gosseyn found himself smiling; for it was . . . surely . . . a subject to which General Semantics had never addressed itself. But he felt secure. 'Not General Semantics,' he said confidently.

During the interchange, brief though it was, the woman must have had time to have a basic thought of her own. For suddenly she smiled.

'My dear friend,' she said, in a voice that had in it the extra sweetness of sarcasm, 'one of these days you must explain General Semantics and tell me all about its God; how he has managed to restrain the passions of the most wilful and sexually determined creatures in the universe: men!'

She broke off: 'Right now I am reluctantly accepting that, for some reason, you cannot adjust to a simple reality of the way of man and woman. And perhaps I shall have to re-evaluate my first reaction to you. But even that can wait. And' — more sweetly still — 'since I accept that nothing is going to happen right now, and I've already been cooled off by this outrageous conversation, why don't you go back into that other room; and I'll join you there presently?'

'Thank you, madam,' said Gosseyn.

Whereupon he turned, and opened the door, and walked through it into the reception or living room.

Vaguely, he was ashamed of himself. But also he felt relieved because really — no commitments until this entire situation was clarified in some reasonable way . . . Right, Gosseyn Two?'

The reply came at once; but it had the same doubtful quality that was there in the back of his own mind: 'We do need more information; but Patricia, here, is shaking her head over you, and smiling.'

'Tell the lady,' communicated Gosseyn Three, 'that women have been rejecting men since time immemorial, and feeling justified about it. And no need for anybody to smile.'

It must have seemed true; because there was no reply.

Chapter Nine

Now what?

He had seated himself in one of the comfortable chairs. He waited there, expecting the woman to appear any moment. But even if she did show, the question remained:

Where do we go from here?

Gosseyn Three was aware of the puffing of his own breathing; and several times in those first restless minutes there was the sound of his clothing rubbing against the soft, luxurious upholstery on which he sat. In between those perceptions — dead silence.

The reception room continued to feed back to him the timeless beauty and costliness of an apartment that had been decorated and furnished to satisfy the requirements of people accustomed to total wealth.

But, somehow, that merely accentuated his feeling of being an intruder, without any real knowledge of his surroundings.

. . . This is pretty ridiculous, he thought.

Incredibly, one of the mightiest events in the history of two galaxies had brought this giant battleship here to this area of the Milky Way galaxy from another island universe out there in space. And had apparently accomplished the feat at the speed of twenty-decimal similarity.

The implications were not immediately analyzable. But surely this wasn't all there was. The colossal meaning of such an Event in Space Time needed to be scientifically studied and understood.

. . . And with, at least, equal certainty, men like Breemeg and the Draydart, representative of the military people, were acting in some way, and not merely waiting.

Something, in short, was happening somewhere on this vast

ship. At the very least keen minds must at this moment be wondering what was occurring between a stranger named Gilbert Gosseyn, on the one hand, and the emperor and his mother, on the other.

Somebody would come to investigate before very long.

With that thought – of an investigating group on the way – it occurred to Gosseyn that the restriction he had imposed on himself in the throne room did not apply here. . . The personal offer the woman made to me makes it mandatory that, if there is trouble, I should be able to come here and help her and the boy –

So he stood up hastily. And quickly, then, he located a place on the floor in one corner, behind drawn-back draperies. And performed with his extra-brain the mental photographing process that would enable him at a later time to come here instantly by the twenty-decimal similarity method.

Moments later, as he sat down, he grew aware that his Alter Ego was manifesting mental activity.

'I told the others what you just did' – the communication from Gosseyn Two was like his own thought, as before – 'and they feel that they should join you, leaving me here to monitor things.'

In the transmitted thought the unstated part of the meaning, the 'what you just did', was the sort of process minds did automatically. The reference was to his action of having his extra-brain 'photograph' a portion of the floor.

'You mean . . . *now*?' echoed Gosseyn Three's answering thought.

'So' – Gosseyn Two's brain was continuing – 'why don't we see if, between us, we can use your location there in that room where you are at this moment, and transmit them there, as you transmitted the young emperor's body into that space capsule. First, Eldred Crang.'

The mention of the transmission of the boy's body brought fleeting memories of other, distant photographed areas . . . still usable? he wondered.

There was a sound off to his left, and slightly behind him. Then, the thought: 'Next, Leej.'

Gosseyn Three had turned. And so he saw, and at once

recognized with his duplicate memory, that Eldred Crang was hastily stepping away from the draperies. As he did so, Leej was there, out of nowhere. She also moved rapidly aside, as Enro, and then the Prescotts, and finally Patricia Hardie Crang, also appeared, one after the other, in the room.

'But — ' mentally, belatedly, objected Gosseyn Three. 'Don't you think we should first . . .?'

He stopped. A thought had come, awareness of the beginning of difference between himself and Gosseyn Two. Obviously, since his Alter Ego and he were at different locations, they had different problems. The concerns at one location did not communicate its full impact to the Gosseyn at the other location.

It was a thought with a significant implication: in terms of experience we're going in different directions, moment by moment. Soon we will not be duplicates, one of the other . . .

No time to think about it now. There were too many things to do. Hastily Gosseyn addressed the new arrivals: 'The emperor's mother will be here any moment. Please go in there — ' he pointed to an alcove that led to a door that he had merely noticed earlier; he had no idea where it went. He finished, 'Give me time to explain to the lady what — '

They were quick. Even the mighty Enro, ruler of the Greatest Empire, after a word or two from his sister in his own language, merely smiled cynically, and then followed the others out of Gosseyn's line of vision.

If several moments passed after they had disappeared from sight, the passage of time was not recorded in Gosseyn Three's awareness. It seemed as if the newcomers were still in the act of departing when, behind him, there was a click. And when he turned the bedroom door was opening, and at once the emperor's mother emerged.

Abruptly, it was evident why there had been a delay in her appearance. She had put on a filmy gown; and the overall effect was of bluish fluffiness. Before Gosseyn Three could really examine the new clothing, the woman said, 'I've called Breemeg. He will take you back to your Palomar.'

It seemed to be a moment for — not truth — but rapid preparation for truth. Gosseyn said, 'Madam, as no doubt has been reported to you, on awakening I found myself in mental communication with someone who looks exactly like me, who at this moment is approximately 18,000 light-years from here.'

The woman was nodding. Her manner and expression were serious, as she said with a small frown: 'Everything that has happened, including the way of your arrival, has been very strange.'

Gosseyn continued earnestly, 'It's a long story. But there's no personal threat in it to anyone. However, that communication with my Alter Ego occurred at a time when he had several important persons with him — important in this area of space; and they would like to come here and talk to you and to your military and scientific personnel.'

The woman said, 'I'm sure it has to be possible. We are here in an isolated condition. One big ship, 178,000 men, and one boy and one woman.'

She added anxiously, 'It may be that it will become apparent to some of the bolder spirits aboard this warship that old rules and old loyalties no longer apply.'

She broke off: 'Tell me, in an emergency what exactly could these associates of yours do?'

It seemed to be the moment — if there ever could be one. The man braced himself, and said, 'Your permission has been mentally overheard, and your authority accepted — and so here they are.'

With that, he gestured toward the alcove. And, though what he had said was a lie, it was surely better that she had now had some advance warning.

As it was, her eyes widened. And she took a single step backward. At which, somehow, his reassurance must have braced her. For she stood, then, silent, as the two women and four men walked into the room.

Something of the shock, nevertheless, remained. '18,000 light-years,' she whispered. 'Instantly.'

Gosseyn said, 'How do you think your ship got here? From an even greater distance? And also instantly?'

All these moments he had been noticing that the frilly clothes were exactly what she should be wearing for a man whose memories seemed to have derived from Earth. So now he spoke softly, 'You're very beautiful. You'll be all right.'

71

But he, also, silently, had another thought: about what the woman had said . . . one ship with 178,000 men aboard.

Voice Four had made a larger story out of that figure: 178,000 *warships*! The transition from manpower to ship totals was evidently the consequence of a swift agreement among the civilian and military commanders of this gigantic vessel: presumably, they believed that if he was in communication with anyone, whoever was out there would be impressed by the larger figure. It would require time to get together a military group capable of defending the Milky Way against so vast a fleet. That had to be the reasoning, and clearly they were unaware of Enro and his swift, enormous super-space-battle-fleet.

But now, the queen mother had unknowingly revealed the truth.

Actually, this huge ship was a big enough Event, all by itself: a single vessel manned by a personnel totalling 178,000.

Fantastic!

Chapter Ten

Gosseyn Three stood gazing at the group. And they stared back at him.

On one level it seemed, in one of the thoughts Gosseyn had, that what he was looking at was not too unusual an assortment of human beings — except for Enro. Five of the individuals were normal-sized men and women, who could be trusted to be law-abiding. They would never cause trouble of their own volition.

. . . But — standing with them, tall, and big, and cynical even in the way he held himself, was Enro. Enro, the emperor-king of the Greatest Empire, who shrank at nothing. He had a fleet out there in the distance with as many ships in it as this Dzan battleship had men.

What was Enro doing here, with that flaming red hair and flaming murderous soul, accompanying his wonderful sister and her peaceful friends? Enro, the killer, the lusting ruler — Good God! . . .

The pictures that came through, now that Gosseyn Three was consulting the duplicate — triplicate — Gosseyn memory, were so numerous and so horrendous that . . .

With an almost physical effort Gosseyn Three ended the useless train of thought. For it was suddenly apparent, from what was in his mind from his faraway Alter Ego, that Gosseyn Two did not know the Great Man's motivation either.

. . . He had suddenly contacted his sister — came the mental message from Gosseyn Two — and since he wanted to come alone, everyone suddenly felt hope —

Enro had been the one who most desired to be transmitted to the Dzan ship.

A mystery! There he stood, tall, sardonic, bearing a small facial resemblance to his sister. But otherwise a strange, dangerous person. No reasonable deduction as to what he hoped to gain by coming here was possible with the data at hand, except –

Watch out!

Worse, there was no time, really, to consider, or even inquire from the man himself. Breemeg was coming, bringing with him all of *that* madness.

Gosseyn turned toward the emperor's mother, and asked, 'Madam, is there any place we can hide these people until we can decide what to do, and who they should talk to?'

The beautiful face relaxed into a smile. 'Through that alcove.' She pointed to where he had briefly hidden them. 'There's a door there which leads to a rather large apartment with many bedrooms.' She explained: 'We use it when Enin and I have relatives as guests.'

It certainly seemed like the ideal interim solution. The entire problem temporarily solved by another whole set of rooms, where the six could wait until necessary preliminary arrangements were made.

'. . . I'll go there with them, take a "photograph" of the floor, and join them there in the event of a threat – how's that, Gosseyn Two?'

The distant Alter Ego replied mentally: 'Sounds like a good back-up idea. I suppose that since I transmitted them there I could also return them here –' the voice in his mind from that enormous distance abruptly changed the subject – '. . . But I'd better caution you. As you have undoubtedly recorded, when I was twenty-decimaling back and forth in my efforts to handle Secoh the Follower and Enro the Red, the extra-brain progressively extended its ability for longer and longer periods the changes in the various "photographed" areas to which I transmitted myself. We may have a similar extended connection with some area in that other galaxy; and since that, so to say, kicked back on you, I suggest that you watch the twenty-decimal process inside your head. If there's any automatic process at all, put your attention at once on some nearby "photographed" location. If you do that each time, it could be that presently the connection with the remote area will come under control.'

Gosseyn Three was nodding grimly. 'I get the idea. Better to similarize to one of my locations on this ship, or even to one of yours out there in our own galaxy, rather than get involved in the complexities of the even more enormous distance.'

'Right,' was the reply. Then, with what seemed to be a smile: 'Please notice that we are mentally separating the two of us. No longer is it "Alter Ego" but "my" and "your". It will be interesting to see how that comes out. Perhaps we shall presently become two different people.'

The mental dialogue had been at the speed of thought; and all the while he had been walking with the recent arrivals into the new set of rooms. And so, as he stood, apparently casual, as the new people walked farther into the big living room of the apartment, Gosseyn Three took his extra-brain 'photograph' just inside the entrance.

Standing there, he was aware that five of the newcomers had immediately started exploring the place, and they essentially had their backs to him. Bedroom doors were being opened.

What happened next would probably have occurred sooner or later. Gosseyn was about to walk away, when John Prescott said something to his wife, Amelia.

That brought a thought; and Gosseyn went over to where the Prescotts had paused, and said with a faint frown, 'Just a minute, my last clear recollection of Mrs Prescott is that she was lying dead on Earth in the City of the Games Machine. The way you knew she was dead was that, when you gave her an injection of what was, presumably, a reviving chemical, her lips remained pale instead of turning bluish.'

Prescott was a husky man with thick, blond hair, and his wife was a slender brunette. Now the man merely smiled, and glanced questioningly at his wife. The slim woman smiled also. 'Mr Gosseyn Three,' she said, 'the wife of a Venusian Null-A, who is playing a game inside the ranks of the enemy, often has to brace herself. What you're remembering was a very unpleasant experience; but remember that a statement such as if-her-lips-don't-turn-blue-then-she's-dead is merely interesting, in terms of General Semantics. Simply saying it doesn't make it so.'

She smiled again, and finished, 'If you'll consult the joint Gosseyn memory you'll discover we had a much shorter conversation about this with Gosseyn Two.'

The memory was there after only moments. Somewhere, during the frantic fight to save Venus, the Prescotts had crossed paths with the incredibly active Gosseyn Two — who was jumping from one twenty-decimal location to another at the time, battling at virtually every stop. So that, when the couple had recently re-appeared in the company of Eldred and Patricia Crang, no additional explanation was requested, or given.

'Oh!' said Gosseyn Three, remembering. 'Yes.' He added, 'I'm glad.'

They turned away, and so did he. But, seconds later, when he glanced back, he saw that they had disappeared into one of the bedrooms, leaving in view only Leej, the Predictor woman.

She had paused, and now she stood looking directly at him. There was a faint smile on her distinctive, even-featured countenance.

Leej, the predictor woman from the planet, Yalerta; Leej, the dark-haired, who might be able to tell him a little about what the future held. Even as he had that thought, she parted her lips, and spoke:

'There's a period of about twelve minutes after you leave here,' she said, 'and then you use your extra-brain again. Which cuts off my view of your future right there.'

The shortness of the time brought a mild shock. 'Twelve minutes!' he echoed.

He was abruptly fascinated. This was his own first experience with a predictor; and here she was, friendly and volunteering information.

He said, 'Any clues as to what leads up to my action?'

'You've left the imperial apartment,' she replied, 'with that man.' She hesitated, then made the identification: 'Breemeg.' She finished, 'You're walking along. And, suddenly, you're aware of something. And that's it. For my special ability, blankness.'

Gosseyn stayed where he was; and the predictor woman must have expected it, because she didn't move either. Gosseyn said, 'I've had another thought.'

She smiled. 'I know. But say it — thoughts are not as clear as words in a prediction situation.'

Gosseyn nodded, and said, 'When you were predicting in

76

connection with Gosseyn Two and the others on the intended big jump, what exactly was your role?'

Once again, the reply was prompt. 'I decided — we decided — that I would try to predict exactly what would be the exact atomic-molecular-particle configuration of some habitable area in that other galaxy. We accepted that nothingness separated the two universes. On the basis of that prediction Gosseyn Two took an extra-brain "photograph" of my entire brain, including the prediction, and tried to similarize all of us over there in one jump. In a way it must have worked.'

Gosseyn Three was thoughtful. 'I had all those memories in my mind, of course. But they seemed so complex that I couldn't quite get the picture. In other words' — with a smile — 'pointing alone, the General Semantics ideal, meaning in this instance my memory of the event, did not quite do the job of picturing the whole event. Words do have their value.'

He finished: 'What do you think went wrong?'

'You.' It was her turn to smile. 'Picture you in that capsule receiving all of those thoughts without anyone being aware of you. So, as it turned out, you were the most receptive part of the whole process.'

'But in reverse,' he pointed out.

There was no answer. The woman just stood there. 'Thank you,' said Gosseyn. With that he went back through the door, and then the alcove, to where the emperor's mother was talking with a strange, excited, little man.

Not wanting to intrude, Gosseyn stopped. At which moment he heard the woman say, 'But I don't understand. What are you saying? Enin what?'

As Gosseyn stood there, out of sight just inside the alcove through which he had taken the others, the little man said in a shaking voice: 'He disappeared! In front of my eyes!' He jabbered on, 'You know how he is when I'm giving lessons. Quiet for a while. Then he becomes restless. Talks back. Jumps up. Gets himself a drink. No manners. But he learns. This time he was just sitting. And, poof! He was gone!'

It took a minute for the meaning to come through from the stuttering voice. But, finally, the picture being verbally presented by this highly disturbed indvidual was unmistakable.

The little guy was the young emperor's teacher. And, during the course of the lesson he had been giving the boy, he claimed to have been actually staring at his pupil when he, literally, blinked into non-existence.

It occurred to Gosseyn Three, as he listened to the account, that the timing of the startling event could have coincided with the arrival of Eldred Crang and the others. Accordingly, Gosseyn Three communicated to his Alter Ego: 'Do you think there was some overlap, whereby Enin was automatically transmitted somewhere else?'

'I seem to remember,' came the reply, 'that at the time of transmission you were recalling several twenty-decimal locations of the past of Gosseyn One and myself. Did you think of the boy as you did that? That I can't recall.'

It was not a good moment for trying to remember those details. Because he saw that the woman had become aware of him, and that she was turning toward him, and that she was in a shaken condition.

'Is it possible,' she asked uncertainly, 'that all this that has happened — '

Gosseyn had recovered. 'It sounds like what happened to him before. I'll see what I can do. I — '

They had both ignored the emperor's teacher, almost as if he did not exist. And if there had been any possibility of Gosseyn eventually taking notice of the little man it ended, because, as he spoke the first word of what might have been another statement, there was a buzzing sound.

'Oh, my God!' exclaimed the woman. 'There's Breemeg, come for you!'

Gosseyn was recovering. 'Don't worry,' he said. 'Let it happen. I promise to be back in a few minutes; but first I should know — we should find out — what's been going on in the rest of the ship.'

Yet, actually, even to him it seemed like the final confusion when, a few minutes later, he walked away quietly with the courtier.

Before, then, he actually got lost in the tangle of garden, he looked back once. The emperor's mother was standing at the door, staring after him with haunted eyes.

Considering what a capable, direct person she normally was, Gosseyn didn't think of what she was feeling as a thalamic reaction. There was such a thing as true emotion.

He was feeling a little of this himself. Because — could he be responsible for the young emperor's disappearance?

Chapter Eleven

Beside him, Breemeg broke his initial silence. 'I'm deducing,' he said, 'that you did not mention our private conversation to the emperor or his mother.'

They were out of the royal garden, and had come to a long corridor, in the desertedness of which the lean-bodied, middle-aged courtier apparently felt free to speak.

'True,' said Gosseyn.

It seemed, under the circumstances, a subject of minor importance; and so he had the private thought that two or three minutes had gone by since Leej's prediction. So that in about nine minutes the whatever would happen that would cause him to use his extra-brain.

In its way nine minutes was a long time. No point, therefore, in dwelling on that . . . for a while.

'I'm deducing it,' continued Breemeg, 'because I would surely not have been called by Queen Mother Strala to come and get you if you had made even the slightest reference to my words.'

This time there were two private thoughts. The first, a simple, personal reaction: . . . Imagine, she invited me into her bedroom without telling me her first name − And now, in this casual mention, there was the name.

'Strala!' He spoke the name aloud, adding: 'I like the sound of it.'

Breemeg seemed not to have heard the comment. They walked on, Gosseyn thinking that her name had a feminine beauty to it.

The second thought consisted of a series of fleeting memories that triggered a sudden hardness. The memories were of Gosseyn Two in action, on the planet of the Predictors, on the planet

Gorgzid, the capital of Enro's Greatest Empire. The awareness brought the beginning of determination that was new to this body. There were things to do. Where was that boy? He should be rescued, and quickly.

Breemeg's next words actually interrupted that train of thought-feeling. 'Obviously,' the man said, 'our most important task is, still, to find out where we are in space, and to discover what happened to bring us here.'

Listening to those words, for the first time Gosseyn had a feeling of relief in relation to this man. Somebody with good sense must have talked to Breemeg in the past forty-five minutes.

The deserted corridor continued to stretch into the distance ahead, as Breemeg enlarged upon his argument: 'Naturally, if there's any chance of our returning to join the fleet, then my statements about a rebellion would have no meaning. That, of course, would be the best solution, since it would ultimately bring us all back to our families.'

It was — Gosseyn conceded silently to himself — not a great moment for General Semantics, as it related to himself. The problem of such a return, according to the data he had, was complicated beyond anything that had ever happened. So it was another lie that the real life situation he was in made it necessary for him to go along with.

But, since the truth would probably evoke swift, strong actions from these people, once more optimum survival for everybody — including the villains — seemed to depend on his not revealing what he knew.

The alternative was to tell the facts, and, if there were repercussions, to fight it out. Obviously, that had to be for later, if possible.

'On the other hand,' Breemeg said, as Gosseyn came to that decision, 'if we are going to be in this area of space from now on, then the sooner we find a habitable planet that we can go to the better. At which time' — grimly — 'our little imperial family will be subject to severe action. The boy' — he shrugged his gaunt shoulders as he walked — 'maybe we can leave him in your care.' He smiled, showing his teeth. 'Eight hundred games of scroob a day, perhaps.'

He shrugged again. The smile faded. 'Whatever — so long

as he's out of the way. As for the mother . . .'

He paused. And there was a sudden stiffening of his body that brought an abrupt return of Gosseyn's feeling of purposefulness.

Breemeg said earnestly, 'Do you realize that this is the only woman on a ship with 178,000 men. So' — a twisted smile, suddenly — 'there'll be several dozen top echelon leaders who may decide among themselves to share her womanly charms.'

The man concluded, 'You can see that these are all afterthoughts, and are somewhat more realistic than what I said earlier.'

So it was going to be a fight, after all. Gosseyn was curious. 'Are any military officers involved in the plan to share the woman?'

There was a long pause. Breemeg slowed in his rapid walk, and simultaneously turned his head and was staring at Gosseyn. Abruptly, he came to a full stop. And Gosseyn, after walking several steps farther, did the same, turning as he did so.

The courtier of His Imperial Majesty, Enin, said, 'That is the damnedest question I've heard recently. It implies some thought of your own, a scheme perhaps to enlist those —'

He stopped. Seemed to brace his body. And said grimly, 'No, the subject has not been brought up to members of the military. Why do you ask?'

It seemed, to Gosseyn, to be the information he needed. So he said, 'It seems to me that you and your associates are all making your plans too quickly. I would guess' — he picked a figure at random — 'that you and your friends should hold back from any private plans for a couple of weeks. Meaning, don't do any irrevocable act that someone else, who is not ready for such a step, might react to.'

Breemeg's expression changed as the meaning of Gosseyn's words evidently ended his anxiety. He was suddenly tolerant. 'The fact is,' he said, 'we have to consider the alien prisoners we have aboard. As a result, the political situation aboard this ship does not permit too much leeway. We have to act, or someone else will act.'

He seemed to have recovered from his momentary shock; for he started walking again. Almost automatically Gosseyn did the

82

same. But he was thinking: 'Alien!' After a long moment he said, 'Just a minute!'

He stopped that reaction with an effort of will, and spoke mentally to his Alter Ego:

'I suddenly feel as if the moment has come for a General Semantics recapitulation. I seem to have been at the receiving end of too many generalizations. And I'm beginning to think I'm assuming a lot that isn't so.'

The answer from the faraway Gosseyn Two was favorable: 'It does appear as if we're taking a lot for granted. The mention of alien prisoners seems to indicate that the Dzan enemy in Galaxy Two is vulnerable like anyone else, and that individuals among them will surrender, and place themselves at the mercy of their opponents, as soldiers have been doing from time immemorial.'

While his mental exchange took place with the duplicate Gosseyn, he had continued walking along beside the gaunt man. Now, Gosseyn glanced at the courtier, and wondered if he had noticed the silence. There was no indication on the long face that Breemeg was concerned.

So perhaps there was still time enough for the recapitulation.

Gosseyn said, 'There's an overall impression I have that this is a warship.'

It required moments only for that to bring a reaction. Once more the man slowed in his walk, and, turning his head, stared with what seemed to be an expression of astonishment.

'What else?' he said. He added, 'You have strange thoughts.'

Gosseyn persisted: 'The very existence of such a large vessel, and your mention just now of alien prisoners, implies that wherever you come from − let us call your place of origin Galaxy Two − you have a mighty enemy.'

The other man seemed to have recovered from his surprise at the simplicity of the questions. He was walking again at normal pace; and he nodded, and said, 'It's a two-legged, two-armed, semi-human race. These beings are both technically and as individuals dangerous to us. For example, it is risky for a human being without some electronic protection to be in the vicinity of a Troog. And we have had to develop elaborate devices to defend ourselves as a group from computer systems that are able to amplify their mental control methods for taking over the minds of the personnel of a Dzan warship during a battle.'

'I gather that such a battle was in progress when your ship suddenly found itself in this area of space.'

'True,' was the reply.

Momentarily Gosseyn tried to picture that battle scene in the remote universe nearly a million light years from the Milky Way galaxy. Human beings there fighting as men had been fighting here since the beginning of recorded history.

He shook his head, sadly. The General Semantics notion that one human being is not the same as any other — Gilbert Gosseyn is not Breemeg, is not Eldred Crang, is not Prescott, is not Enro — while it had a limited truth in terms of individual identity and appearance, did not seem to encompass the character of the race as a whole.

He sighed. And continued with his recapitulation:

'I'm going to guess that the absence of your ship could be an advantage for the enemy.'

Silence. They walked several steps, and the end of the corridor was visibly only a few hundred feet ahead now. Then: 'It will probably take a while,' Breemeg said, 'before anyone becomes aware that we have disappeared. So ours may not yet be a dangerous absence.'

'Your description of the enemy,' said Gosseyn, who had been considering what the other had said, 'suggests that for the first time ever men have met a superior life form. By which I mean —'

He stopped, incredulous.

The floor was shaking. *Shaking!*

It was a vibration that was visible. Literally, under him, the floor wobbled. And he saw that wobble run like a ripple that moved slantwise across the corridor. And, apparently, passed on to other parts of the ship.

And was gone from where he was.

Just ahead, a ceiling bell clanged. And then a man's strident voice said urgently: 'All personnel to stations. An enemy supership has just this minute entered our area of space.'

Because of the intensity of tone, it took a moment to identify the voice as that of the Draydart Duart.

Inside his brain, he was aware of his Alter Ego mentally groaning at him: 'Three,' that distant thought came, 'I think you've done it. You thought of that other galaxy battle location; and I have an awful feeling something big happened — again.'

Gosseyn Three had no time for guilt. Because at that exact instant he felt an odd sensation in his head. It required several split instants for his second-in-line memory from Gosseyn Two and Gosseyn One, since he had no personally associated physical movements, to identify the feeling.

Then: . . . Good God! Something was trying to take control of his mind —

The twelve minutes of Leej's prediction must be up.

That was only one of numerous fleeting impressions. Thought of Leej also brought instant memory of the Crangs, the Prescotts, Enro, and Strala . . . all of whom at this moment must be fighting efforts to control their minds.

So Gilbert Gosseyn Three had better get back there. Too bad because — that was another of the fleeting realizations — I should really be tracking down that boy . . .

Chapter Twelve

A chill wind blew into Gosseyn's face.

As far as the eye could see were snowy peaks. And, directly below the ridge on which they stood, was a swift flowing river with ice-encrusted shore lines.

He saw that the boy was gazing at the scene, eyes wide. A flush of color was creeping into the white cheeks. And it just could be that the chill of that wind was reaching through all the madness and making itself felt on a new level of reality.

There was a long pause. Then: 'Hey, this is really something, isn't it?' The boyish voice had excitement in it.

Even as the words were spoken, the wind blew harder, icier. Gosseyn smiled grimly, and said, 'Yes, it really is . . . something.'

His Imperial Majesty, Enin, seemed not to hear and not to feel. His voice went up several pitches of excitement: 'Hey, what do you do in a place like this?'

It was not too difficult to believe that this boy had all his life been protected from extremes of weather. So Gosseyn's feeling was that perhaps a little explanation was in order. Accordingly, he said, 'Since, because of the battle that's going on . . . back there' — he waved vaguely in the direction of the light-years-away Dzan ship — 'we'll be staying here for a little while, I should tell you that what you're looking at is the winter season of this planet, and it's a wilderness area. Not a sign of civilization is visible from here.'

'There's something over there,' said the boy. He pointed, and added, 'I've been here twenty minutes longer than you, and it was brighter then, and it looked like something when the sun was out.'

Gosseyn's gaze followed the pointing finger, and saw that it was aimed in the direction that the river was flowing. The distance involved was more than a mile. There, at the point where the river and the valley turned leftward out of sight, was a dark area in the snow, seemingly at the very edge of the disappearing stream.

Was it the first building of a settlement that was located beyond the bend?

It would take a while to get there, and find out. But there was no question: if they remained here, that was the direction in which they would go.

Aloud, he said, 'Let's hope so. We have to find a place where we can be warm when night comes.'

Undecided, he looked up at the cloud that hid the sun. And saw that it was part of a dark mass that would presently cover most of the sky. Too bad! It would have been interesting to see what kind of sun it was.

Already the air seemed chillier than at the moment of his arrival. Time they were on their way.

As the two of them partly climbed down, and partly slid down, the icy slope Gosseyn Three conducted a silent debate with himself.

Presumably, the place where he — and the boy before him — had arrived, was a twenty-decimal 'photographed' area of Gosseyn One or Gosseyn Two; an exact location one of them had used for some purpose in the past.

The problem was that his own recollection of the travels of the earlier Gosseyns could not seem to recall a frozen mountain area. The joint memory he shared with the first two Gosseyns did not include a mental picture of a scene such as this, utilized for any reason.

It was merely a mystery, of course, and not a disaster. At any moment he could choose to use his extra-brain — and something would happen; exactly what was no longer predictable.

. . . After all, my intention was to return to the imperial apartment on the ship to help Strala and the visitors, who had been transmitted aboard by Gosseyn Two.

And, instead, he had had that final, fleeting thought

about Enin; and, somehow, his defective extra-brain had worked out those intricate details, and had brought him to where the boy was on this frozen planet.

It could, of course, be Earth itself. Still descending, still holding onto the boy's hand, Gosseyn — with that thought — looked down and around, suddenly hopeful. He drew a deep, testing breath. The air, though chilly, felt exactly as his group memory remembered the air of Earth. The snowy mountain peaks, the flowing stream, half-embedded in ice, were surely a variation of a thousand similar scenes in any of a hundred mountain areas on Earth.

The feeling of hope stayed with him for at least another hundred yards of the descent. By then he was putting first one hand and next the other inside the upper portion of the loose-fitting garment that Voices One and Two had tucked him into.

There was still warm body underneath; and by repeated contact, he was able to keep his hands, one at a time, in a reasonably warm state. But as more time went by, and still they were merely edging down that slope, there was no question in his mind: he was not dressed for this climate.

A few minutes later it seemed as if the time for decisive action had come, as the boy suddenly whimpered, 'I can't — I can't — it's too cold. I'm freezing.'

They had come down to a wide ledge. There they stopped. And stood on the ice, slapping themselves in the manner of freezing individuals trying to force circulation back into their fingers and hands.

The view remained absolutely magnificent. Unfortunately, the fact that they could still see ice and snow in a thousand beautiful formations in the distance below and to either side meant that they still had a long way to go. Gosseyn unhappily estimated that they were still four hundred yards above the river level.

Standing there, not quite sure what came next, he remembered — a Gosseyn Two involvement — when the group was preparing for the Big Journey they had made three preliminary tests.

First, Leej predicted a location on Earth; whereupon Gosseyn Two made his mental 'photograph' of what his extra-brain 'saw' at the particle level in the involved cells inside her head.

Two other tests, one to an unknown planet — the existence of which she predicted — and one to her home planet, Yalerta. And only when that preliminary had been evaluated as being satisfactory did Leej aim her prediction at a location in the other galaxy.

. . . This planet, where Enin and I landed so automatically, could be one of those preliminary test locations that no one ever actually went to — was it Earth? Was it Yalerta? Was it the unknown planet?

Obviously it would not be possible to find out immediately. But if this was Earth — what? There seemed to be several possibilities, all of them vague.

He kept stamping his feet, and rubbing his hands. And he was reluctantly realizing that, if the boy and he were this cold already, there was no chance that they could walk a whole mile to the dark area where the river made its turn. Even getting down to the shore of the river seemed as if it would be too much for their freezing bodies.

Yet he was feeling better about the mis-transmission that had brought him here . . . Have to learn to control that, of course; such accidents would need to be analyzed, and something positive done, but . . . The kid had been in this icy world at least twenty minutes longer than he had. And evidently two things had saved him until now. During those first minutes the sun had been shining. Also, a young boy's better circulation and overall warmer condition had had its good result.

Unfortunately, those special advantages had run out of time. And so — for both of them — the moment had come for one of those vague possibilities.

Gosseyn reached over, caught the boy's cold, right hand, and squeezed it. Holding the hand firmly, and having gained the other's attention, he said earnestly, 'Listen, Enin, you and I have special abilities. And what might be the most advisable special thing for us to do right now is to find some way to trigger one of those electrical charges that you can do.'

Gloomily, the boy shook his head. 'But it has to come from an energy source that already exists. A cloud with lightning in it, or a live wire somewhere.'

Gosseyn nodded. 'That bunch of clouds up there' — he pointed with his thumb — 'and this tree right here, set it on fire!'

The tree he pointed at was a twisted, twenty-foot long, winter-denuded object. With its leafless, spread-out branches it poked out of the side of the cliff just above the ledge, and seemed to hang there at a downward angle.

He waited while the boy looked at it, then glanced up at the cloud; and then: 'Is there lightning in the winter?' Enin asked dubiously.

'Oh!' said Gosseyn.

It was a question which — he had to admit it — had never crossed his, or any Gosseyn's mind. Ruefully, he realized that lightning on Earth was connected with summer thunderstorms.

'I guess you're right,' he agreed. But he was bracing himself with another possibility. He pointed with his free hand. 'If that dark spot is actually a building, and it has electric wires in it, what could you do at this distance?'

Silently, the boy stared in the indicated direction. There was a pause; not long.

Abruptly, a crackling sound, and the tree burst into flames!

Minutes later they were still warming themselves as near the flames as they dared to go. The tree burned with a satisfying intensity; and even when it presently became a blackened ruin, it still gave off heat.

But getting warm ceased to be a principal occupation. Gosseyn grew aware that his companion was gazing off to one side, a troubled expression on his face. 'Look!' the boy pointed, and added, 'I was afraid that might happen.'

What Gosseyn saw, when his gaze followed the pointing finger, was a column of smoke a mile away, where the dark spot had, indeed, turned out to be a habitation.

'The electricity I brought over here,' said Enin, 'set their place on fire when I forced it out of the wires.'

He seemed concerned; and it occurred to the man that the imperial child seemed to have acquired, or was automatically showing — now that he was away from his lifetime environment — moral qualities of a well brought-up twelve-year-old who knew right from wrong.

As he had that thought, the boy spoke again: 'So now if we go there, we may not find any place where we can stay.'

Gosseyn stared silently at the pall of black smoke that reared up into the sky, thinking ruefully: . . . Well, maybe not that moral, after all. Aloud, he said, 'I hope no one was injured.'

The visible damage that was being done to the distant structure abruptly brought his mind back once more to the question: what planet was this? What kind of people were out there in that burning building? What level of technology?

. . . Obviously not possible to find out immediately. Gosseyn had the conscious, dismissing thought. And saw that the boy had ducked under the smoldering tree and was restlessly walking along the ledge beyond it, peering over the edge as he did so.

Abruptly, Enin called, 'I think we can get down better from here.' He pointed to a spot where the snowy slope seemed to be less steep.

'I'll be there in a minute,' Gosseyn called back.

First, his own, next purpose needed to be tested out.

Gingerly he reached down, and took hold of the thickest of the blackened tree branches. Flinched. And let go again immediately. It was more than just warm.

It took a few minutes then. He threw snow on the sections he wanted to grab until they cooled; rather quickly, it turned out. As soon as he could comfortably take hold, he used his feet as a brace, and tore the entire branch loose from the tree.

Carrying the branch, he joined the boy. Moments later they were heading down the slope again. But now they had with them something which, while it held its warmth, would be the equivalent of a portable heater.

The downward journey had its darker aspects. Both his and the boy's hands were soon black from the need to touch the warm spots. Also, they each, several times, stood on the warmer, thicker part of the branch to warm their feet. So there was presently a trail of black ashes in the snow behind, and above, them. And their footgear showed the consequent smears of black.

Gosseyn tried to avoid touching the loose suit he wore; but in those moments that they slid down steep embankments there were accidents.

They came down, presently, to the shore line of the river; and it was encouraging to feel that the tree branch still had some heat in it. Gosseyn was suddenly hopeful that, by walking swiftly on this relatively level ground, they would be able to make it to the inhabited area a mile away.

It was Enin who pointed out the price of the descent. 'We sure look like a couple of dirty bums,' he said. 'You got black on your chin and your right cheek, and I can feel the stuff on me, too.'

'It's principally on your forehead and neck,' said Gosseyn, and added, 'And, of course, our hands are doomed till we get some warm water.'

'Let's go!' said the boy.

It still wasn't quite that settled in Gosseyn's mind. But they set off, while he thought about it.

Snow and ice on every horizon — except for the dark area ahead, closer now . . . The fire there was evidently under control because no smoke was visible.

That relieved Gosseyn, but there was a growing feeling inside him of reluctance to be here on this river shore, tramping along over frozen ground, carrying a tree branch that was now barely warm.

All the minutes that he walked the thoughts of his Alter Ego had made a steady impingement alongside his personal awarenesses. Out there, in faraway space, Gosseyn Two was in motion. Already he had made the jump to the Dzan ship. And the mental pictures after his arrival reported that the computer system in the huge space battleship had automatically put up an energy screen, which cut off the robotic mind control forces of the alien vessel.

From this safer environment Gosseyn Two had time to notice Three's disturbed reaction, and to offer advice: 'You've saved the boy. The fact that that happened as a consequence of a problem with your extra-brain is interesting for the information it gives us; but it should not result in you being negative about yourself.'

Two continued his admonition: 'Right now, remember that human beings tend to have mental hang-ups about a mystery. And that's what your situation is to a slight degree: a mystery. Where are you? What is the strange building ahead? Why not walk on, and clear up that mystery?'

It seemed to Gosseyn Three that the more important truth was that, if this were Earth . . . 'I should be in the capitol city finding out what is going on there.'

'Eventually,' came the reply, 'that's a good purpose. Particularly since you shouldn't come back here until I leave. You and I should not have a confrontation at close quarters until we've analyzed what might happen to a couple of duplicates like us at close quarters. But I deduce from events that I won't be aboard this ship very long.'

And the reason for that had also come through from mind to mind — automatically: why Enro had wanted to be one of the delegates to the ship from another galaxy. It seemed he had brought with him a signal device, whereby units of his fleet could make the jump to the nearest planet with a Distorter system, and then another jump toward, but just short of, the signal device. In all the surrounding space the warships of the Greatest Empire were flicking into view, and taking up positions.

As a consequence it appeared that the alien enemy was having second thoughts. Because he had ceased all aggressive action, and had begun communicating concern and confusion; those aboard apparently didn't know where they were either.

A strange message had come from it: 'Let's negotiate!'

It was a hitherto unheard-of alien concession, and therefore suspect. But Gosseyn Two was in favor of negotiation.

'So' — his direct thought — 'save yourself and the boy. I've already told Queen Mother Strala, and you may believe me when I say she is relieved that it's you that's there with her son.'

Gosseyn Three, still walking, skidding a little, still manipulating the big tree branch so that it did not accidentally knock over the boy considered the implications of the young mother's gratitude, without knowing exactly how he should feel. But one thought came to him: 'It looks, Mr Alter Ego, as if I'm going to be the first Gosseyn to go into a bedroom with a woman for a purpose other than sleeping.'

The reply to that was philosophical. Gosseyn Two responded in the silent fashion of thought communication: 'It just happens that my particular lady has not yet shown up in my life. As you know, both Leej and Patricia had, and have, other commitments.'

His thought continued in the same speculative vein, 'By the time this entire situation resolves itself, we may all have a clearer awareness of our ultimate destiny. In your case, save the son — and you've got the mother.'

Still walking along that icy shore on a world that could be Earth, Gosseyn Three said, 'Let's leave the distant future alone. I'm in a situation that I want to get out of, principally because my feet keep freezing, and my body is chilled to the bone.' His thoughts, still intended for the other Gosseyn's attention, went on: 'The way I analyze my extra-brain is that, if I concentrate, and allow no side thoughts about other locations at the moment of connection, I'll go where I want to go.'

The reply to that was a slight change of subject. 'There may be a problem,' said Gosseyn Two. 'It seems Enro has taken a look at the lady, and having, of course, failed to marry his sister, Patricia, has stated that a marriage between two super Imperial families could be very useful in inter-galactic relationships.'

Standing there in a frozen universe, Gosseyn Three was not exactly clear as to whether he should feel relieved or disturbed. What it came to, finally, was a mild blankness.

And then: 'Has the Lady Strala been informed of the Great Man's interest in her?'

'I believe,' was the reply, 'that she has got the thought. But my own feeling —'

Surprisingly, the mental communication was vague, almost like a pause.

'Yes?' Gosseyn Three urged.

The answer had in it a speculative aspect: 'I think by the time this entire situation resolves itself, we may all have a clearer awareness of our ultimate destiny. In your case, save the son — and you've got the mother . . . that is my belief.'

Gosseyn Three had had another thought. 'We must,' he said, 'do our best to deduce how Enro, the galactic ruler, can utilize this contact to his advantage. And because he's capable of mass murder in the military meaning of the term, we must try to make sure that no advantage occurs.'

He continued: 'I'm sure you will agree that we do not want Enro's fleet to gain access to that other galaxy. So — no marriage for him to the emperor's mother, if I can help it.'

He concluded, 'But that's for later. Right now —'

The firm decision in his mind must have reached across the years of miles; for the Alter Ego faraway thought came, simply: 'Good luck, Three.'

To protect himself from any possible mental hang-ups from the mystery, Gosseyn, there in that winter world, located a section of frozen soil and took his extra-brain photograph of it. And so, at any time in the future, he could return to this location and resume his journey on foot. Naturally, if that ever happened, he would make sure that he was more warmly dressed, thank you.

His final mental comment to the remote Alter Ego was: 'I think I can live with the mystery of what that building ahead might be. And I suppose I can live with my regret that I never got a chance to interact with one of the alien prisoners aboard the Dzan battleship; the first non-human we've ever heard of in all the Gosseyn travels. Though Breemeg did call the aliens semi-human, didn't he? But even that is a unique event. Nevertheless, I'll have to live with both mysteries because, right now, it's getting colder here every minute; and it'll soon be dark. So —'

Chapter Thirteen

Earth!

They stood in the backyard of a small house. The little place was located on a slope, so that there, partly visible below them, was a city. In the near distance Gosseyn could see, principally, roof tops of residences, and the greenery that surrounded almost every visible home.

Standing there, he was conscious of both an outer — the air felt summery — and inner warmth. The inner good feeling seemed to be there so naturally that many moments went by before he identified it:

. . . It's as if I've come home.

It took other moments, then, to argue mildly with himself that, really, a body that had been found floating in space in a capsule could not, except by a considerable extension of logic, establish a legal status of belonging to a specific planet.

Presumably that inward argument could have continued except, at that precise moment, Enin stirred beside him, and said, 'What kind of crumby place is this? Where are we?'

It was a distinctly variant point of view. And, as he glanced down at the boy, Gosseyn saw that the emperor of the Dzan was not looking at the vista of the city below, but at the backyard and the rear of the house that was in the yard.

And, for the first time since their arrival, that reminded Gosseyn of his earlier — light years away — anxiety about where they would end up: at the aimed-for destination, or somewhere else?

. . . I made it! The method of concentrating, and shutting out side thoughts works — 'Hey, Gosseyn Two, got that? I can control that defect.'

There was no reply from his faraway Alter Ego, and, in fact, no particular awareness of the other's thoughts. So — later!

So he looked down at the boy, and said in a chiding tone: 'We're where it's warm. Or, would you rather be back on the ice?'

Enin dismissed that with, apparently, no gratitude for the change. 'How did we get to a place like this?' he asked in a disgusted tone.

Gosseyn smiled. 'Well, it's like this, Enin. What I can do in making those shifts in space — which is my special thing, as you should know — '

The twelve-year-old face that was tilted up to him held in it no criticism of how what he 'could do' had on one occasion affected the emperor of the Dzan in front of his courtiers. The lips merely parted, and said, 'Yeah! So.'

Gosseyn explained: 'It's best to have places to come to where no one sees you arrive. Now, this little house is the home of a friend, and it's located very nicely for what I just said. No one in the neighborhood can easily see how we got here. Right?'

Presumably the boy had already, in his initial disapproving survey, noticed those very drab details. But he seemed to be motivated to take another look. And, evidently, the analysis made sense.

'Hey, yeah,' he nodded, 'you're right.'

'And,' Gosseyn continued, 'if you'll look up, you'll see that it's still morning. And so we've got almost a whole day ahead of us.'

He had already had the realization of the time of day from the position of the sun in the sky. But saying that aloud brought an awareness of an automatic . . . thalamic? . . . feeling inside him. The feeling was a sense of belonging, not necessarily here in this backyard, but here, everywhere, on this planet.

He saw that the bright eyes had narrowed. 'What are we going to do here?'

That was not really a problem. The time of day had evoked a thought: at last report, Dan Lyttle, the owner of the little place, had been a night clerk in a hotel. Which could mean that, at this early hour of the day, he had not yet departed for his job.

Abruptly hopeful Gosseyn walked forward, and knocked on the back door. He was aware of Enin coming up beside him.

The boy's voice came, puzzled: 'You want inside? Why don't we just go in?'

In a way, in this instance, it was not an impossibility. If Dan Lyttle were still the owner, he would probably not be disturbed, if he was out and returned to find who it was that had entered.

But that wasn't the meaning of his Imperial Majesty's words. Shaking his head, Gosseyn turned towards the boy. 'Listen,' he said in a firm tone, 'We're not on one of your planets. Here we have to live by the local rules.' He was gazing into those youthful, unabashed eyes as he completed his admonition in the same firm voice: 'You do not intrude on other people's property without permission. Understood?'

Fortunately there was no time for Enin to reply. Because at that exact instant there was a sound. And the door opened.

The familiar, lean figure that stood there said, 'Oh, my God, it's you!'

It was a sentence that Gosseyn, himself, could probably have spoken. But his tone would have been one of relief. Because the individual who had uttered the exclamation was identified by the Gosseyn memory as the owner of the cottage: Dan Lyttle, in person.

The hotel clerk, who had come into Gosseyn Two's hotel room – and saved his life.

His face was still as lean as it had been before. He seemed more mature than the Gosseyn memory recalled. But that was a subtle difference. Most important, he was delighted to have them as guests in his little home.

'You came at the right time. It's my day off. Or' – with a smile – 'my night off; so I can be of some use to you, maybe. Anyway, right now I can see you two need a bath and sleep. Why don't you and the kid take my bedroom, and any sleeping I do I'll do on the couch out here.'

Gosseyn Three didn't argue. The 'kid' seemed to hesitate; but then he went silently through the indicated door with Gosseyn. However, once inside, with the door closed, Enin said, 'Are we really going to stay here?'

Gosseyn pointed to the far side of the queen-size bed. 'You have your bath first, and stretch out there. And when I've showered I'll take this side.' He added, 'We can decide later what we're going to do here.' At that point Dan Lyttle brought in a long shirt for Enin and a pair of pajamas for Gosseyn. And so, presently, they slept.

. . . Gosseyn came to, drowsily, and lay for a minute with his eyes still closed; and he was having a strange thought: that was the first normal sleep of this Gosseyn body.

The realization held his attention briefly. For some reason, when he had lain down on this bed earlier, it had seemed so natural, so — ordinary — that the uniqueness of it in his own existence had not occurred to him.

Moments after that awareness he was conscious of himself smiling. Because it was obviously a minor reality in a universe of sleeping humans.

With that he opened his eyes, turned over, glanced toward the other side of the bed — and sat up, frowning.

The boy wasn't there.

As he swung his legs off the bed, and started to put on the slip-ons that had served him as shoes all these hours, he was mildly bemused. But there was — he noticed — a small thalamic reaction.

He saw that the shoes were clean. And that his suit, which was neatly draped over a chair, had also been washed while he slept.

It required a few minutes, then. First, he went over to the toilet, and experienced his very first urination. Then he stepped to the sink, picked up the brush that lay there, enticingly, and combed his hair. Next, he washed his face and hands, and used a guest towel that hung on a rack. (The previous night there had only been Lyttle's bath towel for both of them.)

And, as he performed his ablutions he let his attention move purposefully to the other Gosseyn . . . out there.

Immediately the vague memories came of Gosseyn Two's movements, and actions, during the past many minutes. And then – abruptly – direct contact!

They were quick. Two said, 'I know where you are. So I'm not too worried – yet.'

Gosseyn Three replied: 'I can finally review your situation. I observe that the single enemy vessel is still talking peace, but no alien has come aboard. And that what may happen on the Dzan ship from all those angry men is not yet manifesting. And Enro's purposes may affect the overall issue. But it will take time for the problems to develop.'

The distant Alter Ego said, 'Then let's concentrate on you. I was talking to Enro, and missed noticing any purpose you had in going to Earth.'

Gosseyn Three was rueful. 'In a way it was just an accident. But, I think, a good one.' He continued his argument, 'After all, the Gosseyns have a lot of hang-ups about Earth. We need to know what happened there after you left. Who has become the government, after President Hardie was killed? What's the status of Null-A? I could go on.' He concluded, 'I seem to remember that the police and the government forces restored order, but –'

It was a big 'but'. Nevertheless, from far off there in interstellar distances, his analysis evoked a grudging agreement.

'I suppose,' came the reply, 'we should find out a few things, and do what has to be done.' The Alter Ego continued: 'But if you'll think about it, going to what used to be the City of the Games Machine, will present problems. For example, neither you nor the emperor have any money. I presume you can stay temporarily with Dan Lyttle. But you can't expect an hotel clerk's salary to support three people for long.'

Gosseyn Three smiled as a thought of his own came in an instant mental reply to the other's objection. 'Did you catch that answer?' he asked.

'Well' – impression of a responding smile – 'I suppose the Gosseyns could assert an ownership, or stewardship, claim to the Institute of General Semantics, on the grounds that "X" was a secret Gosseyn. But I don't recall it being a place where food was immediately available.'

Gosseyn Three replied, 'The old guy had his quarters there; so there may be a food supply. And, of course, there'll be a caretaker on the premises. Question: who has been paying his salary?'

'What would you do? Take the place over by force?'

'Well —' Pause. Gosseyn Three grew conscious that his was now a grimmer smile — 'It's hard for me to accept that that objection came from a Gosseyn who did not hesitate to force, or dupe, servants to feed him on Yalerta, and who always ate well wherever he went in the universe; and in no case, as I recall it, was local money available.'

Gosseyn Two's answering thought had a touch of resignation in it. 'I can see you're making up your mind to stay.' He seemed to utter a sigh. Then: 'Okay, give Dan Lyttle my best.'

'Well' — wryly — 'that will be a little difficult. He thinks I'm you.'

'Of course,' was the reply. 'I have to admit that's a hard reality to keep in mind: that there are two Gosseyns now. I doubt if "X" ever intended that there would be two of the same age group conscious at the same time.'

The mention of 'X' brought a thought. Gosseyn Three said, 'All these hours I've been vaguely aware of such a person having existed as a sort of ancestor. But it's not been something that's been to the fore of your mind. So vague is the correct description of the way it came through. Tell me more.'

'Wel-l-l-ll!' The mental answer had in it uncertainty. 'There's reason to believe that he was in one of the original migrant ships from that other galaxy. Except — impression only — that little vessel crash-landed, damaging the male body that we later knew as "X". Also damaged was the computer that had the scientific data in it. Anyway, the other man went off with the two women because, as they got out, the damaged vessel was flown by its damaged computer to some other area of Earth. "X" recovered to the extent that he was periodically able to re-enter the little ship and go back into suspended animation for hundreds, even thousands, of years at a time.'

The Alter Ego's account continued: 'Naturally, he presently

began to notice the descendants of his male companion and the two women. There had been a reversion to barbarism, which apparently even included matings with male and female apes.'

The mental voice added, 'As you have been able to observe on today's Earth, it all worked out reasonably well. But it was "X" who had the ancient memory and who, by using male sperm from his own body, eventually created the Gosseyn bodies. It's our task to make sure that the cloning system he developed is carried forward into the future. This should be one of our goals, regardless of what other actions we undertake in terms of personal association.'

Gossyn Two concluded, 'I would guess that "X"s apartment should be carefully searched for hidden rooms, or secret storage places, where he may have kept a set of records, and equipment for doing what he did.'

Gosseyn Three replied, 'I'll certainly take a look. And I'll continue to consult you in any crisis.'

'Theoretically,' came the answer from that faraway duplicate body-mind, 'we're the same person. Your judgment would probably be exactly the same as mine.'

It was true. And yet – somewhere inside himself he felt very much a separate individual.

Two grown men, the same person but, somehow, different.

Once again came his own thought: 'It will be interesting to see how the similarity works out.'

'It sure will.' The response from Gosseyn Two was in his mind almost as if it were his own thought. But not quite.

And it was him here, who was washing his face and combing his hair; not Gosseyn Two – actions and movements which he had not ceased doing during the entire high-speed, mental conversation.

Essentially, it seemed to him, standing there, he had only one reason for worry: Earth was dangerous for a Gosseyn. At least, the part of Earth to which he had come was dangerous.

There were people here who would recognize the Gosseyn face. And it would require only one discharge of any kind of weapon to kill this particular Gosseyn body. If that should happen the fact that the whole memory of the experience would continue on in the mind of Gosseyn Two was not really satisfactory.

The Gosseyn ancestors had unquestionably bequeathed a remarkable personality maintaining technology to the descendant duplicates. But to a particular individual of the long line, the reality was that the me-ness of identity continued to reside in one living body.

Chapter Fourteen

As he used each item, and did each little grooming act, he found himself remembering that similar conveniences had been available for the other Gosseyn on that other occasion.

It was not the kind of fantasy that could hold him long. Because once again he was having fleeting thoughts about Enin . . . out there. With that, he hastily put away the electric razor. And then —

And then, it was just a matter of slipping again into the slip-on shoes. But he had the thought that he'd better get some better clothes, somehow. And some much stronger shoes.

Moments after that he was out of the bathroom, and setting off. As he pulled at the door that led out of the bedroom into the rest of the house, he heard Enin saying, 'Yes, Mr Lyttle, but what's an assumption?'

Gosseyn slowed his action of opening the door, and stayed where he was. As he listened, then, to the voice of Dan Lyttle explain the General Semantics definition of an assumption, he felt awed . . . Of course, he thought — this attempt should be made. How it would work on a brain not yet fully grown, and with no reward that could be offered to someone who had everything — was not clear.

But he drew back, out of sight, pushed the door until it was open only an inch or so. And listened.

'You mean — why do I act the way I do?' The boyish voice showed continued puzzlement.

'Yes.' It was Dan Lyttle's voice. 'A little while ago you came out here and ordered me to get your breakfast ready. And I did, didn't I?'

'So?'

'Well' — the man's tone was ever so slightly insistent — 'you're a guest in my house, and you treat me like I'm a servant. That's what I mean: what's the underlying assumption?'

There was a momentary pause. Then: 'I'm the emperor. Everybody does as I say.'

'You mean, where you come from?'

'Dzan. The universe of Dzan.' It was Enin's voice.

'So,' went on Dan Lyttle, 'one of your assumptions is that here on Earth you should be treated the way you are treated at home?'

'I'm emperor wherever I go.' It was insolently spoken. Gosseyn Three smiled. Grimly.

'And' — continued the man's voice out there in the living room — 'I gather you have a number of underlying assumptions by which you believe that you are better than other people?'

'I *am* better than other people. I was born to be emperor.'

'Your assumption, then, is that, because of an accident of birth, you have a right to lord it over other human beings?'

'Well . . . I didn't really think about that very much before my father was killed. But when I became emperor I just treated people exactly the way he had treated them. And I've been doing it ever since I ascended the throne. What's wrong with that?'

'Well' — smiling tone — 'what we General Semanticists are interested in is what kind of thinking makes people do irrational things. For example, how did your father die?'

'He fell out of a high window.' Belligerently. 'Are you suggesting that his assumptions may have had something to do with that?'

'They might — if we knew all the details of how he got so close to that open window. Were there witnesses?'

'It was a top level government meeting.'

'And he was so busy thinking, or talking, as he wandered near the window, that he didn't notice and fell out? Is that what the witnesses report?'

'My mother says that's what happened.' Pause. 'I never asked who told her.'

'We may make the assumption, then, that everyone who was in the room with him verified that that was what happened?'

'Hey' — exicitedly — 'is that what you mean by an assumption? You didn't see it yourself. So you have to assume that people who did see it are giving you the facts?'

'That's part of it. But the assumptions you should really be interested in are those that you've got sitting down deep inside, and you don't notice that they're there, or what they are. But in life situations you act as if they're true.'

'Well — I am the emperor. That's the truth.'

'How do you treat other people?'

'I tell them what to do. And they'd better do it.'

'Your assumption, then, is that an emperor can act bossy with all the people that he's emperor of — maybe even be mean and nasty.'

'I treat 'em like my father did. And I suppose those could have been his — what did you call them? — assumptions.'

'What you're saying is, you didn't ask yourself what his assumptions were? You were just a copy-cat?'

'Well —' Pause. Then, a different tone: 'Maybe,' said Enin, 'I ought to give you a little taste of my power.'

There was a quality in the boy's voice in those final words that decided Gosseyn that, perhaps, Enin's first lesson in General Semantics had gone about as far as it could.

Abruptly, with that thought, he pushed the bedroom door open, and walked out into the living room.

And stopped, teetering.

Because in that initial instant of emergence he saw, to his left, out of the corner of his eye

Six men sat in a row against that left wall. Four of them were in some kind of uniform.

As Gosseyn turned in their direction he was already aware that the four in uniform held pistols in their hands. They were energy weapons of some kind, not identifiable at this distance; and, though they did not point at him in a fixed way, they were definitely — as the old saying went — 'at the ready'.

It was not an ideal situation for any person to have to confront . . . suddenly. For Gosseyn the thought-reaction was complicated by what seemed to be a contradiction: Dan Lyttle giving Enin a lesson in General Semantics, with armed intruders watching.

The other complication was that, in his interest and response, the boy had acted as if his instructor and he were alone in the room; and, even in his final, threatening reaction against Lyttle he had paid no heed to the onlookers.

It took a moment or two, then, to realize that His Imperial Majesty had behind him at least two years of ignoring onlookers, and of being totally confident that his special mental control of energy was always decisive.

With that realization, he drew a deep breath. And was back to as much normality as was possible under the circumstances.

Normality came just in time.

At that exact moment Enin ran over to him, and grabbed his arm.

'Boy, am I glad you finally came to, Mr Gosseyn.' He seemed to have forgotten his implied threat against their host; and he totally ignored the intruders. His bright eyes peered up at Gosseyn. 'You always sleep this long?'

'Well!' Gosseyn managed a smile, and, since it was his first normal sleep ever — a reality which, fortunately, he had already considered, he was able to dissemble as he said, 'I think it was the icy cold . . . back there . . . and my unusually thin clothing. I —'

That was as far as he got. From off to his right Dan Lyttle's voice interrupted: 'It looks as if this little house has been bugged all this time, Mr Gosseyn,' he said. 'While you two were asleep I went over to the hotel, and borrowed a video game for your young friend here. When I came back these men were sitting where you see them.'

Even as Dan Lyttle's voice gave the explanation, one of the two men in civilian clothes made the first overt move of any of the intruders: he stood up. He was a medium-sized, rather chunky individual. There was a twisted smile on his thick face as he waited politely for Dan Lyttle to finish his brief statement. Then he spoke in a soft voice:

'Mr Gosseyn, as soon as you've eaten breakfast, we'll have to tie you up. The boss wants to come over and take a look at you.'

It was not a moment for anyone to make a swift move. And even His Imperial Majesty must have realized it; for his voice came, high-pitched but controlled: 'Shall I let him have it, Mr Gosseyn?'

That required a reply. 'No, Enin!' Gosseyn had been considering the information in the words of the spokesman for the intruders. He explained: 'I deduce we're going to meet some of the people I want to see while I'm here. So all is well.'

He added, 'We can decide later what we do about it. Okay?'

'Okay?'

During the interchange Dan Lyttle had not moved. Now he said, 'Before I make breakfast, I think I'd better make sure your young friend is not bored while you eat.'

With that he walked to the wall near the outer door, and removed the canvas covering from a shining machine that had not been there before they went to sleep.

It was easy to guess that it was the video game borrowed from the hotel where Lyttle worked as a night clerk.

Both men, and the intruders, watched as Enin walked over to the instrument. The boy peered at the transparent inner works. Then he examined the computer buttons. And, finally, he gingerly reached over and turned a switch. There was a flood of light inside. The appearance was of an underwater city and populace threatened by gigantic sea beasts.

It was quickly possible to deduce that the game player's job was to decimate the attacking creatures with the computer-controlled weapon systems.

As Gosseyn watched, smiling, the emperor of the Dzan began firing. After that it was simply a matter of internally dimming the effect of Enin's delighted cries, and, at the same time, asking questions of Dan Lyttle. And of listening to the answers while he, presently, ate eggs, bacon, and a waffle.

The questions had to do with the government situation on this part of the planet.

The answers were discouraging.

It seemed that supporters of the late President Hardie had somehow managed to inherit his power. And, apparently, they had no awareness that Hardie, himself, had not been responsible for the excesses of his regime, but had been a pawn in an interstellar struggle for control that he never really understood. Apparently, the inheritors were mostly venal men of the type known in politics on Earth from time immemorial. Lyttle named no names; and that was obviously wise. Named individuals had a tendency to get even, on the level where these people operated.

The additional information was that the people on Venus had not been heard from since the attack by Enro's forces a few months before.

On that point Gosseyn had his own thoughts — which he had no intention of sharing.

The fact was that the non-Aristotelian millions of Venus had, for some time now, been emigrating. Groups of them were being taken out to the inhabited planets of, principally, the Interstellar League. They were assigning themselves the task of bringing the philosophy and methods of General Semantics to all those enormous populations out there.

It would take a while.

Equally silently, Gosseyn doubted that Earth was being entirely neglected by the Venusians. Undoubtedly individuals had arrived from Venus, and were evaluating the problem of dealing with the consequences of the earlier secret takeover of the government by the minions of Enro. Currently, that meant dealing with the Earth types who had been motivated to join the invaders, and who were now entrenched in key positions.

It was Gosseyn Three's silent belief that, in the area of dealing with the venal types, he himself might be of considerable assistance.

With that mental reiteration of his purpose, he was about to lay down his fork, when he grew aware that Dan Lyttle was standing slightly behind him, offering a damp towel.

'Clean yourself — your mouth.'

As Gosseyn accepted the cloth, he saw that one of Lyttle's fingers of the hand holding it was oddly extended. Pointing. At something on the table cloth.

As he accepted the towel, and began wiping himself, he looked to where the finger had pointed. What he saw lying on the table cloth was a small, white sheet printed with thousands of computer chips. How it had got there, how Lyttle had managed casually to include it, unnoticed, as part of, or among, the breakfast dishes he had set down, could, presumably, be explained by the fact that, so far as he himself was concerned, he had been busy with his own thoughts. And the intruders had evidently been lulled by the ordinariness of a man eating.

Lyttle was leaning down again, and this time he whispered: '*That* is the Games Machine! Its identity!'

'Hey!' It was a yell from the intruder spokesman.

Both Gosseyn and Lyttle were quick, then. Gosseyn said, 'Some more egg, you say?'

With that, he wiped his mouth as if the whisper had had to do with the grooming act. The cloth he laid on the chip card. Stood up. And turned.

He said, 'Thank you for letting me eat. But it's time to tie me up, and call your — what did you call him? — boss.'

As he walked toward the intruders, he was aware of Dan Lyttle behind him busily cleaning up the breakfast dishes. Surely that would include a skilful removal of the small sheet that had been so undramatically identified as the identity of the most important machine ever to exist on Earth.

The way it was done: they tied his legs with cord at the ankles and at the knees. His hands and arms were handcuffed behind his back. And he was laid down on the sofa, which was against the wall across from where the intruders now re-seated themselves.

'Stay there!' the thick-faced man commanded. 'Mr Blayney is on his way over.'

'Blayncy!' said Gosseyn Three. But he didn't say it out loud.

After hearing that name, there was no question. He would indeed, 'stay'.

Chapter Fifteen

Gosseyn said, 'You've come far, Mr Blayney, since we last met. Head of the government and commander-in-chief of the armed forces.'

There was no immediate reply. The man who was gazing down at him had a grim look on his smooth face, with a suggestion of puzzlement. Blayney seemed older than the Gosseyn memory recalled for Gosseyn Three. And what had been a heavy-set body was leaner. As if a lot of meals had been skipped, or perhaps there had been an internal chemical re-adjustment to a period of tension.

The clothes the man wore were, if anything, even more elegant than last time.

And, still, there was no reply to his opening remark.

Gosseyn lay there during the lengthening silence, recalling somewhat unhappily that the last time Blayney had stood like this, looking down at a tied-up Gosseyn body, he had suddenly, without visible motivation, leaned down and struck several hard blows.

It seemed an appropriate moment for another conciliatory comment. 'I would deduce,' he said, 'from your great success, that my then analysis of you was in error.'

At that the grim look changed into a shadow of a smile. And the unpleasant silence ended. 'I took your advice,' said Blayney. 'I did an elementary study of General Semantics, and corrected certain, shall we say, false-to-facts personality flaws that you called to my attention.'

Gosseyn had unhappily recalled that the personality flaw the earlier Gosseyn criticised had to do with Blayney being excessively worried about future possibilities. At that time the warning given the mighty Thorson was that a man who always expected the worst would sooner or later — usually sooner — take unnecessary preventive actions on a paranoid level.

It would be unfortunate if anything of that remained; for, in a moment of actual crisis, it might cause an unusually violent response. And, in this situation, the victim, of course, would be Gilbert Gosseyn Three.

An effort should be made to try to head off such an outcome.

'If,' said Gosseyn, 'an elementary study could so quickly elevate you to where you could become head of government, it might be worth your while to take more advanced non-Aristotelian training, and dispose of the remaining . . . false-to-facts' — he repeated the General Semantics term after a tiny pause, and finished — 'that may remain from your early life conditioning.'

What there was of a smile on that smooth face faded. The grimness was back. Blayney shook his head. 'The game of politics,' he said, 'is strictly Aristotelian. It has no place for idealists.'

Above him the hard face was changing again. The puzzlement was back as Blayney bent down, and, with his right hand, touched the cords that bound Gosseyn's knees.

'What I've been trying to figure out,' the man said in that soft voice of his, 'is, why did you let it happen — again?'

The question seemed to imply that Blayney had heard of the twenty-decimal abilities of the Gosseyn brain.

Naturally that was a possibility only, and not to be taken for granted. So Gosseyn parried: 'I'm no smarter than I was last time.' He added, 'Who would suspect that you would take the trouble to keep this little house under surveillance.'

He was watching the smooth face as he spoke the words, with their implied praise. And felt pleased as he detected a tiny smugness in the other's expression.

But Blayney said nothing; offered no explanation of his own foresightedness.

In a way, of course, his comment did not need a reply. First, it was doubtful if an honest answer would ever be given by a conniver. There had been a small group of top people involved, secretly backed by the mighty armies of Enro, commanded by Thorson.

Of those individuals President Hardie was dead, and Thorson was dead. Not too surprising that Blayney, who had been a close associate of one or the other, had taken advantage.

And, obviously, when elections were rigged, those who did the rigging — or their chief aides — tried to gain advantages. But even so it was hard to believe that the people of the western hemisphere of Earth had come down to this in the twenty-sixth century A.D.

It showed what secret intervention by interstellar forces could do to the unsuspecting inhabitants of a planet.

Fortunately, except for further action that Enro might take while aboard the Dzan battleship, that conspiracy had been essentially defeated.

. . . And except, of course, for the leftover debris — like Blayney — that still remained to be cleaned up on Earth. Hopefully, there was a possibility that the man knew nothing of the background of what had happened —

Also, it was possible that the question asked by Gilbert Gosseyn Three had averted a violent reaction from the new head of the government in this area of Earth.

Other than that the Gosseyn predicament remained the same. So far nothing basic had been accomplished.

Thinking thus, and still lying there, Gosseyn Three allowed himself a partial General Semantics awareness.

Naturally, first impression was, once more, of the interior of this little house. And secondly, the thought that it was probably significant that Blayney had not yet indicated his purpose in coming to a place like this . . . coming here from the grandeur of the presidential mansion. But the reality that he had come at all indicated that a decision would presently be made.

So the biggest threat had to do with the presence in this room of a very special type of ordinary, old-style human beings: meaning, most of the individuals who had intruded into Dan Lyttle's small house would probably do nothing inimical until they were given a direct command.

Gosseyn, who had already, earlier, taken the precaution of mentally photographing the four gunmen with his extra-brain, decided that at very least he should offer them a way out. Since there was now a person present with the 'right' to give them any order, including 'Shoot him!' — *and they would* — the time of such an offer had to be now, and not at the moment that the command was given.

It was purpose on an intermediate level; and so he turned his head, and spoke to the four:

'I'd appreciate it if you would all put away your guns.' He added, 'They're not needed, now that I'm handcuffed and tied up.'

Interesting, then, that three of the men simply sat there as if they had not heard. The fourth man — at the far end of the quartet — glanced over at, presumably, his sergeant, or equivalent — the civilian who had, so far, done all the talking for this lower echelon group — and said, 'You got any thoughts on that, Al?'

The man addressed replied immediately in his soft voice: 'The Big Boss is here' — he indicated the beautifully arrayed individual standing beside Gosseyn — 'and he'll give the orders when he feels like it.'

The gun holder, who had spoken, glanced at Gosseyn. And shrugged. Whereupon he sank back into silence, gun still in hand.

Gosseyn turned his gaze away from the men, and smiled grimly up at Blayney. 'Looks like there's not a future Venusian in your group,' he said.

The man-who-had-become-the-equal-of-king was frowning down at the prisoner. 'Was that an attempt to subvert men who have sworn to do their duty whenever called upon to do so by an authorized commander?'

Gosseyn gazed up at the other's slightly heavy, frowning face, and shook his head. 'On one level,' he said, 'General Semantics recognizes the rule of law in a backward society. But what has happened here seems to transcend ordinary legal, or criminal, ordinances.' He broke off: 'Am I to understand that I can be tied up in this fashion without any charges being leveled against me?'

Blayney stroked his jaw. 'You're a special situation. And I gave the order.' His lips twisted into a smile. 'And these men obeyed it, as they should.'

'That's why I spoke to them. They are participants in a pre-emptive action. Their role is that of automatons. In coming here, they came as minions and not with any intention of finding out the facts. Later, when they go to their homes, if someone asks them what they did today, what will they be able to say?'

Blayney's smile was tighter, his teeth showing. 'They're bound by their oaths not to reveal to unauthorized persons anything that happens during their period of duty.'

'In other words,' replied Gosseyn, 'if you were to order them to shoot me, they would do so without having to know the reason?'

'Exactly.' Blayney's manner abruptly showed impatience. 'Government by authority will be continuing on Earth for some time. So let's get to the point. What are you here for?'

But Gosseyn had turned his attention back to the four gun carriers. And it was them he addressed: 'As individuals,' he asked, 'do you each, separately, wish to be bound by the minion condition in this specific situation?'

The Gun-holder-second-from-Gosseyn's-left stirred, and said to Blayney, 'Any special orders, Mr President?'

Silently, that individual shook his head.

So there was still time to obtain more data. Gosseyn turned. And called, 'Mr Lyttle!'

It must have been unexpected. For Lyttle, though he had ceased all kitchen work, and had his hands free, merely stood there. And waited.

It seemed a good idea to let the man recover. The recovery occurred in about five seconds, as Lyttle replied, 'Yes, Mr Gosseyn?'

Before Gosseyn could acknowledge that, there was another interruption. Enin, who had been staring, said, 'You fellows just going to talk?' he asked, 'Or' – to Gosseyn – 'you need help from me?'

Gosseyn smiled. 'Not yet, Enin. If I do, I'll let you know.

116

Right now, if you wish, you can go back to your game.'

'Okay.'

Moments later the delighted cries began again.

And Gosseyn said, 'Mr Lyttle, what would you like to have happen on Earth?'

The reply came immediately, 'I'm hoping that you'll stay, and help restore the whole General Semantics preliminary to Venus here on Earth, including' — after a small pause — 'complete rehabilitation of the Games Machine.'

Gosseyn commented, 'It's generally agreed among Semanticians that the Games Machine proved to be unexpectedly vulnerable to interference with its activities.'

'We have to remember,' was the reply, 'that it's basically a computer; and the addition of a few thousand chips, each with its protective programming, would be of great assistance to it in the future. But of course' — he spoke firmly — 'no machine should ever transcend human control.'

Abruptly, with that reply, Dan Lyttle became a special situation. It took a while then. Even for a Gilbert Gosseyn body-and-mind the associations that came required more than one run-through.

What had seemed coincidence . . . back there . . . with both Gosseyn One and Gosseyn Two suddenly became — what?

Suddenly, the hotel clerk — Dan Lyttle — coming up to the room of a Gilbert Gosseyn, and saving his life, seemed to be connected with . . . with everything that had happened.

And yet, how explain a Gosseyn renting a room in the hotel where that Very Important Clerk worked on the night shift?

It seemed such an ordinary job, such a normal young man, with his little cottage out here, accidentally — so it seemed — located in the hills, slightly to one side of, and above, where the Games Machine had talked every day during the games to the thousands who came periodically in the hope that their knowledge of General Semantics would win them the right to migrate to Venus. Each individual taking his tests alone in one of thousands of separate cubby holes . . .

There had always been something about the way Lyttle held himself, his body, his head. True, knowledge of and the daily

117

use of General Semantics did something similar to most people.

But here was the man that the Games Machine had, in its death throes, entrusted with the part of the gigantic computer system that was . . . itself!

And now, from that same individual, a statement with a basic related purpose.

The explanation for the mystery of Dan Lyttle would have to wait. Right now, it was enough to recognize the man's goals as being similar to his own. And that, accordingly, for Gosseyn Three was the moment of decision. Silently he gave four signals, one after the other – rapidly – to his extra-brain.

Then he relaxed back on the couch, his eyes pointing toward the ceiling.

There was a loud sound, then, off to his left. It was the sound of a man's voice emitting a prolonged 'Uhhhh!'

And then: '*Hey!*'

That final yelling reaction came from the spokesman for the six persons, who had, all this time, been off there to one side. Gosseyn was able to make the identification because he had once more turned his head in that direction.

What he saw were the two men in civilian clothes. Both men were on their feet, and they were staring. It was, for them, a sideways look at the four chairs that, moments before, had been occupied by four uniformed, armed men.

All four gun-holders had disappeared.

It was still not a good situation. A precaution, yes. But, despite his success in getting rid of the threat posed by the four gun-holders, it was still far from being a normal condition for a human being.

His legs were tied as tightly as ever; the handcuffs that encased his wrists were of metal. And he was very much acceptant of responsibility for what had happened as a result of his arrival. Though he was not the original Gosseyn, nevertheless he had made the decision to come here. As a consequence Dan Lyttle and his little house were endangered. And so, Enin and he could not just take off in twenty-decimal fashion.

It was — Gosseyn realized ruefully — not exactly the ideal moment to state a basic purpose. Nonetheless, as he gazed up at Blayney, he spoke the great words:

'Why not,' he asked, 'a return of honest government in the City of the Games Machine?'

Chapter Sixteen

Silence!

Blayney stood there, looking down at the man he had evidently considered to be a prisoner, and not, so to speak, in name only.

Gosseyn, having stated his bottom line, a purpose so basic that anything else at this moment — words or action — would, it seemed to him, merely confuse the issue, consciously relaxed and lay quiet.

It was the second of the two aides who broke that silence. He spoke from the other side of the room, where the gun-holders had been, and said in a deep baritone voice: 'Sir, may we step over there, away from this Distorter area?'

Blayney's expression, which had been essentially that of a non-plussed individual, became grim. He said, 'I think we need a more basic solution.' He pointed down at Gosseyn. 'Come over here, and carry this man outside.'

His eyes narrowed as he gazed down at Gosseyn. 'Any objection?' he asked.

Despite his lying-down position, Gosseyn actually made a shrugging movement with his shoulders. 'I see no point to it,' he said. He added, 'I simply wanted to ask you that one question without being in danger of getting a violent reply.'

He shrugged again. 'What about it?'

Once more it was Civilian Number Two who spoke first. 'What about' — the man waved vaguely towards the empty chairs — 'our guys? Shouldn't he, uh, produce them?'

Blayney, who had half-turned toward the speaker, glanced back at Gosseyn. 'What about them?' he asked.

Gosseyn said, 'They're not dead. But' — he added —

they're not on this planet.'

'I've been trying,' said Blayney, 'to guess where the Distorter would be located that could whisk them away. Because,' the man sounded both puzzled and impressed, 'it must have taken some fine focussing to leave the chairs behind.'

For Gosseyn it had been a relieving interchange; for it was now obvious that Blayney knew nothing of the ability of his extra-brain, and merely believed that a hidden machine had done the nefarious deed.

It seemed important to encourage that belief. So he commented in an even voice, 'As you probably know, the interstellar contact brought a lot of scientific refinement to our little planet, along with the dangers and threats.'

The head of the government of what had once been the United States of America nodded. 'I suppose that's a good way to put it.'

But he seemed to accept the explanation. Because, when he spoke again, it was more personal: 'As for your question, let me repeat something I've already said.' The smile grew satirical. 'Have you ever heard of political parties?'

'In what connection?'

'Well' — tolerantly — 'the upper echelon of a party is a gang of insiders. They occupy all the key positions. There's approximately eight hundred of them, and, prior to an election, they meet in that famous, smoke-filled back room that we've all heard about, where the language is four letter words. Each one of them has his own smoke-filled room, with about two hundred cursing followers; and they all get jobs, also. The upper group are alter egos of the president, and if he does something they don't like, they start yelling.'

Gosseyn said, 'Give me the names of the inner group; and I'll go and talk to them.'

If ever a man had an astonished expression on his face, it was Blayney at that moment. '*Talk* to them!' he said. 'You out of your mind?'

'Well, not really talk.' Gosseyn produced his own tolerant smile. 'My real concern is to begin by re-establishing the Games Machine. Maybe you could treat that as a sort of educational thing, or a museum, or better still a way of getting the votes of the General Semantic nuts — you can call them that, unless you have a better four letter word that will be more convincing to your cursing followers.'

'But why would you want to go and see some of these people?'

Gosseyn explained: 'My interest is only in individuals who resist the re-establishment of the Institute of General Semantics, and, later on, the Games Machine.'

'But what would you do to them?' The man's tone had an insistent quality. 'Kill them?'

'No, I'll just get rid of them, as I did your gunmen here.'

Long pause. Finally, reluctantly: 'Well, I have to admit that you can rig up some pretty good disappearing equipment.' He broke off: 'Where would you send them to?'

'I have a place in mind. But I think it would be better if you didn't know where that was.'

Blayney must have beckoned. Because the civilian Number One came over, untied Gosseyn's legs, and unlocked the handcuffs. Gosseyn took them off himself, and handed them over.

As the aide stepped back, he addressed his 'boss': 'Sir, may I ask this gentleman over here a question?' He indicated Dan Lyttle.

'Why not?' Blayney shrugged.

The aid thereupon said to Lyttle: 'That assumption business you were telling the kid — is that for grown-ups, also?'

There was a faint smile on the lean face of the hotel clerk. 'It's for everybody. Why?'

'Listening to you,' was the reply, 'I got to thinking, maybe I've got a few assumptions I could do without.'

Lyttle said, 'Take a course in elementary General Semantics, like your, uh, boss here did. Look where it got him.'

There was no reply. But a faraway expression in the man's eyes indicated that a thought had come, and was staying.

Moments later, he was courteously opening the door for President Blayney's departure.

. . . As Enin and he rounded the corner, Gosseyn had this

body's first direct glimpse of the Institute of General Semantics — or rather, of what was left of it.

What he saw was a building with a rectangular front that, except for its battered appearance, could have been what was left of an old-style bank building. Coming closer Gosseyn saw that the look of being old was not just wear; it was tear.

Since he knew that the decorative façade had been forcibly removed, it was evident — as he gazed now — that the concrete, which had been below and behind the façade, had been damaged also.

Enin and he crossed the street, and so, presently, they were at the main entrance. And he was pushing a button that had above it the word CARETAKER. Next to the button was a small, ordinary door.

At least two minutes went by. And then the smaller door opened; and a middle-aged man stood there.

Neither the man's eyes nor manner had any welcome in them. However, after he had reluctantly read Blayney's authorization on its official form, he stepped aside, and pointed along a dimly lit, pock-marked main floor that looked as if it had once been marble. He said:

'There's a door about two-thirds down, which has on it the word "private".' His voice sounded unhappy, as he finished: 'I guess that's what you want.'

Gosseyn said, 'We'll also need two keys for this door, so we won't have to bother you when we've been out.'

He indicated the front entrance. Another memory came. He added, 'I seem to recall that there's a side door. We should probably have keys to that, also.'

'Yeah, okay,' was the gloomy reply. And, apparently, a thought was finally coalescing inside the caretaker. 'Things going to happen here?' he asked.

'A lot,' replied Gosseyn.

But he spoke that final comment over his shoulder, as Enin and he started walking off down the broad floor.

After they had walked a hundred or so feet Enin said. 'Something funny about that fellow.'

Gosseyn found himself agreeing silently that the caretaker had been singularly reluctant. Perhaps — he pondered — the man's job was a sinecure; whereas greater activity might require him to start earning his salary.

The man should probably be watched . . . though it was not readily apparent what inimical action such a person could take . . . unless there were others involved.

Gosseyn grew aware that he was smiling wryly at the direction of his thoughts. The vague implication was that there might be enemies of General Semantics, somewhere in the background.

But that really wasn't a problem. For the most part, the vast majority of the Earth population couldn't care less. For them Venus — where everyone had to be a self-starter — had no attraction whatsoever.

. . . No jobs there! — Good God, how do they operate the place? . . .

The timeless masses of Earth, on whom the passage of the centuries had made no basic impact . . . except that, with the development of technology, they now pushed buttons which operated the daily machinery of their homes and their transportation on a level of underlying intricacy that the individual normally did not even try to comprehend.

So — Gosseyn's interim conclusion, as Enin and he came to the door marked private — if the caretaker needed to be spied on, it would be for a reason that, right now, was obscure. And not analyzable in advance.

Chapter Seventeen

As they went through the unlocked door, marked private, Enin said, 'Looks like we're meeting nothing but crumby people and going to nothing but crumby places.'

The thought which the comment evoked in Gosseyn Three brought a smile to his lips; whereupon, after a small pause, he spoke the famous General Semantics concept:

'Enin, the map is not necessarily the territory; and, besides, you've got your maps slightly mixed. After all, we've just come from a meeting with the top government leader of this continent.'

There was a pause. Then: 'Oh, him!' Another pause, followed by a frown, and the words: 'What do you mean, map?'

'Later,' said Gosseyn, 'I'll explain.'

But with him, also, and, with or without the aid of General Semantics' concepts, the living quarters he was looking at did not evoke love at first sight.

The apartment in which they found themselves was large enough for their immediate purposes; but it had definitely not been well kept. And it had visibly been stripped of some of its furniture.

There was only one place in the living room to sit down: a couch. No chairs were to be seen, and only one small table, and a cabinet phone; the phone was complete with a videoplate, whereby, if one so desired, one could see, and be seen, by one's caller.

Gosseyn made a single, quick mental survey of the possibilities inherent in himself being seen during a phone call. And promptly walked over, bent down, and disconnected the video modular.

In the kitchen, moments later, he saw that there was a built-in breakfast nook, a built-in oven, and a large built-in refrigeration unit. Missing from the surrounding built-in shelves were about three-quarters of the dishes that must have been there at one time.

There were two bedrooms, one with a single, king-sized bed, and the other with twin-beds; but no other furniture. Built-in clothes closets were available in both bedrooms; so at least there would be a place to store whatever clothing thcy acquired while on Earth.

He was aware of Enin going into the smaller bedroom. So Gosseyn headed for the kitchen. In his initial search of the drawers there he had noticed a pad and pen. So now he sat down, and began to make a list.

It was his first quiet moment since their arrival. Sitting there he became aware of an odd sensation inside his head and body. Gosseyn paused, pen still inches above the pad. He frowned because . . . what, what?

Interruption: Enin's voice reached him from beyond the door: 'Do you think he means it? Do you think he's really going to do it?'

'Do what?'

His awareness of the strange internal feeling grew dim, as he called out the question, and followed it with another one:

'And who do you mean?'

'Mr Blayney! Do you think he'll really rebuild this place?'

Gosseyn finished writing the word 'milk'. Then he laid the pen down. Stood up. And walked out to the living room. As he did so he realized he was experiencing a complexity of thoughts and awarenesses:

. . . Awareness that the strange sensation had been there all these minutes, maybe even hours, damped out by the demanding presence of Enin; thought about how to answer the boy's question; vague consciousness of his Alter Ego, and all those realities . . .

He found Enin lying on the living room floor in what could essentially be called a twisted position. But the kid seemed at ease. Gosseyn walked over, and stood looking down at the emperor of all Dzan, and spoke again in General Semantics phraseology:

'The best answer I can give you is based on a generalized map I have inside me of the way governments work.'

'But you said the map is not the territory.' The boy's eyes were bright.

The man was aware of himself smiling. 'I meant the map is not necessarily the territory. And that's particularly true when we're dealing with the maps we have of the way the world is and the way people are in general. Here on Earth President Blayney has a lot of money at his disposal for public spending. One or more companies will do the rebuilding of the institute; and they'll receive government aid to do it. What's important about that is, it puts the builders on our side. So −'

At that moment the phone rang. Gosseyn walked over, lifted the receiver, and said, 'Hello! Who are you calling?'

A man's voice said, 'This is the Daynbar Construction Company. We understand you have been authorized to rebuild the institute; and we'd like to send a team over to discuss the renovation.'

Gosseyn had his moment of awe, even though he had just predicted something basic like this. His instant deduction was that an associate of Blayney had contacted a builder who, presumably, at some later time would pay the informant for the information.

Since it was, for him, a positive development, his reply was within the frame of business courtesy: 'When can your people get over here?'

It developed that their 'team' would show up at 8 a.m. next day . . . all very normal, Gosseyn realized. But, somehow, not fast enough for the feeling of urgency that was − somehow − reaching into him from . . . somewhere.

After he had replaced the receiver, he grew aware that Enin was up and standing in the kitchen doorway, staring at him. But the boy said nothing. Whereupon Gosseyn commented: 'I hope all this is not too boring for you.'

There was a pause, and then − of all things − a grin creased that youthful face. 'I guess,' the boy said, 'you've got some assumptions about me wanting to be back on that stupid ship with all those suck-ups.'

'More like, maybe you want to be back with your mother,' Gosseyn answered.

But even as he spoke, he was silently adjusting to Enin's analysis. It was not wrong after all those boyish complaints; but he had to admit that the thought — belief — in his mind had been that, to his Imperial Majesty of Dzan, a place like Earth, with no one kowtowing was, well, crumby. And crumby in at least one of its meanings implied that whoever felt that way didn't want to be here.

As that thought was completed, Enin spoke again: 'Things happen around you,' he said, 'and you're not a sissy. Just imagine — you let yourself be tied up back there, and you got rid of those gun carriers . . .' Pause. The boy's eyes grew wider. 'Hey, I forgot to ask. Where did you put those guys?'

Gosseyn smiled. Grimly. 'On that ice world, where we were.'

'Boy!' Another pause. 'You don't think they'll freeze?'

Gosseyn said, 'They had on pretty regular clothes, and there's only about a mile to go to that building; so I'm not worried.'

He thought for a moment. Then: 'It's the price I'm charging them for not being aware of the assumptions by which they operate.'

He concluded: 'You remember, I gave them all a chance to think about it, and one of them bothered.'

There was, if it were possible for a boy of twelve to have such an expression, a pensive look in Enin's face. 'Yeah,' he said then, 'yeah.' He added, 'It's hard to picture us just sitting here while they rebuild this place. Is there anything else coming up?'

It was a good question. The feeling inside Gosseyn of something probing at him was stronger. And it was definitely time to determine what, if anything, was causing such a strange sensation in his head.

The phone rang again, instants after that purpose was born.

Enin's voice came from off to one side: 'Looks like another company wants the job.'

Gosseyn, who was heading toward the phone, made no verbal reply. But he did have the thought-answer that, on this high government level, there would probably be no bidding for specific construction projects.

Any call having to do with rebuilding would have to be about another aspect of the task. And, of course, the truth was there would be many aspects.

However, moments later, as he spoke the same question — as before — into the receiver, there was a far more significant difference in the reply. The man's voice at the other end of the line had a harsh quality, as it said, 'Let me just make it very clear: if you don't get off those premises by the end of this day you'll get hurt. That institute of stupidity is not going to be rebuilt!'

Gosseyn, who had automatically noted that the message, and the voice, were being recorded — automatically — by the cabinet machine, was able to recover from the unexpected threat in time to say, 'Be sure to dress warmly from this moment on!'

There was actually a pause at the other end of the line. And then the same voice, but with a baffled instead of a threatening tone, said, 'What kind of nonsense is that?'

Bang! Down went the receiver at the other end.

'. . . On that call,' Gosseyn analyzed moments later, 'I am inclined to deduce that it is the result of our caretaker advising someone who is willing to pay him for the information.'

Enin frowned. 'I don't get the assumption,' he said.

Gosseyn could not restrain a smile at the use of the General Semantics term — which was not entirely applicable. But all he said was, 'My reasoning is that groups, or individuals, against re-educating the public would have a very inexpensive source of information about any projected activity on these premises, if they bribed the caretaker.'

'Yeah!' The boy spoke his agreement almost absently. He stood there with his lips drawn tight, as if in deep thought. Then he nodded. And said, 'Now, what do we do?'

It was not a question that Gosseyn was able to answer immediately. His head was, figuratively, whirling.

There was accordingly no question. The most important event in his life at the moment was that sensation of something probing at his entire nervous system.

Chapter Eighteen

When, moments later, he was able to attract the attention of his Alter Ego, Gosseyn Two said mentally across those vast distances: 'I've been aware of your sensations, and they're similar to what we get from that alien ship when our defenses are momentarily penetrated. Your problem is you're out there, unprotected.'

Because of the enormous interstellar barrier between him and the enemy, it was a startling analysis. But it was surely the most likely possibility. The alien ship's efforts at mental control could not reach through the electronic defenses of the Dzan vessel or of Enro's warships.

But, somehow, those incredibly accurate instruments had retained contact with Gosseyn Three. And, though they were probably not aware of it, he was, for them, the most important human being: the individual who, inadvertently, was responsible for their entire ship, with all its personnel, being transmitted from their own galaxy to this one.

But they suspected something. Because, though he was multi-light-years distant from them, they were electronically aware of him, and, with their refined instruments, were somehow trying to grab him.

The instant thought in his mind, now that he was considering it, was: why not let them succeed?

He asked the question of Gosseyn Two: ' . . . What would I do, if I went aboard their ship?'

'Well' — the distant thought of Gosseyn Two was accompanied by a grim smile — 'one thing that would, at very least, be delayed would be the rebuilding of the Institute of General Semantics on Earth.'

There was at least one answer for that. Gosseyn stated it mentally: 'When Dan Lyttle gets off duty from his hotel job at midnight, he's coming over here to sleep.' He concluded that message, 'I think I can safely leave him in charge if I go aboard the alien ship – which I really think I should do, provided I first get rid of a potential trouble maker here on Earth.'

The answer seemed to be a resigned acceptance: 'You're a braver man than I am. What about the boy?'

Gosseyn had been intent. Now, he glanced around. And was slightly startled to realize that Enin had disappeared . . . That strange look in his face; he's up to something –

Mentally, he said, 'I think I can leave him here with Dan temporarily. I doubt if he should go back aboard at this time.' He smiled. 'His General Semantics re-education is not yet completed. And right now I'd better sign off, and see where he went . . .'

– A big man in his shirt sleeves. That was the source of the threatening voice.

Gosseyn's swift search for Enin had taken him down the long, grubby hallway to the caretaker's quarters. And there was that unworthy on the floor, babbling information to a boy who had – it developed – 'burned' him several times before the reality penetrated that only a confession would save him from the special ability of this demon kid . . .

The name that finally came from him – Gorrold – turned out to be an individual on Blayney's list of top two hundred cursing back room supporters.

And Gosseyn, who had thereupon gone straight to the man's office, now stood slightly baffled, gazing at the chunky Gorrold body and insolent face. Because it would be wrong to twenty-decimal a person so flimsily dressed to that frozen world . . . back there.

As he thought of other possibilities, Gosseyn spoke glibly, 'President Blayney asked me to talk to you. Perhaps we could go somewhere, and have lunch, or a drink?'

At the very least, going out – for anything – would require Gorrold to put on a coat.

But the smoldering gray eyes merely stared at him from a

131

grim, heavy face. 'I have drinks right here.'

However the man made no move to get the 'drinks'. Simply sat there behind his gleaming desk in his shirt sleeves, smiling sarcastically. It was an expensive looking shirt, but not warm enough for icy weather.

'I'm going to deduce,' Gosseyn continued, 'that you will understand when I say that it's to be a private conversation; not to be held in someone's office where we might be overheard.'

'If,' replied Gorrold, 'the president wants to give me special instructions, he can just pick up the phone, as he's done a hundred times before; and when I recognize his voice, I'll say, "Yes, Mr President, consider the job done." '

With that the face lost any semblance of a smile. 'So I don't get this private message, with the messenger being someone I've never seen before.'

Gosseyn's seeking gaze had suddenly spied the man's coat – at least it had the same cloth color as the trousers he wore. The coat lay across what he guessed was the private bar table of this office in the far corner.

With that discovery made he felt better, and stood up. 'Evidently, you don't appreciate what I've just said: that conversations might be overheard. So I'll simply report back to the president that you would rather not hear his private communication, and he can take it from there. All right?'

Gorrold accompanied him to the door, opened it, and called to his secretary, 'Miss Drees, let this gentlemen out.'

The way Gosseyn passed him to go out required Gorrold to step back partly out of sight behind the door. At that exact instant Gosseyn transmitted him to the ice world.

Gosseyn grasped the door knob firmly, and said as if speaking to Gorrold: 'See you again, sir.' Almost simultaneously his gaze flicked over to the coat lying on the bar. With his extra-brain he made his special mental photographic copy. And moments later transmitted *it* also to the location on that distant world of ice.

Whereupon he closed the door gently behind him. And, moments later, walked past the secretary to and through the partly open outer door.

As he headed for the distant exit he was unwarily thinking about something to which he should not have given a moment's attention: it was a vague hope that Mr Gorrold had his help so well trained that there would be no chance of Miss Drees entering her boss' office without being called.

His vague feeling was that it would be better for the rebuilding of the Institute of General Semantics if there was never any connection suspected between the visit of Gilbert Gosseyn and the disappearance of Gorrold.

Unwary moment. At that exact instant the sensation in his head became a whirling blackness.

Chapter Nineteen

Gosseyn opened his eyes in pitch darkness.

Remembering what had happened — the whirling sensation — he lay still. And it actually took at least a dozen seconds before the thought came that . . . Could it be, was it possible?

His sudden startled realization was that this was exactly the way the Gosseyn Three body had awakened after the space capsule had been taken aboard the Dzan battleship.

. . . I'm lying here naked (that was the feeling), covered by a thin sheet.

He moved his hands and arms slightly. And there was no question: it was a sheet, and it was cloth-like and not heavy; and, except for it, he seemed not to be wearing any clothes. His fingers touched warm skin.

Slowly, carefully, he pulled at the sheet; drew it down, and away from, the upper part of his body. Then, equally slowly, he raised his hands upward, probing.

He touched a flat surface. Less than a dozen inches above his chest, he estimated. And when he braced himself, and pushed against it, it turned out to be a smooth, solid substance with no give in it.

. . . *Exactly as when he had come to in the capsule* . . . only a couple of days ago in terms of how long he had been conscious since then.

He sank back to a relaxed position, and wondered: . . . are my actions being observed here, also?

. . . Or am I cut off from the outside?

With that sudden feeling of uncertainty, it was definitely time for a test.

'Alter!' It was a directed mental call. 'Do you have any idea

134

what happened to me? Was that' — he hesitated, shaken by the possibility — 'another death in our group?'

There was a pause. A sense of emptiness . . . out there. And then, abruptly, contact, almost as if a door had been opened. 'All these seconds,' came the thought of Gosseyn Two, 'I've been only vaguely aware of you. Even your thought just now was dim. So it could be that someone is letting this communication happen. Everything is suddenly clearer.'

It did not seem to be the moment for analyzing who that someone might be. And in his next 'words' the Alter Ego seemed to have had the same thought; it was an answer to Three's question:

'I don't think,' said that faraway mental voice, 'that you, Gosseyn Three, were killed. So this is not another Gosseyn body awakening.'

The statement had its relieving aspect, but there was also a chilling quality. Because what had happened and was happening implied that the someone who was performing these remarkable technological miracles knew about the earlier awakening.

Because it was a similar type of capsule he was in.

Which triggered a sudden additional thought: That first time — all those connectors?

He could feel none of the physical sensations of rubber tubing or penetrating needles, of which he had so swiftly become aware on his first awakening. And, as he now probed cautiously with his fingers and hands, and with arms reaching all the way down to his lower extremities, there was only bare skin.

He called out mentally to Gosseyn Two: 'It looks as if you got it right. This is not Gosseyn Four coming to consciousness. As you, apparently correctly, analyzed, it has the look of a captured Gosseyn Three.'

For some reason he felt relieved. And many moments went by, then, before the realization came that proof that here was, in fact, a captured Gosseyn body, was not exactly a reason for he who was the captured one to feel better.

Suddenly unhappy again, he resumed his thought communication with the safe Gosseyn . . . out there: 'It would seem these aliens were able to reach across tens of thousands of light-years, grab me, and take me somewhere.'

'Wel-l-l-ll!' There was a reluctance in the reply from the faraway Alter Ego, with overtones of unhappiness rather than rejection. 'Remember, they got some sort of hold on you, electronically, before you left the Dzan ship. And evidently they finally worked out the problem of distance control, and took action.'

Lying there in the darkness, Gosseyn Three agreed that it was very evident indeed.

'After all,' Gosseyn Two concluded, 'we have to remember that the Gosseyn extra-brain has proved that at some level of reality distance has no meaning.'

It was true. But it was not a happy thing to realize that somebody else had now used a similar method to capture a Gosseyn body. Since the alien-controlled ship had not hesitated to attack the Dzan battlecraft, the question was: why hadn't they simply killed Gosseyn Three?

Gosseyn Two's answering thought came through at that point in an odd, matter-of-fact fashion:

'I think we can finally analyze the situation. They're probably studying you. They'd like to reconstruct what happened to them. Here they are in another galaxy; and they have now got the villain responsible for causing the disaster. So any minute be prepared to go on trial for the crime of illegal alien transportation.'

It was, somehow, not a reassuring comment.

The recollection came to Gosseyn Three that, while still on Earth, he had actually expressed the wish that he go aboard the alien-manned ship, and confront the semi-humans.

Presumably such a confrontation would now take place under circumstances somewhat less favorable: they knew where he was, but he didn't know for certain where either they, or he, was.

What bothered him — he realized as he continued to lie there — was that, perhaps, he should be on his way. And never mind waiting here in the hope of finding out what anyone else might want to do with him.

. . . The private thought, with its implied purpose, must

136

again have transmitted itself to Gosseyn Two; for the Alter Ego mind was suddenly manifesting relevant thoughts:

'Whatever you do should be very carefully considered. As I said, your captors may be studying you, and that means studying the Gosseyn extra-brain potentialities. And since, as you just recalled, you were trying to figure out how you could get aboard, don't dismiss the potentialities of that too rapidly.'

'You're presuming that I am aboard the alien ship?'

'It's not the only possibility, but, considering what has happened so far, the most likely one.'

'True,' Gosseyn Three acknowledged from his darkness. 'So what is your recommendation?'

'Wait!'

. . . The waiting grew long.

His feeling finally was: perhaps those who were observing him were wondering what *he* would do next. It occurred to him that one of those nexts should be the Dzan battleship.

Going there would place him again within the frame of the big ship's protective screens. So it would be important to determine if his captors were prepared to let him escape to a location where they could no longer control him.

As he reached that point in his analysis, he realized that the other Gosseyn was mentally shaking his head.

'It's okay to come here,' telepathed Gosseyn Two, 'provided you first transfer Enin back to his mother's and his apartment. The lady thinks the boy is with you; and so, you'd better not come here by yourself.'

'Okay. That tells me where I should go first.'

It could have been the moment of decision. Gosseyn could feel himself bracing; his extra-brain doing that special focussing necessary for the twenty-decimal similarity transmission to work, when —

At that moment a voice said: 'Get him out, and the . . . (meaningless word) will talk to him!'

A pause; then, from the faraway Gosseyn Two came an admonishment: 'Watch it, Three! They obviously let you hear that intentionally. And so, although the whole notion of a talk would normally be reassuring, after their instant attack when they arrived, as a reminder that they're not friendly, I advise you to be ready to jump if that's merely a ploy.'

Under his body he suddenly felt a movement. As on that first occasion two long days ago, the movement was in the direction towards which his head pointed.

Gosseyn sighed inwardly. But, after moments only, he noticed it was not a feeling of relief that he had so automatically – thalamically – expressed. It was tension. Which intensified as that steady motion brought him closer to – what.

Flickering memories came of how – last time – he had actually been brought out of the capsule into the virtually total darkness of the Dzan laboratory.

Maybe the Troogs would make a similar attempt to conceal themselves from him while, by way of their instruments, they looked him over.

Should he let them? After a rueful moment he realized that the real question was: *could* he stop them?

He recalled that . . . back there on the Dzan ship . . . he had felt a sudden freshness because, then, what was apparently either a greater amount of air, or a slightly different temperature in the laboratory, had affected the nerve ends of his naked body.

Shall I? Shall I not?

He actually thought of where he should try to go first, and he actually did what was necessary to 'set up' his extra-brain for the twenty-decimal similarity jump to that location.

But the indecision, he realized, had a basic, underlying, unresolved uncertainty that was relevant only to the Gosseyn condition.

Things were happening, and would continue to happen, to the Gilbert Gosseyn duo that was currently alive. And on one level – the level where the two of them operated as a team, whereby it didn't matter if one body was killed so long as there was another one to carry on, with duplicate memories and abilities . . . on that level, it might be a good idea to confront these people before he had any real understanding of what they could, or could not, do.

. . . On the other hand, if this body is killed – that's really *me*, gone forever.

Guilt came . . . Here we are, we Gosseyn bodies, with this great similarity thing in our heads, whereby memory equals identity, and similar bodies go on and on — that group of eighteen-year-olds were still waiting out there somewhere . . .

In spite of that reality, I am the one — maybe the first one — who's beginning to think like a separate person.

In terms of General Semantics, of course, he was a separate being: an intricate complex of particles and energy flows arranged in the shape of a human being, different from all the other similar shapes in the universe, including Gosseyns One and Two.

Something of the implications of that rapid reasoning in this stress situation must have reached out to the faraway Alter Ego. Because, suddenly, the thought came: 'Hey, Three, wait a minute! Let's talk!'

Presumably, with that other Gosseyn mind reaching out to him, and at that very instant a door opening, and light glaring in on him from a room, where — instantly — he could see several twisted looking, two-legged beings standing, staring at him with round, lidless, black eyes . . . presumably, it was a moment of confusion.

Enough to trigger a reaction.

Chapter Twenty

He arrived naked, still on his back, and face up.

Gosseyn Three lay very still, orienting himself to a sunlit room. Not easy; for there was the confusion of those last moment mental pictures of what he had seen of the aliens.

And there was the instant concern about them, and what they might do; and, simultaneously, a quick attempt at awareness of his own body feelings:

. . . Were there any sensations that would indicate that they still had contact with him?

The several seconds required for him to realize that he was lying on the carpeted floor of the bedroom in the Institute of General Semantics went by. Relief came when he saw that the door was closed, and that he was alone. And then, finally . . .

He grew aware of a vague, slow, spinning sensation.

Deep inside him.

Even though he had expected it, he was disappointed.

'Okay, okay,' he thought glumly, as he climbed to his feet. 'At least now I know what it is and what it can lead to.'

After several seconds of adjusting to the standing position, he was suddenly hopeful: maybe they would observe him for a while. See what he did. Find out why he had come here.

And, of course, there were obvious firsts for a human being to do.

Blayney had sent over half a dozen men's suits, with all the necessary complements; and five of them – Gosseyn discovered with relief – were still in his clothes closet.

As he slipped hastily into, first, undershorts, and then a pair of dark beige trousers, and a brown shirt, socks and shoes, he found himself wondering what had happened to the suit he had been wearing at the moment when he was transported to the capsule duplicate aboard the alien ship.

Was there a crumpled coat, trousers, shorts, shirt, tie, socks and shoes lying in the corridor outside the office of businessman Gorrold?

That was the most likely possibility. Hard to believe that the spinning sensation, which had preceded the moment of transmission, had affected anything but his living body. In his own twenty-decimal similarity extra-brain transport, clothes accompanied him only if he consciously took that special mental photograph of them . . .

His small awarenesses about that ceased abruptly, as he grew more consciously aware of his surroundings, and of the fact that, during those final moments of getting dressed, he had the realization that Gosseyn Two was manifesting . . . out there.

In effect, then, he looked up, and spoke silently: 'Okay, Alter Ego, any suggestions?'

The reply was peaceful: 'No. You're the one that's out there. I seem to be sitting out this entire experience. I gather you want to do something about Enin before anything else happens.'

It was true. Though − now that he was back on the scene − the purpose did not seem quite as urgent as it had earlier. He realized that Two's comment about not being involved had brought a whole new train of thought.

'Does that mean,' he asked, 'that we're getting to be sufficiently dissimilar that you don't have any of that spinning sensation inside you?'

'Apparently,' was the reply, 'they seem to be able to differentiate between us. Or it's a focussing device they use, and they've got it pointed at you.'

The second thought seemed, instantly, to be the most likely possibility. And so, Gosseyn Three telepathed: 'If that's the truth of the matter, then, if necessary, you can either come and get Enin, or transmit him on the basis of the mental photograph in my extra-brain.'

'We have some fine reasoning to do,' came the reply, 'and maybe even some testing. But in anything to do with Enin and you, we must include in our logic the effect on the Queen Mother Strala of anything you do.' A faint smile seemed to accompany the concluding thought: 'If you're going to be the first Gosseyn to make love to a woman, you'd better not muff the emotional preliminaries any more than you already have.'

Gosseyn Three did not argue with the analysis. He finished putting on his shoes. And then he was up, opening the door.

He saw at once that Enin was there in the living room with Dan Lyttle. The boy saw him, and said, 'Gee, I'm sure glad you're back. This guy is worse than — ' He spoke an unfamiliar name.

It was one of those delayed hearing processes; but presently it seemed as if what he had heard was 'Traada!' And, equally important, it dawned on him that that must be the name of the emperor's teacher on the Dzan battleship.

The disgusted hand movement seemed to mean that Dan Lyttle was worse than Traada.

The situation seemed to call for a question. 'What's the subject?' Gosseyn asked.

'Names.'

'Oh!' acknowledged Gosseyn.

'He says a chair is not a chair.'

In spite of himself, Gosseyn found himself smiling. Evidently Dan Lyttle had been continuing the boy's General Semantics education. And this was the latest.

What bothered him was the feeling that he didn't really have the time for things like this. His logic said the Troogs, not being semantically oriented, would swiftly become impatient if he involved himself with the homey details of human existence.

Nevertheless, there were things he should know. Quickly.

He turned to the man. 'Any problems while I was — ' At that point he hesitated, with the realization that Dan and Enin believed him to have been interviewing business people who were against General Semantics; there were no suitable words that could possibly describe the awesome reality of what had happened, so he completed the thought with a stereotype — 'out?'

The phone rang.

Whereupon Dan Lyttle smiled, and said, 'I think we have the answer to your question. That's the fourth call since I came in. The first three were from outraged businessmen. Shall I take it?'

'No. Let me.'

As Gosseyn hurriedly walked over to the end of the couch, sank into it, and picked up the receiver, Enin said, 'And there were two calls when I was here alone.'

Gosseyn said, 'Hello.' In his best baritone.

There was a long pause at the other end. Then the sound of a man forcefully inhaling. And finally a familiar voice said, 'This is Gorrold. In case you don't remember my name, maybe it will help if I tell you I'm phoning from an observatory in the Andes. And there are four President Blayney guards here. And we'll be back this evening. Three of us have plans for you.'

So it had been Earth.

Gosseyn was aware of mixed feelings as that reality penetrated. Presumably he should feel relief; since, of course, he had never intended permanent harm to any of the men. Also, it seemed reasonably logical that his extra-brain had, during those moments of confusion, selected the known location from the unknown. Split-instant interactions would have been involved. And at that speed the familiar had automatically synchronized more swiftly.

They were split-instant, fleeting thoughts; and, even as he had them, he was making his decision.

'I have the feeling,' he said into the mouthpiece, 'that we ought to have a face-to-face conversation. And, now that you have experienced the basic nothingness of the universe, maybe right now would be a good time.'

The voice at the other end of the line made a sound. It seemed to be an expression of puzzlement. The word uttered, if it could be called that, had in it a combination of h's and n's, and a vowel, or two, or three. And it came through something like:

'Huhnnuhhn?' The tone implied a question.

Gosseyn did not attempt an exact translation. In the moments that followed its utterance he, first, made an extra-

143

brain photograph of a location on the floor a dozen feet away; and simultaneously recalled his mental photograph of Gorrold.

As he did so, there was a sound and a gasp. It came from the business executive he had seen so briefly — was it the day before? — who was now lying on the floor across the room.

Gosseyn replaced the receiver, and said in his calmest voice, 'The difficulties we find in our dealings with other people is that they have an overall simplistic idea in their heads about how things are. To such people the world is a series of fixed mental pictures. They look at what we call a chair, and they think of it as exactly that — no more, no less.'

His self-control was evidently catching. Because Enin, after one startled look at the writhing body on the floor, seemed to recover. He said in a challenging tone, 'Well, isn't it? Chairs are for sitting down in.' The boy was shrugging. 'I'm beginning to think maybe I'm on their side.'

'Each chair is different from all other chairs,' Gosseyn explained. 'Even in a factory, where they make a single style of chair by the thousands, the grain of the wood — as one example — is different in each. But that's a superficial aspect of what we're talking about in General Semantics. What's important for the mind is that we should at all times be essentially aware that *any* object is a complex structure in terms of physics and chemistry. In this instance, we have given the structure the name ''chair'', and we generally use it for what you said. But I've also seen it used for holding open a door. What it's called is okay. But we should be aware of the underlying particles, atoms, molecules, energy flows etc.' He smiled. 'Got that?'

There was no immediate answer from His Imperial Majesty of the Dzan. Gosseyn grew aware that Dan Lyttle also had a faint smile on his face. The younger man glanced at him, and then, without a word, walked over to where Gorrold was climbing to his feet.

The sturdily built business executive seemed to be uncertain. Finally: 'Where the hell is my jacket?' he asked in a sullen tone.

For Gosseyn it was a moment of mild surprise. He hadn't

noticed in a meaningful way that the man had arrived coatless. Vaguely, the awareness had been there at the back of his mind. But he had had — he realized — so many other things going on in the observational side of his brain that, in fact, the automatic truth of the extra-brain had not transferred its meaning.

Belatedly he recalled that originally he had transmitted Gorrold to the icy mountainside, and had then transmitted the jacket to the same location as an act of kindness — not really wanting the man to suffer any more cold than was minimally necessary.

Presumably the coat was now lying on the floor beside the phone in the observatory over there in South America.

Under the circumstances it was no greater problem for the extra-brain to transfer the coat than the man. And so, bare moments later, Gosseyn warily walked past Gorrold and Dan. Reached down. Picked up the jacket. And handed it to the owner.

There was silence as the chunky man put on the coat. His fifty-ish face reflected a whole series of inner reactions. Then, as he completed the act of dressing . . .

'I have to admit — ' began Gorrold.

. . . Hopeful beginning, thought Gosseyn.

' — that,' continued the man, 'however you're doing what has been happening to me — '

The words seemed to indicate that caution was moving in behind all the basic outrage and anger.

' — maybe I'd better think things over before I do anything further!' With those words, the super-executive completed his thought.

For Gosseyn, it was undoubtedly the best outcome he could hope for. For the time being.

He saw that Dan Lyttle had walked over, and was opening the corridor door. And then he waited while the older man walked over to it, through it and, turning, moved off out of the line of sight.

Gosseyn was prepared to deduce that the man would leave the building as swiftly as possible; but Enin trotted over to the door, and peered around it. The boy presently reported, 'He's heading for the main door.'

Then: 'He's gone.'

During the half-minute involved Gosseyn had closed his eyes, and transmitted President Blayney's four guards one by one to a street location that the earliest Gosseyn had once used.

Enin was coming back into the room. He asked, 'Going to do anything about those other guys who called?'

Gosseyn drew a deep breath. 'No,' he said.

A strange thought had come — strange for him. It was time to take a break; that was the feeling. There had to be a pause in the ceaseless driving existence in which this Gosseyn body had been involved since that first moment of awakening inside the capsule aboard the Dzan battleship.

True, he had slept in Dan Lyttle's little house. But though a sleep of exhaustion had its place, and its own necessity, that was not what he needed.

A break.

He said, 'Listen Enin! Listen, Dan! President Blayney put a billfold with money in every one of the suits he sent over for me. So let's leave right now, and go to the nearest restaurant, and eat. And talk.'

As he mentioned the money there was fleeting memory in him. It was a fragment of information, automatically known to the dead Gosseyn One's brain, and of course, therefore, automatically a part of the memories of Gosseyn Two and Three: about the five times, in five hundred or so years since the death of Korzybski, that an inflated dollar had had to be brought back from the level where a dozen eggs cost $500. At each deflationary time, thousand dollar bills, beginning on specific dates, were exchanged for $1 each. Five such inflationary periods had now come back to the rational condition whereby his billfold contained, of course, a few fifties and hundreds, but also, ones, fives, and tens.

. . . The restaurant had one of those dimly lit interiors; but there was a video game room, from which Enin had to be rescued twice; both times he came dutifully when Gosseyn went over and reported that food had arrived. Each time he ate his share, and then departed at speed.

146

In between, as Gosseyn and Dan Lyttle each ate a sandwich and salad, the subject of conversation was Dan Lyttle himself.

Gosseyn's first question: 'Why, after your training in General Semantics was accepted by the Games Machine as being adequate, didn't you go to Venus?'

The younger man's answer was, in view of the subject matter, obviously straightforward: 'As you know, I'm a night clerk at a good hotel. Despite the advanced state of computer technology for such places they still need human beings; and I got the job at a time when work was temporarily scarce. I immediately discovered that it removed me from the normal condition of a human being.

'Working all night, and sleeping eight hours some time during the following day, quickly ended the few associations I had formed when I first came to the City of the Games Machine from the east coast. I thought about that, and, after taking two different young ladies out during my days off — separately, of course — I decided I could not subject a normal young woman to marriage with me. Now, General Semantics, as you know, and as I discovered later, merely provides guidelines in the direction of survival within the frame of any life situation.

'Before I ever took my GS training, there was a woman who had seen me late one night when she visited an out-of-town friend who was staying at the hotel. Naturally, I found this out only later. But what happened: she checked in one night, and called me at 3 a.m., and asked me to come up to her room and make love to her. Well, I was a young fellow; I still hadn't made any decisions about things like that. It turned out that her husband had died; and she had resolved to be his wife forever, and never marry again. But she saw me and called me, and I went up. And thereafter, once a month, she would pray for her husband's forgiveness, and check into the hotel, and call me.

'As I said, I started getting involved in that situation before I took my training in General Semantics. And, when I later discussed this relationship with the Games Machine, apparently human sexual activity was something it could not evaluate. Believe it or not, after it discovered that I was awake

147

all night, the Games Machine occasionally phoned me in the wee hours, and talked to me.'

Gosseyn waited. It was a minor item, but interesting, implying that the Machine was busy thinking even during off hours.

Dan Lyttle continued: 'Maybe it was also phoning other night clerks; but I think not. Because, after you showed up for the Games, and it started evaluating your situation, and the meaning of the great armies that were arriving in the vicinity of Earth, it used me as its outside ally in case of an emergency. So one day I went over, and that was when the Machine gave me a duplicate it had made of itself.'

'That was the small transistorized plate you showed me?' Gosseyn asked.

'That's it. Believe it or not, until you came along with your duplicate body, it had not thought of such a solution as a duplicate of itself.'

'Well' — Gosseyn was thoughtful — 'that still doesn't entirely explain your not going to Venus.'

'I became its special agent.' The eyes on the other side of the restaurant table gazed at him earnestly. 'You'll have to admit that was a worthwhile status. As for the woman, after I became GS oriented I urged her to take the training. She did, and, after a while, I discovered that something inside her was beginning to adjust to her husband's death; and that in fact a male acquaintance had suddenly noticed her, and had asked her to go out to dinner with him. Not too long after that she stopped seeing me. But there was a change in her. She held herself differently, somehow.'

Gosseyn had no additional question, or comment. What he had heard gave him a new view of the late, great Games Machine. As for the woman, and her association with a hotel clerk — there had always been a human problem to solve in that area.

It had been observed that men normally preferred women who had a good outer appearance, and who, as a consequence, showed some kind of inner strength. Interesting that, perhaps, the inner strength was all that was needed.

He stopped. Because . . . inside him . . . an odd, tugging

sensation had started suddenly.

He rose hastily to his feet. He said, 'You take Enin back to the Institute.' By the time he finished those words he had hastily taken out the Blayney billfold and tossed it on the table. 'You pay for the dinner out of that.'

He was thinking: this time it was not the earlier spinning feeling but —

He wondered vaguely: . . . tugging — to where?

Chapter Twenty-one

On a planet of a sun in the Milky Way a man named Neggen stood gazing down at a machine — a small, cigar-shaped spaceship.

The spacecraft was below him in a natural hollow that was half garden and half smooth marble. It was man-smoothed marble and a man-made garden, which provided a decorative setting for the little machine.

The man was thinking with a dark regret: 'All these years, these millenia, that ship has been down there — and we didn't realize what it was.'

And now a message had come from a Gilbert Gosseyn on distant Earth. It was a message authorized by the Galactic League, stating that many such craft could probably be located, at least one each on tens of thousands of planets. The message had described exactly what he was looking at.

The accompanying photograph showed the interior of the ship, with its four containers. Two of these were large enough to hold, each, one male adult human. The other two were slightly smaller, and each was designed to hold a woman.

The details had been described in Gosseyn's message, which concluded: 'Advise at once if such a vessel has ever been found on your planet, and where it is now!'

So he had sent the information requested . . . and now here was the man himself, who had been shown in an accompanying photograph; except that now he was walking up the marble steps toward Neggen.

. . . What bothered Gosseyn Three a minute or so later, as he stood beside Neggen and gazed at the photographs, was a feeling of overwhelming. And every instant that now went by he had the strong conviction: he should have some purpose of his own.

But what?

Naturally, there was always an obvious goal in every situation: *stay alive!* However, that really led nowhere in terms of the specific situation he was in.

What bothered him most was the precision of awareness the Troogs were displaying. Somehow they had become aware of how mankind had originally, perhaps as long ago as a million years, come from that other galaxy.

And they had used League authorization and his name in their attempt to locate one of these four-passenger spaceships. And, when a reply came, they had immediately had available a twenty-decimal method of their own to transport Gilbert Gosseyn Three to a location where neither he nor any other Gosseyn had ever been; transport him at twenty-decimal speed from a restaurant near the Institute of General Semantics on Earth.

And the fact that he had arrived fully dressed indicated that they had taken note of what he had done with businessman Gorrold's jacket with a precision that did not simply derive from Gosseyn's own mind. Because he himself had not yet taken his extra-brain photographs of this new suit of clothes.

When he had come up to the level of the man in the Roman toga-like garment, who stood at the top of the steps, Gosseyn had had the thought: 'Maybe just noticing how skilful they are is the only purpose I need right now.'

All the details might tell him something eventually.

Neggen said – in English: 'What do you hope to gain from discovering such machines as this?'

As he heard the familiar language Gosseyn was aware of a tiny purpose forming inside him. For later. Incredibly – again – these Troog must now know how *they* had learned English, because here they had utilized a method of transmitting it to someone else.

All by itself, during a later confrontation, that would enable him to find out how 178,000 Dzan had automatically spoken English, the language of the sleeping Gosseyn body in the space capsule they had found in space . . . after the Dzan and their ship were mysteriously transported at twenty-decimal speed from their own galaxy a million light-years away.

. . . Should I leave? Should I return and pick up Enin?

And head for the Dzan battleship, and whatever protection it could give?

'What do you think, Alter . .?'

It was a spontaneous question, with no advance thought about it; simply acceptance that perhaps he should have some advice. What startled him, then, was that there was no reply; and, worse, no sensation of that other Gosseyn mind . . . out there.

It was not clear why the Troogs were taking the trouble to keep the two Gosseyns mentally disconnected in this situation. If it was another attempt to demonstrate their capability, that had already been established earlier; though − the thought came − not for such a long time.

His rapid speculation was interrupted. Footsteps. He turned, with Neggen. And saw that a woman, also dressed in a toga-like outfit, was approaching from a long, squat building visible through heavy brush in that direction. In terms of Earth age she seemed about forty, which was also the age appearance of the man.

The women stopped about ten feet away on the slightly higher level of steps at that point, and said something like:

'. . . N'ya dru hara tai, Neggen?' Her voice sounded troubled, and had a question in it.

The man's eyes widened. 'Good God!' he said. 'Rubri, what kind of gibberish is that?'

The shock waves of the interchange had also reverberated through Gosseyn. It required several moments to come to terms with his instant feeling of being somehow responsible for what had been done to these people.

Addressing Neggen, he asked, 'Your wife?'

The man nodded, but his face still had a critical look on it. 'What's the matter with her?'

Gosseyn was recovering from his own dismay. He pointed at the photographs and the accompanying message. 'Let's take her to your computer,' he said. 'If it could accept a message from me before − uh − I learned your language, then it can

152

translate for your wife. In fact,' he added hastily, 'all these interstellar computer-communicators automatically translate about a hundred thousand languages — I'm told.'

'B-but — but — '

'It's a long story,' said Gosseyn, 'and right now I don't know how it will be rectified. But, quick! Before anything further happens.'

The urgency in his voice came from a sudden feeling inside him — the tugging sensation was back.

He was conscious of a vague thought of his own: somehow the Troogs had brought him here so that *they* could have a look at one of the small craft that had long, long ago brought two men and two women from their galaxy to this one.

In that time long ago hundreds of thousands of these tiny spaceships had crossed the colossal distances of intergalactic space. And evidently they had wanted to see one —

. . . Into one of the smallnesses of the universe, into a restaurant, turned out to be the next place to which he was transmitted.

But it was actually not until he came cautiously out from the small anteroom, in which he had arrived, that Gosseyn saw that he was, in fact, in a rather fancy Earth-type restaurant.

As his gaze, in a manner of speaking, absorbed the elegantly dressed maître d', what diverted him was . . . he was remembering that he had taken Enin and Dan Lyttle to a restaurant. What could be the purpose of the Troogs in duplicating such a situation?

The memory remained a small distraction to him during the next minute, as the maître d' came forward, and said in English, 'This way, Mr Gosseyn. They're waiting for you.'

'This way' led to the door of one of those small private dining rooms. And it was not until he started across the threshold that he saw the, approximately, dozen people — first glance impression — who were inside, already seated around a long table.

In that group, in that dimly lit room, a head of red hair caught his eye; and so the first individual Gosseyn recognized was — shock! — Enro the Red, king of the planet Gorgzid and conqueror of the colossal empire that Gorgzid controlled.

President Blayney sat beside Enro, and so he was second to be identified. Swiftly, after that, the faces, figuratively, leaped out at him: the Prescotts, Eldred and Patricia Crang, Leej, Breemeg, the Draydart — in uniform — and three more men who, since they faced away from him, Gosseyn took a little longer to identify. They were the three scientists, whom he had identified as Voices One, Two, and Three. They were the ones who had originally brought him out of the capsule.

The fact that these were all persons who had been aboard the Dzan battleship was surely significant. They were all individuals with whom he had been in verbal contact aboard the great vessel, and in addition there was President Blayney of Earth.

Missing was Strala. Missing were Enin and Dan Lyttle, and — a significant omission indeed — Gosseyn Two.

The flickering thought came: the aliens were not yet ready to deal with both Gosseyns at the same time . . .

Gosseyn Three had the impression that the roomful of people had been engaged in a very minor and subdued conversation just prior to his arrival.

. . . They must surely, each and every one, be startled by the implications of what had happened . . . what technical mastery it must have taken to bring them here; and yet, also, the fact that they were alive, and not murdered out of hand, had its own significance.

He had already noticed that at the far end of the table was an unoccupied chair, with a place setting on the table in front of it. He was not surprised that it was to this chair that the maître d' guided him.

During the half minute required for him to walk over to the unoccupied space, there was verbal silence from those who were already seated.

Gosseyn did not sit down. He waited for the maître d' to depart, meanwhile gazing at the assembled guests, and he saw that they were staring back at him expectantly, perhaps even hopefully.

The implication seemed to be that they were anticipating that a purpose would now emerge for them. Somehow, everybody's presence in this room would, with Gosseyn's arrival, be explained. That must be the hope.

Gosseyn felt a small sinking sensation. Because he still had no purpose, himself.

His feeling: he needed more information. And, since he believed that, with the Troogs, time — for him — was short, he spoke . . . a question:

'Anyone here have a significant thought to express in relation to the possibility that the aliens brought you people here?'

It was Enro who put up his hand, and who said — in English: 'I believe that they probably know that if they do damage to me my fleet will destroy their single ship.' He added, 'Right now, Admiral Paleol is in direct contact with me.'

Gosseyn wondered if Enro had noticed that, on his arrival aboard the Dzan warship, he had needed his sister to translate the language of Gorgzid into English, but now he had not only understood Gosseyn's question, but had answered him.

So he smiled as he spoke the obvious question: 'In the English language?' he asked.

Pause. Then, with a grim smile, the super-leader commented, 'There's automatic translation in the interstellar communication lines; and the major Earth languages were added after my dear sister' — he paused and glanced at Patricia Crang — 'came out here and, uh, found herself a husband.'

The young woman raised her eyebrows, but said nothing. And Gosseyn was not about to make a comment on personal matters.

But inside his head that aspect — Enro and his special situation — abruptly took on a special, no-delay meaning . . . 'I should do something right now about that, just in case . . .'

It was a moment of interim decision. With his special ability he made a precise extra-brain photograph of Enro, noting — as he did so — that a tiny object attached to, or somehow inside, the big man's clothing had a special quality.

'. . . He's carrying a tiny distorter,' Gosseyn reported to his Alter Ego, 'and that's how he's staying in touch with his fleet, and they with him.'

155

'I'm sure you're right,' was the reply.

At once Gosseyn Three made a separate second-brain picture of that remarkable little device. It was a precaution for the future. Completed now. To be utilized at a key moment.

Standing there, he continued his role as intermediary.

'You've given us a major reassurance that you, at least, will not be damaged.' He glanced around him. 'Anything else that will make us all feel safer?'

Eldred Crang held up his hand. 'Mine may not be reassuring, but I notice that you, also, seem to be assuming that the prime mover in this situation has been the Troogs.'

Gosseyn nodded. 'I believe the Troogs used the knowledge they gained of my extra-brain to bring you people here. So it would appear' — he used the GS qualification phrase — 'that they have a plan.'

He thereupon described what had happened to him when he had suddenly found himself back inside the capsule, except that this time it was aboard the alien ship.

He concluded his account, 'Maybe I should have stayed for that interrogation, but I opted out.'

No one said anything. The faces at the table seemed more serious, but that was all.

Except for Leej. Something about the way she held herself seemed significant.

Gosseyn, who had a somewhat greater feeling of urgency, had been aware of Leej the predictor woman sitting off there to one side. In a small way, she had avoided looking directly at him. And so, for him, it was time to utilize her special ability.

He glanced at her, and said, 'Leej, how much time do we have?'

'Your question,' she said, 'implies you yourself do not have anything more in mind besides what you did a minute ago.'

So she had noticed; not surprising, but he hadn't thought about her; had been too intent. 'True', he said now.

Pause, then:

'About four minutes,' said the woman, 'and then there's that blankness.'

It could have been a special moment. But bare instants after

156

the woman spoke a rear door of the dining room opened, and three busboys came in with drinking water. They spent about a minute filling all the glasses. As they went out, the one who must have been head-boy turned and asked, 'Do you want the waiters to come in?'

'Later,' said Gosseyn.

President Blayney spoke for the first time, firmly. 'We'll call you.'

The boy went out; and Gosseyn stood there.

It was a special moment. The fact that everyone at the table, including the two government leaders, Enro and Blayney, *were* looking at him, evoked in Gosseyn a visualization of what they were seeing:

Himself, standing here! Physically strong, lean-faced, and tanned, a medium tall — just under six feet — determined man who felt calm and capable; and somehow that showed in everything he did: the way he held himself, every movement he made, reflected the power of the extra-brain and . . . General Semantics.

Where the tan had come from he could only speculate. But he deduced that a source of mild radiation inside the capsule had been part of the life support system tending to his needs.

During those seconds of self-awareness, it seemed to him that there was no point in doing anything else but what he had already been doing. So he said, simply: 'Any more comments?'

Prescott who, with the appearance of being in his forties and, therefore, along with Blayney, one of the two oldest persons in the room, indicated with his fingers, and said, 'What do you think is the basic purpose of these creatures?'

'I believe,' said Gosseyn, 'they want to get back to their own galaxy; and I believe they're studying me to see how I might have participated in helping to bring them here.'

Prescott made a small gesture with his hand, indicating the other people at the table. 'If they were technically skilful enough to bring us all here, why haven't they been able to accomplish that basic goal?'

Gosseyn explained about the damaged nerve ends in his head. 'They'll be studying me carefully in connection with that,' he said. 'What I'm afraid of is that, when they're ready to leave, they'll kill everybody they can reach — and that probably includes all of us — unless we can establish that Enro's fleet will hit back before they can get away.'

There was silence in that small, private dining room. And so, after a small pause, Gosseyn continued, 'We probably need everyone's reaction. So, I'm going to go around the table, and when I name you, or point at you, give your comment or suggestion for this situation.'

There was one obvious person who had to be first on a list of direct requests; and Gosseyn, after a small inward groan at the waste of time involved, named him:

'President Blayney?' he said.

The elected head of the North American Continent said, 'I was, fortunately, alone in my office when I felt a peculiar sensation. And the next instant I was out there in that restaurant alcove without my guards. As soon as I walked farther into the place, there was that maître d', evidently already briefed; for he said: "This way, Mr President."'

Blayney added, 'I've naturally asked him to advise my office; so a small army will probably be here shortly, if that's any help.'

He concluded, 'I'll have my people find out from the restaurant staff just how this luncheon was set up.'

Gosseyn said courteously, 'Thank you, Mr President.'

And, since time was pressing even harder at that four minute deadline, his gaze went hastily down the table. 'Patricia,' he said.

The young woman, who was Enro's sister and Eldred Crang's wife, seemed momentarily taken aback at being named. But after a pause she said 'I suppose you could say I've been in this whole business from the beginning. Yet I have to admit that the arrival of the Troogs leaves me blank.'

Having spoken, she leaned back in her chair, and shrugged.

Since Crang had already spoken, Gosseyn indicated Mrs Prescott, who sat at Patricia's side.

The woman sighed. 'I was virtually killed once in this nightmare, so I know that death is blackout; and I guess I can take it if I have to, hoping that there will be no preliminary pain.'

The words were spoken quietly, but they had a grimness to them that brought Gosseyn a sense of shock. He braced himself hastily, drew a deep breath, swallowed, raised his hand and indicated the scientist who sat just beyond Mrs Prescott: Voice Three.

The Dzan scientist said, 'I think you shouldn't waste another moment here. Get yourself back to the protection of the energy screen of our battleship, and let the other Gosseyn come out here, and rescue us. I —'

If there were other words spoken after that, Gosseyn did not hear them. There was a tugging inside him . . .

Chapter Twenty-two

'They're probably studying you . . .'

That seemed truer than ever, as he looked around at his new location. This time he was on a street which, by no stretch of the Gosseyn memory, resembled anywhere that a Gosseyn had visited.

He stood there. And looked slantingly down into the upturned face of a young woman. She was a complete stranger. Presumably, there must be something in his reaction to her that the aliens wanted to observe. What could it be?

The young woman said hesitantly — in English, 'I received a photograph of you.'

She had a fine, well-balanced face, brown hair and brown eyes. It was not an Earth face . . . somehow. He estimated her height at about five feet five inches. Her clothes seemed to consist of a pale beige cloth that was wrapped around her body from the top down like a series of scarves. On her feet she wore brown sandals and around her neck was a thin, leathery looking necklace.

Hers was a reasonably slender female body; but she was not, by Earth standards, a beauty. And there was no way for him to deduce, from what he was looking at, what the aliens had in mind for this meeting.

There she stood, an attractive female, seemingly about twenty-two or three in terms of Earth years. Beyond her, a street was visible — he presumed it was a street because it was a level, grayish in color, that was about four hundred feet wide, and stretched straight for several miles to where he could see the beginning of a city of solid, yellow-brown masses: buildings, he assumed.

On either side of that straight, gray level were tall trees. And a curtain of shrubbery that made it difficult to see the vaguely visible low-built structures that he assumed were residences.

Everything looked . . . different. Not of Earth, nor Venus, nor Gorgzid, nor other familiar scenes. Standing there, Gosseyn accepted that it was another human-inhabited planet somewhere in the Milky Way galaxy.

He was simultaneously remembering: in those final moments at the dinner-to-be, as he felt the tugging sensation, it had been a flash decision to let a Troog transmission of him happen at least once more. Let it happen despite the fact that his reason had immediately agreed that Voice Three was giving good advice about going back to the Dzan battleship.

Unfortunately, what he had allowed to happen seemed a minor, almost meaningless meeting. And, sadly, the individual involved had now been damaged in that she was no longer able to communicate in her native language.

Gosseyn sighed. And realized that this time he had really let his own thoughts take over. At the very least a long minute had gone by since his arrival. Belatedly, now, he recalled what the young woman had said at the beginning of that minute. And he echoed one of the words:

'Photograph?'

'Yes.' She reached into a fold of that unusual dress, and drew out a small, flat print. She held it out to him, almost anxiously.

As he gazed down at the print of himself, apparently taken when he was standing with a wall behind him, it seemed to Gosseyn that it was a picture that could have been taken in the restaurant where he had been about two minutes before, in terms of inner time elapsed.

What could the Troogs have in mind for a meeting between Gilbert Gosseyn and a young woman from another planet?

Out of his bafflement came a second question. This one he spoke aloud: 'You seem to have been willing to receive such a photograph. Why?'

'I decided very early, after I heard about all those other places out there' — she waved vaguely towards the sky — 'that I didn't want to spend my life on Meerd. And,' her voice was suddenly tense, 'and the message said that you might be interested in me.' She finished anxiously, 'I've been a member for more than two years without anyone like you showing up.'

And those words also seemed to have no meaning, except — the implication came to him suddenly — that maybe what she belonged to was an interstellar marriage club.

The young woman was staring up at him beseechingly. 'I'm supposed to tell you my name,' she said, 'and then all will be well between us. They said' — pause — 'that you are absorbed with the meanings of words, and that my name will have a very special meaning for you.'

'Words?' echoed Gosseyn.

He could almost feel himself sinking into some depth of Troog analytical point of view. Was it possible that the aliens were puzzled by the fleeting, so to say, glimpses they had had of his interest in General Semantics? And this meeting on this planet was designed to take advantage of a suspected weakness in him?

He was conscious of an automatic tensing inside him. He actually separated his feet slightly, as if to give himself better balance and a firmer footing. His feeling was suddenly that he might be staying here longer than he had during the previous times that the Troogs had controlled his movements.

But all he actually did was to ask *the* question: 'All right, will you tell me your name?'

'Strella', she said.

He could have thought about that a long time. Because, words. And a basic General Semantics concept being involved. Strella and Strala being similar names . . . I did comment, back there, that I liked the name Strala — and so, maybe to the aliens the word *was* the thing; which was the exact opposite of the General Semantics concept: 'The word is not the thing.' In this case, it was not the woman.

His mind went back again to the realization that this young woman might possibly be permanently damaged in relation to her home planet. And, again, the faraway amazement that the Troogs must believe that any woman with a similar name would be equally attractive to him.

With that — decision! Simply and directly, Gosseyn acted.

He made his instant mental, extra-brain photograph of Strella, and at once transmitted her to the floor location in the Institute of General Semantics on Earth, where he had brought the businessman Gorrold, from the Andes in South America.

It was a location where, at least, she would be able to make herself understood — up to a point.

As he completed the best saving action he could think of for the young woman . . . something stirred in his brain.

Sudden awareness, after all these minutes, of Gosseyn Two — out there.

It must have been a simultaneous realization; for his Alter Ego addressed an urgent mental message to him: 'I have bad news. The moment you left the restaurant, the people there were taken aboard the Troog battleship.'

The shock of guilt inside Gosseyn Three faded quickly. The truth was, even if he had stayed to help them, the aliens would have been able to capture the majority; so far he himself had operated at the rate of only one twenty-decimal transport at a time.

His immediate thought-purpose must have reached out. Because Gosseyn Two said across the light-years in a resigned mental voice: 'The truth has to be that you're the one they really want. If anyone can help them return to their own galaxy — the method is probably available somewhere in that tangle of nerves in your head.'

He concluded, 'Good luck, brother — I guess that's what we are: twin brothers.'

. . . Not quite twins, thought Gosseyn Three.

He did not pause to reason out the details of their difference; but at once transmitted himself to the laboratory aboard the Troog warship.

Chapter Twenty-three

The final struggle was about to begin.

That was Gosseyn's impression as he realized he was lying on a floor. Lying face down; not standing.

So, somehow, in those split instants before transmission occurred, the Troogs had been able, with their mighty science, to modify one aspect of the twenty-decimal transport method, whereby he had always, in the past, arrived in the physical-muscular-body position that had existed at the moment of departure. On Meerd, he had been standing. Here —

Gosseyn stayed where he was. Did not even turn his head immediately.

'. . . I could have been killed as I lie here,' was his thought. But he realized that he believed the aliens still needed him. And in every way had proved it in three separate control actions. On each occasion death could have been administered; but it wasn't.

Here he sprawled, face down. His nose was actually pressed against what seemed to be a soft, smooth floor. His eyes stared directly down at the grayish-white, slightly gleaming flatness. He was, he realised, still presuming that this was the laboratory floor toward which he had aimed himself from the remote star system, which the young woman, Strella, had called Meerd.

. . . Time to show awareness, and to move carefully. What he did, he raised himself to his knees.

And saw that, though he had only glimpsed it fleetingly as he was emerging from the capsule, it was, in fact, the room which he had originally thought of as a laboratory.

For some reason, the identification — the recognition —

evoked a strong reaction of relief.

'. . . I am where I wanted to be.'

Even as he had the awareness, he was lifting himself in the same unhurried fashion; it was still his assumption that any quick movement could bring an unpleasant reaction.

Standing, he looked around a bright, large interior. Visible were numerous gleaming machines and instrument boards projecting from wall and floor.

However, there was no sign of the space capsule inside which his body had lain while the Troogs duplicated his original awakening as it had taken place – earlier – on the Dzan ship. Not that he had expected it still to be there. It had obviously been brought aboard through some wall opening. The most likely wall was the one with the least instrumentation built into it, and with a long, dark slash right down the middle from ceiling to floor; that was where it must divide and slide back. It was through such an opening that large objects could be brought into the laboratory or taken out.

It seemed a shame that time was being wasted. Because here he was, the man with all the answers to everybody's questions. . . . Surely they knew that he was here –

It seemed to him there must be something he could do while he waited for their reaction . . . The truth was, the more he found out – now – the safer he'd feel when the moment of crisis came.

Perhaps, contact Gosseyn Two?

It was a passing impulse. The fact was, he had already noticed that the ether was silent. There was absolutely no mental awareness of his Alter Ego. It was a case of complete cut-off. Again.

Perhaps he should try to decide what the Troogs had in mind for the other prisoners? That would require leaving the room, with the intention of looking for, and locating, Crang, Patricia, the Prescotts, Enro –

It was staring at what looked like a door – off to his right – that brought that thought. Without hesitation, he headed for it.

Whatever it was, the flat surface that looked like a door had several metallic attachments that undoubtedly had some

165

purpose. Gosseyn pulled, pushed, twisted at each separate piece. Two of the items made a clicking sound when thus manipulated; but there was no give to the door, if that was what it was.

He stepped back, suddenly more determined . . . Okay, maybe if he made a twenty-decimal connection between the energy feeding one of the instrument boards and the door mechanism . . .

The failure of the Troogs to acknowledge his presence was beginning to be a little irritating. A waste of time.

Above everything else he needed an audience that would hold still for what he had to say.

The wry thought was still in his mind, and he was still there, moments later, when a tenor voice said, in English, from the ceiling:

'Gilbert Gosseyn, we have you completely in our control. Here you cannot even use your extra-brain method to escape.'

Although the words conveyed a possibility that had already occurred to Gosseyn, hearing the meaning spoken aloud brought a thought: '. . . This is what they learned how to do during those three trips they sent me on —'

So there seemed to be no question about it: this whole madness was about to enter its decisive stage.

Despite his instant hope, there he still stood at least a minute later, waiting — he realized ruefully — for the self-appointed enemy to provide him with the opportunity to act.

During that minute his environment was the same gleaming metal room with the same grayish floor, and all those instruments jutting out and up.

He had been assuming that the Troogs could, to some extent, read his mind. But since they had missed a decisive aspect of his General Semantics orientation, perhaps all they could essentially study was the brain itself, with occasional thoughts available in some connecting situation.

Another fifteen seconds — at least — went by . . . They're waiting, and I'm waiting. For what?

After several more moments of consideration, he walked over and once more tried the door mechanism. This time, when the two clicks sounded, the door swung open.

Gosseyn wasted no time. With not even a single backward glance he walked through the opening into a wide, high-ceilinged hallway.

Momentarily, then, the rueful feeling came back: '. . . Okay, okay,' he thought, 'I was reasoning some human way, and they had their Troog approach to logic.'

The Troog way seemed to anticipate that, after a conversation, friendly or unfriendly, if a human being had once tested a door to see if it would open, he would then test it again, without waiting for instructions.

The human way — the Gosseyn version at least — had been to await further instructions, once verbal contact was established. A courtesy approach was what he had intended.

The conclusion seemed to be: the enemy automatically expected aggressive — or, at the very least, purposeful — behavior from him.

Even as he had these thoughts Gosseyn turned to the right, and walked along the wide, dimly lit corridor. He could see a barrier about 150 feet ahead; and, presumably, that would be the moment of truth.

It turned out to be a door that wouldn't open. Still following his new theory, Gosseyn turned and walked rapidly in the opposite direction. The barrier that way was about 400 feet distant. And there was another door, yes. With the familiar looking mechanism. Two of them clicked, one after the other; and, when they did, the door swung open.

What he was looking at, then, was another corridor at right angles to the one he had already traversed. Another decision to be made: he chose a right turn again. It was a wrong choice once more. But when he went back in the other direction, and that door opened on still another cross corridor, he had the opportunity of going left as his first decision. Went that way; and this time *it* was the wrong direction.

But that was his journey through more than a dozen silent corridors. At the end of each corridor a door either opened, or it didn't. It was, in its fashion, a good test for discovering how much of the Leej-style predictor ability he had. His conclusion: he either had none, or very little. His choice was correct four times only; eleven times it was wrong. And in all those latter instances he had to retrace his steps, and then go the distance of another empty hallway, silent except for the soft sound of his shoes on the cushioned floor surface.

Not once did he see a Troog. Empty, deserted, silent, huge spaceship — so it seemed; and solidly locked against intruders, except for the doors that opened, and presumably guided him towards where someone wanted him to go.

There were some diversions. Along each side of each corridor at intervals, not evenly spaced, were wall shapes that — he assumed — were doors that led to rooms like the laboratory from which he had started on this tiresome journey.

At first he passed them by, but presently he paused at each one and tried to work the mechanism.

They were all locked, and stayed locked.

After a while he had a thought: '. . . I suppose this could be a way of exhausting me physically.'

And, still, he could not persuade himself to test whether or not he could escape to some twenty-decimal location.

The continuing ordeal brought another, and unexpected response: he felt less willing to help. As the minutes and the miles — it seemed like — went by, a thalamic reaction began. He had started along that first corridor accepting that when he was finally able to confront his captors he would do his best to help them to get back to their own galaxy. Now, the memory came that General Semantics rejected most automatic acceptances.

True, it seemed obvious that the aliens were entitled to return to the place they had come from. But it was not necessarily true. And so it was interesting that by way of exhaustion and irritation had come the realization that perhaps he had better re-examine his automatic decision.

Fortunately, he recognized those negative speculations for what they were; and so his irritation never grew into the huge rage that might have festered inside an old-style he-man.

The end of that long harassment came suddenly. It was as he glanced along what could have been another meaningless corridor, that he saw a splash of bright light about 250 feet to his left.

168

The appearance was of a doorway . . . open, not closed. And, in fact, after he had walked rapidly towards it, and then slowed, edged forward, and stood there carefully peering in, what he saw was a duplicate of the earlier private restaurant room, except — instead of the recognizable human beings — sitting around the table in that dimly lit room there were about a dozen Troogs.

It took a little while then. But presently Gosseyn realized that they were aware of him. His hesitation ended. And, remembering they expected aggressiveness, he walked in. He had already in that first look noticed that there was an unoccupied place at the table.

It was on the far side of the table. And he went around behind a half-dozen Troogs, and over to the empty place. What was different from that earlier restaurant meeting, and, in its fashion, more respectful, was that instead of continuing to stand as if he were the important person, he sat down.

But his faraway thought was: how close to the end can you be? . . . And how fantastic that they would have a dinner meeting like this!

Chapter Twenty-four

Think positive! — Gosseyn admonished himself.

Despite the negative feelings that still lingered from the long walk through empty corridors, the truth was he was here to solve everybody's problem . . . if they would let him.

No one said anything; but the room was dark enough in that dim-lit way of many restaurants that the diners could be aloof from each other. Thus he had his chance to glance around at the strange beings, who had been so busy causing trouble ever since their arrival.

The positive approach suffered an immediate diminishment. They looked awful. It was the same reaction as when he had had his initial glimpse that time in the laboratory.

Gosseyn fought a silent battle against that automatic human tendency to apply human standards to appearance. Beauty — he recalled the ancient adage — is in the eye of the beholder.

After all, there was humanness. Except that their faces were almost round, and purplish in color. And that the part of the neck that he could see was almost skeleton thin; but there seemed to be some fairly large bodies below. All arrayed in uniforms that glinted as if they were constructed of bits of metal.

The head, like the face, was round. And almost bald. There was an ugly something that resembled hair; a cluster of what seemed to be bristles poked up from the top center.

But that face: a small, almost lipless mouth, a strange little nose, and above, dominating everything, were two large, round eyes, with black pupils, but without eyebrows. There did seem to be several folds in the skin immediately above and below. His impression: the eyes could be closed.

Before he could look further a door to his right opened, and five Troogs and one human being entered, carrying platters. The human being – a youth – came around to Gosseyn, and set in front of him what looked like an omelette, and the Troog waiters supplied all eleven of his tablemates with a dark glop of some kind.

As the waiters started to leave, for just one moment Gosseyn's gaze and the human youth's eyes met. What he saw was a haunted expression: darkness of soul, hopelessness. Then they were gone out of the door, all six of them; but the memory remained.

Everybody, including Gosseyn, ate. There was the scraping sound of his fork, and of the slighlty different, almost knife-thin utensils of his hosts . . . for that smaller mouth.

Since they could have a human being aboard, presumably they could also have genuine eggs; and that's what the omelette tasted like – the product of a real Earth chicken.

What puzzled him was that he seemed to be hungry. Did the body experience more time in these journeys than was outwardly apparent?

Something to think about later.

Gosseyn Three put down his fork, and leaned back. Sitting there he saw that his dinner companions were, each separately, taking the final bites that completed the intake of whatever it was they had been eating.

And they, also, thereupon leaned back in their chairs.

There they were, then: all of them in that dimly lit duplicate of an Earth restaurant. And his thoughts went back to the fact that they had made an effort to get him Earth food. Somehow, the deeds of those millions of chickens back there . . . out there . . . had been observed: still surviving, although most of their eggs had been stolen from them day after day from earliest times.

. . . I wonder if I went to a Troog planet, would I make a point of noticing where they got that glop from that they ate here today?

Looking back, he could not recall Gosseyns One and Two ever paying attention to the origin of the food on the planets where they had been: since other humans ate the stuff, so had they also.

His after-eating survey had been swift, but long enough. And so he had a strong feeling of relief when, directly across from him, one of the bulkier bodies stood up. For a long moment the individual – presumably a leader – gazed at Gosseyn with those round, black eyes. And then the tiny mouth under the tiny, slitted nose, said in a surprisingly normal, medium tenor voice:

'As you are undoubtedly aware, something unfortunate happened. An entire shipload of the people who matter arrived in this galaxy, and in the process lost their ability to speak their own language, and instead acquired an equivalent ability to speak English, one of many languages spoken on the planet Earth: but – and very significant this – your language.'

There was only one sentence in those introductory remarks that gave information Gosseyn did not already have:

. . . *The People Who Matter* . . .

It was an automatic acceptance of being better. All through human history on that singularly important planet of the solar system, there had been similar self-laudatory judgments by groups and by individuals, whereby the conclusion was forced upon them: somehow, they were superior.

Odd that, with all those brains, the Troogs had made such a huge project out of getting the help of the one person who possessed, somewhere in his head, the ability to assist them in their basic purpose.

As soon as possible he would tell them he was ready and willing. But even as he reiterated that thought within himself, the feeling came that the positive approach would run into problems.

Hard to know what. But if anyone could do it these people would find a way to negate what anyone from another race might try to do.

Fortunately, there were verities still.

The room, the table, the dishes, and those who had eaten – including himself – remained as they had been. The hidden source of light continued to shed the same dim illumination. The speaker was still standing; which seemed to promise more words would be spoken.

In fact, even as Gosseyn had the awareness, the human-like alien continued:

'Many of these developments are new, and have never before been observed. The implication is that our theory of the nature of the universe needs to be re-examined, and we shall seek an understanding that will include the new data.

'Our study,' he went on, 'of that special section of your brain has not yielded as much information as we need. Fortunately, you yourself have evidently finally realized that you could not escape from us; and so you have come here, presumably with one of those devious schemes, which we have noticed to be a common behavior of those members of your kind in this galaxy, whom we have observed in their daily activities. I must warn you, therefore, that we are not easily deluded, and urge that you cooperate without mental, or other, reservations of any kind.'

With that, he performed a dangerous — it seemed to Gosseyn — physical feat. With only that thin neck to support the movement, he nodded the large head at the prisoner-guest, straightened the head again until it was once more balanced evenly above the body, and sat down.

Gosseyn remained were he was. He had a small feeling of overwhelming. So many words had been spoken that he was aware of a need arising inside him to counteract, to defend, and point out, and, among other realities, to ask about the aggressive behavior of the Troogs; and other questions.

It took a long moment, then, to brace himself against those numerous little impulses. But he was finally able to exercise the necessary control, and to say simply, 'Sir, and gentlemen, you may count on my fullest cooperation.'

The silence that greeted his words was finally broken by a stirring movement: the old, human habit — it sounded like feet changing position, and making a shuffling noise in the process.

Then . . . the spokesman leaned forward. He did not get up; but when he spoke his tone was accusing: 'Don't think for one minute that you can fool us with this pretended cooperation. We are perfectly aware that you do not know

173

how to deal with the damage that was done to that special part of your brain, whereby a reversal of some kind took place — and brought us here.'

Gosseyn's first reaction: it was definitely not a gracious acceptance of his offer. It also seemed to him that he could not entirely agree with the negative analysis of the situation. Surely, in those instants when he had been extra-careful, he had been able to control the deviant tendencies of the damaged nerve endings; and had, as one example, arrived safely aboard this ship, his intended destination; and had done so without deviation.

That part, of course, could be explained. But what additionally disturbed him about what the Troog had said was a feeling that the speech was only partly for his benefit.

'. . . For some reason he wants these onlookers to believe that he's on the ball; that he's handling one of those cagey characters from Earth — me — in a no-nonsense manner, please notice, everyone.'

It was an oddly tense moment. And, sitting there, Gosseyn yielded to an impulse to shift his own body position before he spoke again.

He said, 'I'm sure there must be a way by which we can convince each other that we actually need to co-operate for mutual benefit.'

He concluded as simply as possible, 'Why don't we set up a step by step program? And then, as we achieve each step in turn, we shall progressively gain confidence that all will be well.'

There was silence. The spokesman stared at him. His huge eyes had an odd, baffled expression in them. Sitting there, Gosseyn experienced a strange thought: could it be that this individual was not the chief authority?

Somehow he had taken for granted that the top officers would be talking to him. Was a higher-up monitoring this meeting? Were the minions at the table waiting for an expression of approval, or for a decision authorizing further action?

As the silence lengthened, Gosseyn waited with them. Waited unhappily; because his situation seemed to be worse, not better.

174

A thought came: '. . . It could be that unless I figure out how to break down these barriers, this could go on —'

Another thought, a memory related to General Semantics: '. . . That business of believing that I would be interested in a woman named Strella because I liked the similar name, Strala —'

It was a vague direction to take. But surely better than just sitting here in this dim room with the people who mattered. With that sudden motivation he straightened a little, shuffled his feet — a little — and, addressing the spokesman, said:

'Do you have a name which distinguishes you from these' — he gestured vaguely toward the other Troogs at the table, and completed his question — 'from these friends of yours?'

The big eyes stared. The little mouth said, 'We all have names.'

But the speaker did not volunteer his own name. He continued to sit there, a glop version of a human being.

'The impression I have,' said Gosseyn, 'is that your friends are not your equals.'

'We are Troogs.'

The tone of voice had in it, suddenly, an imperious quality. The expression of personal power evoked from Gosseyn his next question:

'Are you the' — he hesitated — 'emperor?'

There was a distinct pause. The face and eyes continued to fix Gosseyn. Finally, almost reluctantly — it seemed — the alien said, 'We Troogs do not have emperors.' Another pause. Then: 'I am the appointed leader of this ship.'

'Who appointed you?' Gosseyn asked.

If possible, the great eyes grew even rounder. Then, impatiently: 'I appointed myself, of course.' The sudden irritation abruptly produced more words: 'Look, our authority system is none of your business.'

Gosseyn rejected the meaning with a gentle shake of his head. Then: 'Sir,' he said politely, 'you've made this entire situation my business by your relentless pursuit of me and your attempts to control me. I should therefore comment that I find your system of government significant. Are you saying, in effect, that no one else was motivated to appoint *himself* commander-in-chief?'

Pause, then: 'Several.' The big eyes stared into his.

'What happened to their acts of self-appointment?'

In front of him the small mouth twisted slightly. Then: 'They never reached the appointment stage. When they spoke of their ambitions, nobody listened. So they got the message.'

'I gather that, somehow, you had put yourself over?' Gosseyn spoke the comment in a questioning tone.

The impatience was still there. 'Mr Gosseyn,' the leader said, 'you yourself manifest many qualities of a commander. I feel certain that, among the human beings we have aboard, there is not one, considering the particular predicament they are all in, who would not accept your orders. Automatically.'

Particular predicament!

It was a relation-to statement, and therefore within the General Semantics frame of reasoning.

The words that had been so casually spoken had an additional revelatory meaning: . . . other human beings aboard –

Aside, of course, from that poor dumb youth who had served his omelette, it was now fairly certain that the reference was to Mr and Mrs Eldred Crang, the Prescotts, Leej and Enro, and the others. They were still alive. Captured but undamaged.

Suddenly, it was sad. Self-appointed leaders. These semi-human-looking people had evolved what had the implication of being an emergency-style system of living with each other. Somehow, in spite of their physical deformity, they had simultaneously achieved a mighty science.

Self-appointed government could work. There was a pragmatism involved that, in most situations, had a potential for almost sensational success.

The self-appointed whatever arriving at a cul-de-sac in his own forward drive-plan-purpose-research; and so not offering a resistance when an assistant asserted leadership by asserting that his – whatever – *would* work.

There was a sort of things-get-done momentum in such an idea. At least a partial certainty of nothing ever slowing down because a single individual could never for long fool his colleagues. Observably, the project he was working on would either be going forward, or it would not be.

Such a system could conceivably work best in the area of physics and chemistry. The results were always visible; and if a research-leader lagged, there were eager usurpers waiting down the line for the slightest sign of slowdown in creativity.

In fact, the leadership system could explain the superiority of Troog science, on the one hand, and a misuse of it, on the other.

Because, obviously, psychology, and the so-called social sciences, as well as humanitarian ideas, could never be observably true. In those fields, there could, as on Earth, be 'schools' with the usual variant beliefs. It was in such areas of study that General Semantics offered the individual a method of avoiding the *need* for certainty.

Nothing like that here, was his feeling-thought.

He was aware of other, similar thoughts crowding up from some equivalent of an inner well of ideas. But before they could take form, the two doors to his right opened again. The five Troog waiters and the human youth entered.

The Troogs were carrying tall, transparent glasses containing a liquid; and in the youth's hand was a cup and saucer, and a cream pitcher. Coffee? Gosseyn wondered.

It was. Quickly set down in front of him by hands that, thereupon, reached over and removed the empty omelette plate. Presumably, particular Troogs picked up the same plates they had set down earlier. Interesting, then, that the human boy, as he withdrew with his alien companions, did not look at Gosseyn.

But his predicament had made an impression. And so Gosseyn gazed after him, and, just before the poor, little guy disappeared, took a twenty-decimal mental photograph of him.

His thought was: 'As soon as I get this whole situation clarified, so that I can be sure, I'll put him somewhere on Earth.'

Chapter Twenty-five

It was a slightly flabbergasted Gosseyn who poured in a tiny portion of cream, stirred it, and took the first sip of what tasted like genuine coffee.

In picking up the cup, he saw that there were half a dozen sugar cubes at the edge of the saucer; but the Gosseyn bodies did not use sugar in coffee; so the cubes remained where they were.

It was evidently another instance of a self-appointed Troog studying human needs, and even coming up with coffee. It was the kind of thoroughness which assured that no other Troog down the line of command would be taking over his job.

That was probably why they had brought the human youth aboard. To help with the finer details.

In such small matters, and in relation to science, the system had its points. But otherwise . . .

He put his cup down, and gazed at the leader, who, he saw, was sipping liquid from the glass that had been set for him. Gosseyn shook his head at the alien.

'I find it difficult,' he said, 'to visualize such a leadership system in relation to important matters. Apparently, back in your own galaxy, the self-appointed super-leader maintains a state of continuous warfare against the Dzan humans.'

Another one of those pauses. All the other Troog eyes stared at their leader expectantly.

Gosseyn waited, as one shoulder of the big body below that head made a movement that could have been described as a shrug. The small mouth said:

'Our Great One,' said the ship leader, 'ordered the lesser race to submit itself to his commands.'

Pause. Silence. Finally: 'When was this ultimatum given?' Gosseyn asked.

The huge eyes stared at him; and there was a small note of surprise from the voice that issued from the little mouth. 'No one has ever asked that question before.'

There were so many implications in the reply that Gosseyn almost literally had to control consciously the wild way his thoughts leaped in every direction. Finally, he said with a gulp: 'Was the ultimatum already in force when you were born?'

'Y-yes!' The hesitation this time was followed by sounds from other Troogs.

He was getting answers, so Gosseyn did not waste time.

'We, here in the Milky Way galaxy, were surprised to discover, when we went out into space, that human beings of various color combinations, inhabited most of the habitable planets – everywhere!

'Recently,' he continued, 'we learned that we are descendants of long ago immigrants from your galaxy. The story was that some malignant energy field was moving in upon that galaxy. At the time millions of small spacecraft were constructed. Each contained two men and two women in a state of suspended animation and with life support systems for the long journey from your galaxy to this one.

'Now, with the arrival of the Dzan battleship and your battleship, we deduce that those persons who stayed behind – because there were not enough spacecraft to transport everybody – that, I repeat, those who remained were not destroyed, as was believed would happen.'

He drew a deep breath, and concluded, 'Have you any explanation for the fact that, apparently, two human races – the Troogs and those who are like us here – survived the threatening catastrophe?'

Silence. They were staring.

It was no time to stop. Gosseyn pressed on: 'When I look at you, Mr Leader, and your colleagues, who are sitting here in this room with you, I see a human shape that appears to have been modified from the original standard human like myself. You are mutants. It would seem, then, that it was your ancestors who were caught in that cloud of malignant energies.

'And, of course,' he finished, 'by the defensive mechanism, well-known in psychology, you thereupon concluded that what had happened made you superior; and here you are calling yourself the people who matter.'

The leader was staring upward, seemingly at the wall behind Gosseyn. And the other Troogs were staring at him.

Abruptly, then — action! A Troog, whose body was easily the largest at the table, stood up — almost leaped up, actually (his chair scraped noisily) — and said in an almost yelling voice:

'Veen, you are no longer qualified to be leader. So I, Yona, appoint myself leader in your place!'

There was no sound from the alien, who had so suddenly been identified by name. He seemed to sink down in his chair; and, what was sensational, did not argue with the evaluation of him by his fellow Troog. Apparently it was unwise, in this super-competitive society, to be surprised or caught off guard.

So Gilbert Gosseyn Three was now an individual who had been instrumental in overthrowing a Troog leader. There would be repercussions; and, in such a logical society, it would be interesting to see what they were.

Chapter Twenty-six

Sitting there, Gosseyn had a sudden surge of hope. At once he addressed the new leader, while the alien was still standing there in his moment of triumph.

'I'm now deducing,' Gosseyn said, 'that this entire dinner, and what happened here, has been broadcast to the crew and officers of your ship. And so they are now aware that . . . (brief hesitation) — Yona is now the appointed leader of this battleship.'

If it were possible the little mouth of the huge man tightened in what, in a human being, would have been a belligerent firming of the jaw section.

'That is true.' The alien's tone had a challenging tone as if he dared anyone to criticise.

Gosseyn leaned back in his chair once more. This time it was not a relaxing action, he realized. The thought that the new leader's verification brought was too huge.

At this instant — that was the sudden awareness — all the way down the line of subordinate leadership; and their waiting-to-pounce aides. Troogs would be thinking what *they*, as individuals, *should* do to fit into the new situation.

The astonishing thing then was, that he was so busy trying to analyze what might be happening, that other intruding thoughts did not penetrate until, suddenly, a directed message came at the mental yelling intensity:

'. . . Mr Gosseyn Three' — it was the mental voice of Gosseyn Two — 'I've been getting your thoughts for at least thirty seconds now; and you're still so busy concentrating on your own situation that you haven't received mine . . . *Wake up! We're connected again!*'

In that dim lit Earth-style dining room Gosseyn Three straightened in his chair. He was conscious of relief but, at the same time, did not lose momentum in what was happening in front of him.

He directed one quick, mental message to his Alter Ego: 'Bear with me, brother!'

To Yona, who was still standing, he said, 'I hope that you will accept the offer I have made, of total cooperation.'

The big man looked at him grimly. 'We have your promise that you will do what you can to help us get back to our home galaxy?'

'One hundred per cent cooperation,' said Gosseyn.

'Do you have any explanation' — it was an accusing tone, still — 'of how all this happened?'

It was obvious from the aggressiveness of the question that the new Troog leader was clearly trying to maintain his momentum of control.

Let him! There was nothing to be gained by opposing him.

Gosseyn said cautiously, 'Sir, whatever I can do — you give the orders.'

'. . . I'm really sucking up,' he thought. But his belief was that he had done all the attacking that was necessary on Leader Veen; and what he needed now was to benefit from the transfer of power to the self-appointed Yona.

Somewhere off to one side of his mind he was also wondering if anything else in his favor had already been done somewhere down the chain of Troog command: he presumed that all that had resulted would not immediately be apparent.

Yona seemed to stiffen. His tone seemed even grimmer, as he said, 'Obviously cooperation involves trust on both sides . . . So' — accusingly — 'what do *you* expect to gain in this situation?'

What bothered Gosseyn about the question was the instant impression it imparted of someone parrying for time; as if the new leader did not quite know exactly what to do next. How to answer? What program to propose?

And the Troog leadership system did not allow for delays or inadequacies. Yona needed help — now!

'In the long run,' Gosseyn said glibly, 'I hope for personal freedom, with goodwill on your side, and continuing communication.'

He broke off: 'But right now I would like to have you call a special meeting that I can talk to. Since I want to explain the exact situation — as you requested a few minutes ago, the audience should include your top officers and best scientists. And I would also like to have present my human associates, whom — I gather — you have aboard.'

He continued, 'Naturally you will, during such a talk, exercise all the necessary security to ensure that no one is endangered.

'And,' he concluded hopefully, 'it is my belief that, after my explanations, we will all be in a position to go on to make final decisions, and take final actions.'

As, once more, he leaned back in his chair, his feeling was that for the time being, at least, he had saved the entire situation — for Yona, for himself, for the captive human beings, and for all the down-the-line sub-leaders.

Was it possible that a General Semanticist could survive in the incredible Troog competitive psychological environment . . .?

Chapter Twenty-seven

It was as strange a lecture meeting as, surely, any Earthman had ever attended: eighteen guests — eight of them Troogs. And the other ten, besides himself, were human beings who had played key roles in this entire affair of inter-galactic transport: Enro, Leej, the Crangs, the Prescotts, plus Breemeg and the three scientists from the Dzan battleship.

Interesting that even those persons present, who were familiar with General Semantics, believed that they were now going to hear new General Semantics data: information or analysis that transcended what they normally would have considered to be adequate knowledge of the subject.

What astonished Gosseyn Three, as he stood there on the platform of that small auditorium in front of the unique gathering, was his belief that their expectation was correct.

He had, not exactly new data, but new awareness . . . And he had actually parted his lips to begin his account when — a hand and arm were raised in the second row.

It was Enro the Red. The big man's hair, as usual, looked only partly combed, and his face was twisted into the now familiar, cynical smile.

Standing there, Gosseyn had a feeling that General Semantics would not be a factor in what the other was about to say; but surprisingly it was.

Enro began: 'I've been getting second-hand information on this system of thinking; and so let's see if you and I can resolve the issue of who marries the mother of the emperor of the Dzan by reasoning the matter in terms of General Semantics.

'The way I visualize this reasoning method,' Enro went on, before Gosseyn could say anything, 'is that General Semantics requires an individual to take the larger view; that is, to include all the possible factors.'

'That,' said Gosseyn, 'sounds as if you have heard at least a part of the system.'

'For example,' said Enro, 'recently, I sentenced a former aide to twenty years in prison for being too busy with his own affairs instead of doing his job. Now, I'm sure that if he had taken into account what it would feel like to be in jail for twenty years, he undoubtedly would not be there today. Similarly, I believe if you were to take into account all the aspects of our future relationship, you would realize that the emperor's mother should marry me.'

He paused, perhaps to catch his breath; and Gosseyn said politely: 'First, the subject matter is very probably a matter you and I should discuss privately. Second, I have a feeling the lady will probably have her own map of the situation; and, thirdly, I have a feeling you have not taken into consideration some of the factors which I am now about to describe.'

The cynical face gazed up at him . . . cynically. 'I'm listening,' said the great man.

'Thank you,' said Gosseyn, politely.

But, somehow, it was no longer quite the same meeting. People were exchanging glances. Even the Troogs seemed to be less relaxed.

— The 'realities' underlying existence or non-existence are not a concern of General Semantics (said Gosseyn in his lecture.) General Semantics begins by accepting what is perceivable, and operates within the frame of what every normal human, animal, or insect can perceive by way of the perceptive system of each individual.

But the Gosseyn extra-brain seems to function on the 'level' of the underlying nothingness. For the extra-brain, operating with twenty-decimal similarity, there is no distance, no time, no universe . . . at the no-time that the extra-brain manifests.

It is agreed (said Gosseyn) that the universe cannot possibly exist. There is no explanation for it. Simply and directly, it just cannot be.

Yet — here it is, around us, through us, and stretching out

. . . scientists say . . . to an enormous but finite distance in every direction.

That ought to be something to perceive, where that 'finite distance' 'ends'.

A definition of 'nothingness' (went on Gosseyn) does not refer to a condition of emptiness. In short, it does not mean an empty space, large or small. It does not even consist of a dot, or a mathematical point.

Nothingness is . . . nothing.

It is non-existence, non-being, without time or space . . . nothing.

It has been estimated (continued Gosseyn) that there are three thousand languages spoken on Earth alone. Inside all those visible heads — observable on the level of consciousness where perception operates — is a neural structure arranged so that each individual could, if he were educated, express all possible nuances of observation and philosophy available for that language.

A normal Gosseyn similarization action merely moves the individual from one location to another. Such a twenty-decimal transmission normally takes him as he is and moves him — as he is. No internal structural transformation takes place.

However, the Dzan battleship, and all its personnel, were not simply moved from one location, as memorized by the Gosseyn extra-brain, to another memorized location.

They came to Gosseyn direct, as if he were the location to be arrived at. And the reason there was no collision between the huge ship and the small capsule (which contained the Gosseyn body) was because the great vessel had automatic energy barriers and screens that prevented it from striking objects in space.

Nevertheless, the basic similarization process was not cancelled. The Gosseyn extra-brain, which operated within the nothingness of the universe, was, of course, the activating force, and therefore was not a part of the neural similarization of a portion of the rest of the Gosseyn brain.

And so the brain of each arriving Dzanian was transformed on the various levels that were most closely connected to the extra-brain. This included all the neural structures involving language — because they were actively receiving messages from Gosseyn Two.

But the messages themselves were stored in a different part of the normal brain.

. . . So the Dzanians — and later the Troogs — instantly had the language neural complexes of their brains slightly altered. The original Dzanian — and Troogan language neural pattern was shifted over to an equivalent in English.

At twenty-decimal speed: instantly . . .

Neither personality, nor education, nor information of any kind was involved.

The English language of Gilbert Gosseyn Three . . . was!

And now (Gosseyn concluded his lecture) are there any questions?

. . . Enro presently raised his hand, and his sister translated his words: 'It has been my observation that women are even more elite-minded than men; and in that connection I have furnished the emperor's mother with visual materials that will show her my palaces on Gorgzid . . .'

Gosseyn Two's faraway thought came: 'I think you should find out what those visual materials consist of besides pictures of palaces.'

'Maybe another little distorter, you mean?' Gosseyn Three replied.

'At least,' said his Alter Ego.

'Under the circumstances,' said Gosseyn Three, 'I think — '

After a pause, and a careful effort at concentration, so that there would be no mistake, he twenty-decimaled Enro into the capsule, to which the Troogs had brought the Gosseyn Three body after a number of initial experiments.

It should be an interesting interim problem for Enro to deal with; so it seemed to Gosseyn Three; and there seemed to be no objecting thought out there in remote space . . .

Chapter Twenty-eight

Back on twenty-sixth century Earth; all of the human beings except Enro . . .

Gosseyn, who had done the twenty-decimal transmitting of everyone, was the last to arrive. As he straightened from his arrival position he saw that the others were waiting for him: the women were already seated in the chairs and on the couch, and the men were standing.

They had all been instructed – again – to leave the location of arrival quickly; and they had obviously done so.

He grew aware that President Blayney was on the phone, saying at that moment: '. . . And get over here at once!'

As Blayney replaced the receiver moments later he saw Gosseyn. 'It's fifteen minutes after twelve noon,' he said. 'I've been missing for three days.'

He added, 'My security people will be here in a few minutes.'

Gosseyn said, 'That's interesting information, sir.'

He wondered what day it was in relation to when Enin and he had originally arrived. But actually that was incidental.

Quietly but quickly he walked over and glanced into the bedroom he had shared with the young emperor. Empty. But the bed was unmade.

Moments later he saw that the other bedroom was also unoccupied.

Swiftly he strode over to the hall door, and opened it. Addressing Eldred Crang, who stood beside his wife – the former Patricia Hardie was sitting in the chair nearest the door – Gosseyn said, 'I'm going up front to talk to the caretaker. I'll be right back.'

Crang seemed to realize his concern. 'I'm guessing they'll be all right.' he said. 'There's no sign of violence around here.'

He added, 'I think it's still basically you they're after.'

Gosseyn said, 'Thank you.' And went out into the wide hallway of the empty shell of a building that had been the Institute of General Semantics.

A minute later, after he had rung the caretaker's doorbell several times, there was that wrinkled face and those sneaky eyes looking up at him; and presently showing comprehension of his question.

'They went out to eat.' The face twisted. 'That friend of yours must have brought some woman in here; because that's who he and the boy went out with.' He finished in a disapproving tone: 'Dressed strange, if you ask me – that woman.'

Gosseyn, remembering the young Interstellar Marriage Club's Strella and her wraparound dress, but already feeling relieved by the information, said, 'Probably one of the new styles.'

He cautioned: 'You'd better get organized. The president's personal guard will be here shortly.'

'Huh!'

During the seconds that the caretaker stood there absorbing what seemed to be a feeling of shock, Gosseyn's eyes turned slightly and located a spot on the carpeted floor half a dozen feet beyond the twisted shoulder nearest him.

He made his extra-brain mental photograph of the floor surface just inside the alcove, paying no attention to the room beyond – but fleetingly aware that it was probably the living room of the caretaker's apartment.

Then: 'Thank you,' he said politely.

As he stepped back the door closed with a click. Gosseyn turned and walked away. That was in case he was being watched through a peephole.

He counted to thirty, because it would take a minute or so for the older man to get to the phone. Made a mental picture of the corridor floor in that location. And then he did his twenty-decimal jump to the alcove position.

As he grew aware again, he heard the caretaker's voice

189

saying: 'Tell Mr Gorrold that . . . that fellow Gosseyn is back.'

He seemed to be listening to a reply because, after a few moments more, his voice spoke an acknowledgment: 'All right, all right.'

At that point Gosseyn made his jump back to the hallway location, and returned to the apartment.

As he entered Blayney was shaking hands with the men, and bowing to the women. His back was to Gosseyn as he said, 'Anything you need, I'll be in touch with Mr Gosseyn.'

As he finished speaking he turned and saw Gosseyn, came over, and said, 'You can get through to me any time. And I suggest' — his tone was suddenly grim — 'until we get those people out of this galaxy we'd better stay in touch, and on the ball.'

Gosseyn said, 'Sir, Mr Crang and I will walk you to the front door.'

Outside in the hallway he made his only comment on Blayney's admonition: 'I'm sure that at this moment nobody can guarantee how all this is going to turn out. Just about everybody is primarily and with total determination concerned with his own situation.'

With that, as they walked along, he asked a question that Gosseyn Two, out there on the Dzan battleship, wanted an answer to.

Blayney was amused.

'We picked up, and stored all the jewels and precious metals,' he said. 'What's left is this uneven floor surface and the torn walls.'

Gosseyn said, 'I'm still hoping it can be rebuilt; and although I, personally, never saw any of the valuables, I gather that what you're saying is that they were never disposed of; never sold at auction, or to individual collectors.'

'They're in a government security building.'

Gosseyn said, 'My brother out there in space would like to have them available again. He thinks they should be returned to their legal owner: a rebuilt institute.'

Blayney's strong face relaxed into a faint smile. 'It's a very complicated subject,' he said, 'I'll think about what's best, from my point of view.'

As, a minute later, Crang opened the front door, a roboplane was sinking to the pavement fifty feet away. As it touched the surface a door opened, and a dozen uniformed men leaped down. They loped over and took up position beside the door. In the time-honored fashion each man clicked his heels, and snapped his hand up to a salute.

A smiling Blayney acknowledged the salute; and then stood there with Gosseyn and Crang another four minutes, before five gleaming limousines came charging down the street and through the gate into the Institute grounds. More men leaped out.

And, evidently, the time had come.

Blayney turned to Gosseyn. 'Do you want me to have Dr Kair brought over to you?'

With so many observers present, Gosseyn made his reply formal: 'No, Mr President. I'm sure I should go over to his office. That, if anywhere, is where the earlier brain photographs will be, and the equipment to deal with the situation.'

'Very good. But don't waste any time.'

'I understand, sir. We don't want any more incidents, or three day absences.'

'Exactly right.'

As, moments later, he watched the beautiful machines drive off, what bothered Gosseyn was: it seemed too easy.

All those violent people out there were being held motionless, so to say, by some equivalent of a psychological trap that they were in. There was Enro, the only human being left aboard the Troog warship because, if he were free, he could launch his huge fleet against anyone.

So there he was, apparently a prisoner, but actually in touch with his admiral who — if the prisoner were harmed — would know it instantly. It was presumed that, in such an eventuality, the great space fleet would at once attack and destroy the alien vessel.

Therefore the Troogs, out-numbered thousands to one, would — so it was believed — restrain themselves from doing anything harmful; in fact, that was the agreement.

191

Here on Earth the outward appearance was that he and the others had the support of President Blayney and all his forces. It was hard to credit that the Big Business people, who were opposed to the rebuilding of the Institute and the Games Machine, would act in some violent fashion during the next two hours.

'. . . So I can go and see Dr Kair.'

That was what Yona had agreed to; and, since no Troog had objected sufficiently to try a self-appointment leadership gambit, evidently all the way down the chain of Troog command there was silent acceptance that something had to be done.

And, of course, here on Earth was Breemeg and the trio of scientists from the Dzan battleship, each thinking their private thoughts; but having to bide their time.

As Crang and he walked back toward the apartment, Gosseyn told the Venusian detective the words he had overheard the caretaker speak on the phone to someone in Gorrold's office.

He concluded unhappily, 'My first thought is, it looks as if, when Gorrold thought it over − as he said he would do − he finally decided to get involved again.'

Crang shook his head. 'It's too soon to be sure. This could all be debris from the earlier commitment. The caretaker, once paid to make reports, is still making them.' He concluded, 'It could be that when that message is transmitted to Gorrold, he may remember to call our little guy here and fire him.'

It was true, in a way. But Gosseyn had a feeling that Gorrold, while thinking things over, might still keep his communication lines open.

He made another evaluation: 'It seems to be a situation whereby we take no action until there are additional developments.' He finished his thought reluctantly, 'It would be sad if one of the developments was a bullet or energy burn for one of our people. And, right now, I'm thinking of Enin and Dan Lyttle and that young woman out having lunch.'

Crang said, 'As soon as we've reported to our friends, so they'll know where we are, we'll do a test on that. We'll go to the restaurant, and escort the luncheon trio back to the comparative safety of that special apartment, formerly occupied by the mysterious Mr "X", who turned out to be an earlier generation Gosseyn in disguise.'

It was a low level of reality. But it evidently fitted with the thoughts of those who now waited in the apartment; for no one offered any objection. Patricia said to Crang, 'Hurry back!' Crang smiled, and nodded; and that was the end of conversation.

A few minutes later, as they came again to the door where they had parted from Blayney, they paused to survey the exterior. The caution was an indication that they were back on Earth.

The view was, by now, familiar enough. All around the devastated building were small parks. From where they stood, the near view was of one of the parks and a driveway, and, beyond that, a business street.

What they could see were the exteriors of a series of one-storey plastic structures, each with transparent front wall for display of goods; at this distance the goods were not visible. In those rows of stores on either side of the street was only one two-storey building.

From where they stood, just inside the institute, both men scanned the street and the buildings. There was a man on top of the two-storey structure; and what was wrong with him, was that he was not in work clothes, but wore a dark gray suit and jacket.

More significantly, he wasn't doing anything relevant to rooftop repair. He simply stood there, close to the roof's edge, peering down at the street below.

'Where's the restaurant?' asked Crang, after a pause.

Gosseyn did not attempt to verify which restaurant. The only one on the street was the Eating House, where he had taken Enin and Dan Lyttle, and where — he presumed — they were having lunch with the Strella from distant Meerd.

The Eating House was two doors beyond the two-storey building; and on the same side of the street. After Gosseyn had given that small detail to Crang, the other man's comment was simple enough:

'Let's face it. If that fellow has anything in mind, either for us when we go over, or for them when they come out — what can we do?'

Gosseyn shook his head. 'He's too far away for my extra-brain to take a mental photograph; and besides I can only see a part of him. So that means I'll have to use the energy from that big light socket just outside the door here.'

Crang must have noticed the reluctance in his tone. 'What's wrong with that?' he asked.

'It could really burn him.'

'Death?'

'No. Not where I'd hit him.'

'Well.' The smaller man was shaking his head. 'If he's up there to kill — which is all we're concerned about — then he's a lost soul, and we'll just do the best we can for him in a crisis.'

With that he pushed the door open; and they went out.

Chapter Twenty-nine

All those minutes, while walking along the corridor, Gosseyn had been aware of his Alter Ego . . . off there, in the remoteness of space, aboard the Dzan battleship. And, because of what was happening, he now addressed the other Gosseyn:

'So far I haven't killed anybody.'

'Lucky you!' came the reply. 'You didn't have to fight off Enro's attack on Venus.'

Thus reminded of Enro, Gosseyn Three commented: 'He's up there, now, on the Troog battleship.'

The reply had in it a satirical overtone: 'I have a feeling that when Enro was telling you about his understanding of General Semantics, about taking all possibilities into account, he believed he knew how to do that better than anyone. But' – smile impression – 'I'm deducing he forgot about your ability.' A mental shrug, then: 'I say, good riddance.' The faraway communication concluded: 'Remember, as things stand, the emperor's mother is all yours – no competition now.'

'It's interesting,' said Gosseyn Three, 'that he never said a word when he discovered he was to be the hostage.'

The reply was the equivalent of a mental shrug: 'I couldn't care less.' He added, 'And while I'm still here on the ship I'll see if I can get hold of those visual materials Enro gave to your future bride.'

That was obviously a good purpose. The material should very definitely be examined. But Gosseyn Three was remembering something else.

'I doubt,' he said 'if we can dispose of Enro in any casual

fashion.' He added, 'Remember, you and the others used *his* ESP ability when you attempted the big jump. We'll need him again for that.'

'We can worry about that later,' was the reply. 'As I see it, it's to Enro's advantage to participate. We can trust him to continue his scheming.'

Gosseyn Three, who had paused to take his extra-brain photograph of the electrical outlet, and then walked hastily forward to rejoin Crang, spoke mentally again to Gosseyn Two: 'Are you sure that kind of dismissal is wise? He's the get-even type, and I see him just biding his time until he can hit somebody. We need to figure out a way to mollify him.'

He sensed a grim smile from the other Gosseyn. The message was: 'Tell Eldred to watch out when Enro is finally let go. I'm sure Enro is still scheming to marry, in the Gorgzid royal tradition, the sister whom we knew as Patricia Hardie, and who is now Mrs Crang.'

It was Gosseyn Three's turn to smile. 'That analysis implies that you're hopeful that things will work out here. You think I can do what everybody's counting on.'

The reply was straightforward: 'We're all trusting that the solution is buried somewhere in the damaged nerve ends in your extra-brain. We hope Dr Kair can use the pictures he has of my brain to fix up yours. Or, at least, that he will be able to tell you the exact problem. The aftermath we'll face when we come to it.'

At that point in his silent interchange with Gosseyn Two there was an interruption. Beside him Crang said, 'The fellow just saw us, and he stepped back out of sight.'

Gosseyn sighed. 'Too bad. So now it looks like a crisis coming, and that he is somebody's hireling.'

Crang said grimly, 'And, for good measure, a man, a woman, and a boy have just come out of the building two doors beyond the two-storey one, and they're coming this way.'

Gosseyn made no additional comment, nor did he glance in the direction indicated. His attention was on the roof of the two-storey structure, where the man was now crouching behind the small abutment that overlooked the street; whoever

196

he was, he was peering over, and down.

Since he was keeping his head visible, he was evidently assuming that no one would be suspicious of his motive for being there; and, of course, since it was still possible that his suspicious actions did not really portend anything, nothing could be done against him until he made a significant move.

Beside Gosseyn, Crang said, 'You may be interested to know that the name of the restaurant is the owner's idea of what General Semantics is all about: plain talk; telling it like it is.'

It was one of those comments that men make to each other in moments of stress. So it was no problem to stay alert, and simultaneously reply, 'Eating House?' Gosseyn spoke the name with a faint smile, but did not for an instant cease watching the man on the roof.

'Here he was,' continued Crang's voice from beside him, 'with the only restaurant near the famous Institute of General Semantics, a subject having to do with the meaning of meaning; and so he evidently thought about it, and came up with another over-simplification.'

They had crossed the park by the time those words were uttered, and were coming to a store with the sign: BUY YOUR SEMANTICS MEMENTOES HERE.

Further along the street Enin had seen them; for he waved. Gosseyn said, 'In terms of to me-ness, I thought the food there was good.'

On the roof the man's hand came into view. The hand was holding a round, metal object. He raised the ball-like thing above his head.

Gosseyn took his extra-brain mental photograph of the metal object; and as he did so, was thinking: 'He's planning to throw it as we all come near each other.'

And still he could not take any counter-measure until the act of throwing took place.

'And here,' said Crang beside him, 'is a store offering video games that teach General Semantics.'

Gosseyn said, 'I was wondering what had happened to those. We'd better buy all that are available to take back with us to the Dzan battleship for Enin, and,' he added, 'any other educational video games we can find, because —'

. . . On the roof the hand was moving forward in the throwing act; and there was no such thing as waiting any longer. As he acted, Gosseyn's feeling of regret was strong. Because electricity on the move was all too visible. This particular movement came from the socket 150 feet away in the form of a lightning bolt; and there was no possible way of modifying its impact.

The details of what happened were not even clear to Gosseyn, although he was the only witness; and he was watching closely.

The metal ball — as he observed the scene — was already in motion when the lightning bolt coruscated against it. The ball exploded not more than four or five feet from the hand that had thrown it from the roof; but that was evidently too close.

The man screamed, and fell back out of sight.

It was one of those small periods of time of several things happening almost simultaneously.

Enin came running forward, and grabbed Gosseyn around the waist, yelling, 'Gee, Mr Gosseyn, I'm sure glad to see you.'

Dan Lyttle was looking up toward the roof of the two-storey building. 'What was all that?' he asked in a puzzled tone.

The young woman, Strella, also spoke to Gosseyn: 'Thank you for sending me here.' She took hold of Dan Lyttle's arm in a possessive way. 'It's going to work out.'

Crang hurried in through the door of the two-storey building. He came out again presently, 'I told the guards inside to call an ambulance.'

Gosseyn hoped the ambulance would come quickly.

He had already, among numerous fleeting awarenesses, noticed that it was an oversized men's clothing and shoe store. Now, he saw the name of the place lacquered into the transparent plastic wall beside the entrance: KORZYBSKI MEN'S CLOTHING AND FOOTWEAR.

. . . Presumably featuring semantically-styled suits, shoes, shirts, ties, pajamas, socks, slippers, and underwear.

It was all a little ridiculous. But it fitted, alas, with the nature of human life everywhere.

– Go aboard the Dzan battleship; and there was a rebellion brewing against a child emperor, who took it for granted that one behaved like his father; at that age there was no thought of the possibility that his father had been murdered because of the behavior that the son was now imitating . . .

– Go aboard the Troog battleship and there was the tense, self-appointed leadership situation . . .

– And now, here on Earth, two aspects: on the one hand, outraged Big Business executives reacting against a philosophy that had raised their costs by depriving them of cheap labor; and on the other, individuals like the ones on this street, trying to cash in on various business aspects of Semantics.

Involved were problems of life, and more than one solution. Among these latter was surely: be aware, moment by moment!

One of those awarenesses came through at that exact instant. The distant Gosseyn Two said, 'I've just checked with the film department of this ship; and they were naturally given Enro's visual materials by my future sister-in-law, because – naturally – she doesn't deal with things like that herself. And as we suspected there was a tiny distorter under a false bottom of the container; and that has been disposed of. So things are lining up.'

They were, indeed.

Chapter Thirty

Back at the institute apartment there were the usual details to see to. Crang phoned Dr Kair, found him in – and willing to cancel his other patients immediately . . . 'Come right over!'

It was agreed, then, that Prescott and Crang would go with him. While they waited for the arrival of a car dispatched by the office of President Blayney, Gosseyn became aware that Dan Lyttle was beckoning him.

The two men went into the master bedroom; and Lyttle closed the door. Lyttle's lean face was twisted into a mildly embarrassed smile, as he said, 'I thought I should tell you. About this woman, Strella . . .'

What he reported was, in a way, amazing. All these years Dan Lyttle had hesitated about subjecting an Earth girl to being the wife of a hotel clerk who worked on a night shift. But, apparently, as he evaluated Strella's predicament, suddenly there were more possibilities. Because – Lyttle pointed out – the girl from Meerd was trapped. Speaking only English she could never again fit into the society of her former friends on her home planet. No one there would understand. It was even possible that she would be considered mentally deranged.

Being a stranger on Earth, with no way to turn, or return – unless she specifically requested this latter solution – she would, presumably, automatically tolerate being in a daytime-only wife situation. It could be that, as the years went by, it would slowly dawn on her that hers was a special marriage.

'That is,' Dan concluded, 'unless I can find a daytime job – which I now may consider doing. But that could take a while.'

. . . As he listened to the account Gosseyn Three conducted one of his silent conversations with Gosseyn Two:

'It would appear,' he analyzed, 'that people still expect that the poor will automatically tolerate more severe conditions than the rich —'

The distant Alter Ego was calm: 'My dear idealistic brother, there will — let us hope — never be a time when everybody reacts exactly like everyone else. The time may come when we have disposed of criminal behavior; but human beings will probably continue to have different life experiences, depending on where they were born; and will tend to choose friends and work that is congenial to the tens of thousands of small personal memories inside their heads; memories — which I will now point out — that General Semantics has no intention of eliminating, even if at some future time science can do the job of memory erasure.'

The distant Gosseyn Two concluded: 'My suggestion is that, as soon as you have taken care of people like Gorrold, and found out why that Gung-ho company that called the first day didn't show up to make an estimate for rebuilding the institute, that you get Dan appointed to be in charge of rebuilding the institute and, of course, the Games Machine. You don't want to see to these details yourself; but he may now be motivated to take on such a daytime job.'

'I can see,' Gosseyn Three replied mentally, 'that a local hotel owner is about to have the job of finding himself another night clerk.'

He concluded his communication, smiling: 'Be seeing you — very soon now, I believe, after Dr Kair interviews me.'

The answer came, accompanied by misgivings: 'I suppose it is, finally, going to happen. You and I meeting face to face —'

Gosseyn Three replied: 'I'm due to leave in a few minutes.'

. . . As he sat in the rear seat of the limousine with Crang and Prescott, Gosseyn Three silently confronted the reality of what was about to happen:

'. . . Am I going to do everything that's expected of me?'

That was definitely a basic question. But, in terms of General Semantics, there was an even more fundamental consideration. It seemed, as he, memory-wise, glanced back over his behavior, that the outward appearance was that he had, somehow, felt automatically committed to help the Dzan and the Troogs to return to their home galaxy.

But why return?

It seemed like a reasonable question. With their equipment, and their great ships, they would probably be acceptable colonists on any number of planets. And colonists seldom felt the need to go back to their homelands. The people who had settled North America in those early days for the most part never did, as individuals, return to Europe. Some of their descendants were occasionally, casually, interested to visit the land from which their forefathers had come. But theirs was a vacationer's curiosity, without strong feeling, and certainly without a homing instinct.

'. . . If they stayed, I'd have to take on a lower profile, and cease to be a target for bomb throwers.'

Perhaps he could move out to the middle west of Earth, buy a little farm, and live there with Enin and Queen Mother Strala?

Gosseyn found himself smiling again, as he visualized that improbable outcome of what he had got himself into. Not easy to realize that Gosseyn One had originally arrived in the City of the Games Machines with the hypnotically-implanted belief that he had been a farmer living just outside a little town called Crest City, and had been married to Patricia Hardie.

What a confusion that had been — for a while.

The train of thought evoked from him another communication with his Alter Ego: 'How is Queen Mother Strala?'

An instant smile impression came through. 'She's waiting for Enin to show up. That's the only thing on her mind. I think she's still mad at you.'

There was abruptly no time to consider that. The beautiful machine was pulling over to the curb in front of a familiar, large, white bungalow.

. . . Dr Lester Kair turned away from the viewing device, walked over to a chair, and sat down. Those piercing gray eyes of his were wide, and seemed to stare at the opposite wall.

There was silence, as they all looked at him expectantly.

Even though he radiated a special inner excitement, he seemed unchanged from what the joint Gosseyn memory recalled: long body, strongly built, face still smooth, the overall impression of an intelligent man in his early fifties.

Awareness of his audience came suddenly into his face. With that, he gulped, and spoke.

'That damaged nerve complex seems to have been only partly disconnected, and so it did get minimal support from the energy source to which, of course, it should have been firmly attached, but wasn't. The result of that partial connection looks fantastic.'

'How do you mean?' Eldred Crang sounded puzzled, as he asked the question: 'A damaged nerve end, as I visualize it, is merely a minute gray extension, which only an expert would be able to identify as being unnormal; but that word "fantastic" is too dramatic.'

Long pause. The tall man in the white doctorial over-cloak, so common in laboratory work, climbed to his feet. 'Gentlemen,' he said, 'I refuse to apologize for my reaction. I thought I had learned to accept the Gilbert Gosseyn extra-brain philosophically; but what I found myself looking at brought new awareness that we have here a neural interconnection with something basic in the universe. And, somehow, the damaged nerve group is in a state of over-stimulation.' He swallowed, and then finished the thought: 'It's like an actual light in there. If we opened his head a brightness would pour forth.'

He beckoned to Crang. 'Come and take a look.'

Gosseyn was still firmly held in the special chair; his head was virtually embedded in machinery, as Crang walked over, and out of his line of sight. He assumed that the Venusian detective was peering into the viewing lens.

Silence. Then there was the sound, and the feeling of someone carefully backing away. Off to one side, Dr Kair said, 'Mr Prescott, would you care to look, also?'

Prescott's answer was in his gentlest voice. 'I have no related medical qualifications; so, I think, one of us peering in is a sufficient witness for your statement.'

Crang walked into Gosseyn's line of sight. 'Well, Doctor,'

he said, 'how do we deal with this situation?'

The psychiatrist who had, on their arrival, been given a detailed account of everything, said, 'I think we'd better get the other special people over here; and then get Gosseyn Two.'

As Crang phoned Leej, and Prescott went out and dispatched the limousine to pick her up, Gosseyn said to Dr Kair, 'I deduce that by the special people you mean the persons who participated in the collective attempt to reach that other galaxy. And that, therefore, I should bring Enro here.'

'Yes.'

Since there had been agreement on that point with Yona, the Troog leader, Gosseyn took his extra-brain photograph of a floor area in one corner of the physician's laboratory and did his transfer. Moments later a huge figure was lying there. Enro the Red picked himself up, looked around, said nothing; but he was presently briefed on what was about to happen.

'You're going to send those Troogs home?'

In spite of his earlier argument with himself, Gosseyn Three said, 'I'm sure you'll agree it's the best solution: get them out of the Milky Way galaxy as soon as possible.'

'True. So now what?'

Gosseyn told him of the meeting that would now take place between two Gosseyn bodies, as a preliminary to the finale.

The war lord's face twisted into a frown. 'You're sure the place won't just blow up?'

Gosseyn Three replied, 'We're already different in many ways.'

'But you're still connected mentally?'

'Yes. Thought-wise. But I would guess,' he continued, 'that if there's ever going to be a mental telepathy between the average people of the universe, it will merely be a scientifically similarized portion of some part of the brain that the individual gives his or her permission to have aligned.'

The big man was shrugging. 'I think I'd like to be in the next room.'

It was interesting, then, to Gosseyn that the others, also, retreated through the door. When they had gone Gosseyn Three wasted no time, but immediately addressed Gosseyn Two:

'Well, Alter Ego, it looks as if our big moment is here.'

'It sure does,' was the reply.

'Do you need any help?'

'No, I think I have the location where Enro arrived in the necessary exact extra-brain imprint. Hold still! Keep your thoughts neutral!'

Holding still consisted of blanking out his own extra-brain. He was still doing that moments later when there was a small noise. Gosseyn Three, who had his eyes closed, was aware of the door opening; and then came the voice of Leej, sounding as if she had not actually entered the room.

'It's all right,' she said, 'I see no problems during the next fifteen minutes at least.'

Gosseyn opened his eyes, and saw that the man who had arrived had his back turned. He was fully dressed, and, when he slowly turned, he had the appearance of a tanned, lean-faced, strong-looking man in his middle thirties. But it was himself in another suit.

Dr Kair entered, and without a word released Gosseyn Three from the examining chair. He remained seated, with the thought that even a different position might be of value.

And so, there they were – together – gazing at each other; one standing, one sitting down. Two human beings, duplicates of each other.

Twins? No.

Some similarity, of course, existed between twins. But the diversity that began immediately after conception, and the variation of experience after birth, quickly created innumerable differences; first, on a minute level, but finally they were merely look alikes, with their own personalities.

The similarities between Gilbert Gosseyn Two and Gilbert Gosseyn Three as they faced each other in the office of Dr Lester Kair included a whole series of interacting energy flows. Brain to brain, body to body.

They were not twins in any ordinary meaning of the term. They were the same person in ten thousand times ten thousand ways.

Gosseyn Three realized that he was almost unconsciously bracing himself against an interflow that tended to tug him out of the chair and toward the other body.

Gosseyn Two seemed to be having a similar struggle; and he actually took several small steps toward Three before he, abruptly, braced himself. A tiny, grim smile relaxed the strong, even features of his face. He had the appearance of a man in control, as he said:

'Looks like it's going to be all right, and that we will be able to collaborate at close quarters, or otherwise.'

As he spoke the words his thoughts seemed to be coming through, also, and his body movements. To Gosseyn Three came the realization that he had a strong impulse to stand up, and that his face held the same tiny smile. He found himself wondering if Two was fighting the impulse to sit down.

And, though he did not speak that aloud, the other man said, 'Yes, I'm resisting the impulse; and I can deduce that if, for any reason, we ever have to stay together for a long period of time, we'll have to work out a system.'

It was a long speech, and Gosseyn Three was slightly resigned to realizing that, although he made no sound, his lips were moving and somehow saying the same words, but under his breath.

He thought: 'It really has been a case of duplicate memories.'

. . . The same thought, the same feeling about that thought. The same experience. The complete recollection of having walked along a street, or on a planet's surface . . . the muscular sensation recalled by both minds – exactly.

It could even be that, all those years while the mental images of Gosseyn One and Two were being recorded in the sleeping brain of Gosseyn Three, all neural responses and muscle mechanisms had operated in unison in some limited way; perhaps a twitching.

Thus it was, at that long, later moment as the eyes of the third Gosseyn blinked open, that the impression of being the second Gosseyn had been that of a sleeper awakening the morning after, with the automatic acceptance that it was I, who had all those experiences, who was waking up after a night of restful sleep.

Chapter Thirty-one

At Dr Kair's request Gosseyn Three had sat down again in the special chair with all the equipment attached. This time there were no straps; he merely agreed to maintain the correct motionless state at the key moment. Sitting there, he was aware of the viewing device being adjusted slightly behind and to one side of his head.

He did not move, or acknowledge as the dark-haired Leej walked past him, and took up a position whereby she could lean forward and peer through the viewing device at the damaged nerve inside his head.

Off to Gosseyn Three's right Enro sat in an upholstered chair, and stared at the wall across the room. Presumably he was ready to contribute his special distance seeing ability.

Gosseyn Two sat at Dr Kair's desk. His task: he had all of Gosseyn Three's memorized areas carefully catalogued in his extra-brain, ready to do his part.

It was Gosseyn Two who broke the silence. He said in a soft voice: 'What we did that time, when all this kicked back on us, and did the reversal whereby the Dzan ship was transmitted here from another galaxy — Leej actually predicted a location in that other galaxy. And so, now, as she gazes into the viewing device, she's going to predict again where that location is, and what it's like.

'Enro,' Gosseyn Two continued in that same soft voice, 'will use his special ability to perceive the predicted location. When he has done so, I will do for my brother what we have agreed will be the safest method for him to handle the situation.

'I have to admit,' he concluded, 'that what will happen here

207

in this room at the moment Enro perceives Leej's predicted area in that other galaxy is not obvious to me.'

As he completed his summation, Enro raised one of those strong hands of his, and wiggled his fingers for attention.

'Perhaps, I should report,' he said, 'that what happens when I have my distance perception, is that I seem to see it as on a screen in front of me, or, if it is an individual, I see him standing on the floor.'

He concluded, 'Until this key moment I've never thought of that method as being anything but an illusion, which is actually taking place inside my head. But if there is any reality to it, in this very unique circumstance, I suggest that no one walk anywhere between me and that floor and wall area I'm looking at.'

Gosseyn Three realized that the last moment explanation seemed to evoke a feeling of relief; as if something that had been vague, and lacking concrete reality, had suddenly come into focus.

. . . Interesting that the otherwise grim Enro, who normally kept his own counsel, had been motivated by the mounting tension to reveal a hitherto unsuspected aspect of his special ability.

The voice of Gosseyn Two came again: 'Any other comments, or information?' he asked.

Silence.

'Then,' Gosseyn Two said, 'Leej, do your best.'

Silence. And then a faint hissing sound.

And a brightness. It was on the floor near the wall at which Enro was gazing. As Gosseyn Three continued to hold himself still, he saw that the bright area was neither quite oval, nor quite round, nor square; but a mix of all three. His extra-brain was reacting to it; and his instant evaluation was: something . . . connected . . . this five foot uneven shape with an equivalent space and object across the immense distance between two galaxies. Connected it in a manner that fell infinitesimally short of similarity.

The voice of Gosseyn Two intruded on those thoughts: 'Three, it's your turn.' He evidently leaned forward, and spoke into a microphone. His words were: 'And Yona, of the Troogs, do your part!'

. . . He was lying on his back in darkness.

In spite of knowing that this time he had come purposefully, and, with the help of the Troogs, had arrived in exactly the right position, Gosseyn was aware of a small thalamic reaction.

As he lay there, and after he had recovered from his momentary anxiety, he made the same checks that, on the first awakening . . . had been so puzzling – and on the second, when the capsule was aboard the Troog battleship, had evoked bafflement.

This time his purpose was to make sure that he was, in fact, inside the capsule. It seemed to be so. Because, when he put his hands up, there was the expected hard, steely ceiling about twelve inches above him; and he appeared to be lying on the same type of padded material that he remembered.

There were several differences, of course, between those other occasions and now: this time he was warmly dressed, and not naked; and this time nothing at all was connected to him. There were no soft wires attached to his head, and no rubber-like tubings poking into his body.

Having verified his condition as well as possible, he permitted one more flow of thoughts; permitted it, and them, because they should be out of the way, and not intruding at the key moment:

. . . Here he lay, the man who could make the jump for them all. Here, in Gilbert Gosseyn Three, was the decisive ability that, it was hoped, would resolve a puzzle two million years old.

Across the endless miles human beings had escaped from a doomed galaxy. But, because of the nature of the doom, they had planned to return *if* they ever discovered how to reverse that doom: one point here, and one there. One predictor and one extra brain, one person who could 'see' into distant places; one logic system to keep them from destroying each other. Perhaps there were other such groupings scattered over a thousand planets, blindly seeking to come together; and then, when each fulfilled his function, the whole was a unit capable of acting.

Lying there, Gosseyn Three thought:

The basic reality was, nothingness should reassert.

Matter and mass had no 'right' to exist, but were held together, and continuing, by awareness.

Mind over Matter was Meaningful.

The reason they had to go back to the second galaxy was that nothing was re-asserting there because of unending wrong thought: the incredible Troog leadership system, whereby no one ever had had the thought of ending the war — so the Troogs constantly attacked, and the human beings constantly defended.

. . . For two million years!

With the return of Yona, he would make a statement asserting his leadership in terms of ending the war. And the encroachment of nothingness would be reversed.

It would take time; but here and now was the beginning. Having had his reassuring thoughts, Gosseyn uttered the triggering words:

'I'm as ready as I can be.'

The reply came promptly. A voice spoke almost directly into his ear: 'The capsule is out in space, floating alongside our Troog ship. The next step is up to you.'

Gosseyn drew a deep breath. Then: 'My first act will be to transfer this capsule, with myself in it, to your galaxy.'

With that, and with his eyes closed, he recalled the five foot shiningness that Leej and Enro, with the help of the damaged nerve ends in his head — with *their* connections — had brought into focus.

As he, next, did his extra-brain complexity, he told himself: it had to work!

It did.

First went the Troog ship. And then, after the Dzan battle-craft moved near his capsule, it also was instantly returned to where it had come from.

Two million light-years away, in another galaxy.

Thus the distances between a hundred thousand million billion stars was, essentially, conquered; the method could be utilized in future at will.

Chapter Thirty-two

'I really don't know,' said Queen Mother Strala. 'This whole matter of the Gosseyn bodies is too strange for me.'

They were sitting in a fabulously furnished room in the palace on the Dzan planet Zero, in Galaxy One. It was day outside; and he had arrived after completing all his actions – except that he had not taken away the English speaking ability of the Dzanians when he returned to them their knowledge of their own language.

Sitting there, facing the beautiful Strala, Gosseyn Three calmly acknowledged that her statement was correct. Weird it was.

She sat there, in a golden chair across from the upholstered sofa to which she had motioned him. Her eyes had a faraway expression; and, finally, as evidence that she had been thinking, she looked at him again, and said:

'As I understand it, your Alter Ego will remain in the Milky Way galaxy; and you will stay here.' She sounded suddenly distracted to him: 'Are you still, uh, connected to your Alter Ego?'

'Moment by moment I'm aware of him out there, and I can get his thoughts, or what he's doing, if I concentrate on him.'

'At two *million* light-years.'

'Distance has no meaning in a nothingness universe.'

She said, 'He will take care of things there, in your home universe?'

It was an unfortunate wording. It evoked a thalamic reaction. It was as if he had left his home town, and home country; and would never see them again.

Recovery took moments only. The truth was – he

reminded himself — that he was not a man who had ever had a country. He had grown to adulthood inside a space capsule, and had no planet of his own, and no relatives in the usual meaning.

Gosseyn gulped — and recovered, as the woman, who was now staring off to one side, said, 'I'll have to think about all this.'

Gosseyn could only gaze at her pityingly. He was not qualified to evaluate the ways of women; but the fact that it was she who had once made a proposal of total intimacy to him gave him control of this moment — so it seemed — in view of what else he knew.

He said, gently, 'My dear, there's no escape for you. You're my lady from now on; my future wife, with all that implies. You're destined to be with me for all the rest of my life.'

The eyes in the perfect face were staring at him. 'I suppose,' she said, almost stiffly, 'there must be some explanation for such a positive approach. My own feeling is, you had your chance — and rejected it — forever.'

She finished her thought: 'Rejected it in a way that I can never forgive.'

Gosseyn drew a deep breath. 'I have to point out to you that you're a mother.'

'Enin's mother.' She nodded. She seemed puzzled.

'Does he know I'm here?'

'No.'

'Call him.'

A pause. Her eyes appraised him. Abruptly she stood up, and walked over to a door, from which tiny, significant sounds had been coming during their entire conversation.

She paused in the open doorway, and called out, 'Enin, can you come in here for a moment?'

Enin's voice sounded, muffled, but clear enough: 'Ah, gee, Mom — let me have this one shot . . . *Got him!*' Jubilant scream. Then: 'Okay, now I can come for a minute.'

The woman returned to her chair, and sat down without a word. She seemed suddenly tense, and she did not look around. And then, although Gosseyn had also kept his eyes averted, there was, first, a sound of footsteps, and then a boyish squeal of total joy.

Fortunately he turned in time. Because bare instants later he had a twelve-year-old in his lap, whose arms reached up and grabbed him around his neck.

There were many words, including: 'Mr Gosseyn, Mr Gosseyn, where have you been? Oh, Mother, Mother, it's Mr Gosseyn!'

It took a while.

Gosseyn gazed benignly down at the excited boy. 'Any problems,' he asked, 'with the, uh, suck-ups?'

'Nope. I called a meeting when I got back aboard the ship, and another one here on this planet where the government is, and I told 'em what you and I discussed.'

'. . . If there are any problems, a committee will review each one — that discussion?' Gosseyn asked.

'Yep.' The impish face grinned. 'Not just me making up my mind like my dad used to, and burning anybody who didn't like it.'

'If,' thought Gosseyn, as he heard those words spoken by a boy who had inherited one of the largest empires ever to exist anywhere, 'there is such a thing as a great moment in history, this has got to be it . . .'

The very heart of a system of absolute power modified to include democratic procedures.

Once more, impulsively, Enin reached up with both arms and hugged him. He said, 'Boy, it's sure going to be great to have you around. It's going to be forever now, isn't it?'

'That decision is entirely up to your mother,' said Gosseyn. He turned toward the stiff-looking beauty sitting in the chair across the room. 'Will I be staying?' he asked, in his most innocent sounding tone of voice.

A moment later, a somewhat resigned voice said, 'You go and play, dear, while Mr Gosseyn and I discuss his future.'

Gosseyn picked up Enin and carried him to the doorway from which he had emerged a short time earlier. As he put the boy down, he glanced into the second room; and he was not surprised to observe that a video game had been interrupted. The screen was brightly lit.

Gosseyn said, 'I hope you're playing the General Semantics games also.'

A pause, a grin, and then: 'There's a good possibility that I am playing those games about as often as, I believe, you would approve of; you being you and I being me.'

Gosseyn was straightening. 'Well, son,' he said, 'your mother and I have a few things to talk about; so you and I will get together later.'

'Oh, boy, you bet.'

He stood, then, watching the boy race off; and then he turned, walked over and stood in front of the woman.

'Naturally,' he said. 'I am aware that you have received another offer.'

'Yes?' She was staring off to one side.

'You have your own interests to pursue,' he continued. 'A woman doesn't have to remain a mother-oriented individual all her life.'

He waited, then, not looking directly at her. There was a pause, then: 'I have been listening to your conversations with Enin, and – '

Another pause. 'Yes?' said Gosseyn.

'They make a certain amount of sense,' said the woman. 'Your philosophy,' she hesitated, 'General Semantics. I can see that, because of what you've taught him, Enin has become a more stable, normal person. As for myself . . .' Another pause, then: 'I finally looked myself over as a woman in relation to the royal environment, with its numerous individuals vying for power and position, and others very honest and sincere, and protective; and I can see that in such an environment what you evaluated when I first proposed to you was correct.'

She was still staring off to one side. Then: 'There is now another aspect we can take into account. Many of the top leaders are aware of the role you played in bringing us back here. They respect you.'

She smiled suddenly, as if her own reasoning had brought a sudden inner release. 'So I think conditions have changed. What do you think?'

He said simply, 'I hope you realize that I'm the only father he'll ever accept.'

With that, without a word, the silken, beautiful female being stood up, silently came over and, exactly as a mother should, who was not trained in General Semantics, put her arms around him. The kiss he gave her was accepted in a way that telegraphed adequate acceptance.

When she drew back she said, 'I think we'd better go into my bedroom and close and lock the door. I don't think we should wait until the marriage ceremony.'

It was a triumph of one level of reality over another – Gosseyn deduced, as he followed her across that beautiful room into a fantastical, elegant bedroom.

He directed his thought at his Alter Ego: 'Mr Gosseyn Two, turn your attention somewhere else!'

The reply, on one level of reality, came from a distance of two million light-years. But, in relation to the reality to which his extra-brain related, was as close as the inside of his head.

The meaning was: 'You both have all my best wishes . . . brother!'

In a future world of strangers,
the hunter and the hunted are one . . .

ROGER ZELAZNY

Winner of 3 Nebula and 3 Hugo Awards

William Blackhorse Singer, the last Navajo tracker on a future earth, has stocked the Interstellar Life Institute with its most exotic creatures. But one of Singer's prizes preys upon his mind: a metamorph. The one-eyed shapeshifter Cat, whose home planet has been destroyed. Singer offers Cat freedom to help him defend Earth against a terrible predator, and Cat accepts. The price: permission to hunt the hunter. And the deadly game begins. In a fierce, global hunt, Singer flees his extra-sentient killer. And suddenly, he is pursuing not life, but the mysteries of his people, and the blinding vision of his own primeval spirit . . .

SCIENCE FICTION   0 7221 9442 0   £1.95

From one of Science Fiction's most acclaimed writers comes an outstanding new edition to the popular DORSAI series

LOST DORSAI

Gordon R. Dickson

WINNER OF THE NEBULA AWARD FOR THE BEST NOVELLA OF 1981

Revolution gripped the mighty kingdom of El Conde . .

As the gap between rich and poor yawned cavernously wider, the massed ranks of the Naharese exploded into bitter rebellion. Men who had been trained by the galaxy's most famous warriors, the Dorsai, now took up arms against them. And into this chaos were flung a handful of noble Dorsai warriors, whose innate honour bound them to secure El Conde from the rebels. Their might was pitted against the most impossible odds: but one of their number faced battle first of another kind entirely, forced to grapple with a sudden, terrifying loss of conviction in the ways of warriorhood central to his whole existence . . .

SCIENCE FICTION   0 7221 30201   £1.95

A selection of bestsellers from SPHERE

FICTION

MONIMBO	Arnaud de Borchgrave and Robert Moss	£2.25 ☐
KING OF DIAMONDS	Carolyn Terry	£2.50 ☐
SPRING AT THE WINGED HORSE	Ted Willis	£1.95 ☐
TRINITY'S CHILD	William Prochnau	£2.50 ☐
THE SINISTER TWILIGHT	J. S. Forrester	£1.95 ☐

FILM & TV TIE-INS

SPROCKETT'S CHRISTMAS TALE	Louise Gikow	£1.75 ☐
THE DOOZER DISASTER	Michaela Muntean	£1.75 ☐
THE DUNE STORYBOOK	Joan D. Vinge	£2.50 ☐
ONCE UPON A TIME IN AMERICA	Lee Hays	£1.75 ☐
WEMBLEY FRAGGLE GETS THE STORY	Deborah Perlberg	£1.50 ☐

NON-FICTION

PRINCESS GRACE	Steven Englund	£2.50 ☐
BARRY FANTONI'S CHINESE HOROSCOPES		£1.95 ☐
THE COMPLETE HANDBOOK OF PREGNANCY	Wendy Rose-Neil	£5.95 ☐
WHO'S REALLY WHO	Compton Miller	£2.95 ☐
THE STOP SMOKING DIET	Jane Ogle	£1.50 ☐

All Sphere books are available at your local bookshop or newsagent, or can be ordered direct from the publisher. Just tick the titles you want and fill in the form below.

Name _____

Address _____

_____

Write to Sphere Books, Cash Sales Department, P.O. Box 11, Falmouth, Cornwall TR10 9EN

Please enclose a cheque or postal order to the value of the cover price plus:

UK: 55p for the first book, 22p for the second book and 14p for each additional book ordered to a maximum charge of £1.75.

OVERSEAS: £1.00 for the first book plus 25p per copy for each additional book.

BFPO & EIRE: 55p for the first book, 22p for the second book plus 14p per copy for the next 7 books, thereafter 8p per book.

Sphere Books reserve the right to show new retail prices on covers which may differ from those previously advertised in the text or elsewhere, and to increase postal rates in accordance with the PO.

A.E. Van Vogt is one of the classic names in science fiction and one of the genre's most widely read authors. He was born in Canada in 1912 and made his initial impact with short stories for *Astounding Science Fiction*. He moved to the States, where he wrote his first novel, *Slan*, in the 1940s. That was quickly accepted as a staple in any worthwhile sf diet and van Vogt has gone on to write a string of successful books.

Also by A. E. Van Vogt in Sphere Books:

TYRANOPOLIS
THE WORLD OF NULL-A
THE PAWNS OF NULL-A